Hooked

catherine greenman

Delacorte Press

Text copyright © 2011 by Catherine Greenman
Jacket art copyright © 2011 by freshsugar.com

All rights reserved. Published in the United States by Delacorte Press, an imprint of Random House Children's Books, a division of Random House, Inc., New York.

Delacorte Press is a registered trademark and the colophon is a trademark of Random House, Inc.

Visit us on the Web! www.randomhouse.com/teens

Educators and librarians, for a variety of teaching tools, visit us at
www.randomhouse.com/teachers

Library of Congress Cataloging-in-Publication Data
Greenman, Catherine.
Hooked / by Catherine Greenman. — 1st ed.
p. cm.
ISBN 978-0-385-74008-1 (hc) — ISBN 978-0-385-90822-1 (lib. bdg.) —
ISBN 978-0-375-89888-4 (ebook)
[1. Teenagers—Fiction. 2. Teenage pregnancy—Fiction.
3. New York (N.Y.)—Fiction. 4. Domestic fiction.] I. Title.
PS3607.R464H66 2011
813'.6—dc22
2010023542

The text of this book is set in 11-point Classical Garamond.

Book design by Angela Carlino

Printed in the United States of America

10 9 8 7 6 5 4 3 2 1

First Edition

For my parents

acknowledgments

There were hundreds of moments when I wanted to bury this book deep inside folders within folders on my computer, like a little Russian doll. I would like to thank Jonathan Rabb, Ellen Horan, Martha Chang, Brendan Kiely, Esther Noe and Rob Weisberg for keeping me going. I'm also deeply grateful to Jennifer Rudolph Walsh, Erin Malone and Alexia Paul for their early insights and support, and to Polly McCall for her bottomless well of encouragement. My heartfelt thanks go to my agent, Alice Tasman, and to my editor, Stephanie Lane Elliott, for their willingness to ride the bumps with my characters and to ask the prickly questions I might otherwise have avoided. Thanks also to Krista Vitola and Jen Strada for their watchful eyes and to Hilary Weekes for her kind help. I'm forever indebted to Julie Moore, who set me free to write this by looking after my kids with amazing dedication and love. And finally, thank you to Richard d'Albert, my husband. When I give it my best shot it's always with you in mind.

part one

1.

I met Will Weston during a fire drill on a gray, freezing February Monday, a few days after I turned seventeen. I was in metal shop when the bells went off, and had to go outside in my smock. Why didn't they have fire drills during homeroom, when we still had our coats? I hid behind a tree to block the wind, and as I studied the gloomy, red-bricked façade of the school for any signs of real fire, I spotted him. Will was leaning against the stone wall, hugging himself in a thin, black sweater. He was tall and he had large, square, hulking shoulders that reminded me of Frankenstein—an aberration in a sea of boys with shoulders so narrow you could lift them off the ground by grabbing their knapsack straps together in one hand. This guy looked too old for high school. His chin was ducked toward his chest and he stared at me forever, and it was clear that he didn't care that I noticed. I remember looking around, wishing there was someone to talk to, but I was surrounded by the dicks from metal shop. Metal shop was the great dick-alizer—we all behaved like we were in preschool, cutting each other in the soldering lines, hogging the drying shelves, all for the easy As Mr. Blake was famous for doling out. It was not lost on me that an A from Blake would finally kick my average up to an A-minus, a longtime hurdle. Anyway, one minute Will was undressing me from afar, and then he just appeared, as if in a blink.

"Blake or Dolan?" he asked, peering into my face.

"Uh . . . Blake," I said, cursing my telltale gingham smock.

"I had him. A girl in my class lost her eye."

"You were in Lisa Kwan's class?" I asked, marveling.

3

"I was." He nodded modestly.

"What happened? He told us she poked it out."

"Her vise was loose," he said. We both tried not to smile. "You don't use them anymore, vises. Right?"

"No, everything's on the table," I explained. "He helps you when you need to make a cut. He's sick of me. I'm always recutting." I realized then that there was something weird about *his* eyes: the left eye was looking at me, but the right eye drifted off toward the Hudson River. It was both off-putting and death-defyingly hot. It also somehow made him seem too smart for me. I wondered if he was a brainiac, like everyone else at Stuyvesant High School, where I'd somehow landed like an alien on the wrong planet. In math and science, at least, which Stuy held sacred above all else, I was the opposite of a brainiac. Not quite a dumbass, but close. I felt like I was working twice as hard to do half as well as anyone else.

"You'll get an A," he said, rubbing his forearms for warmth. "Don't worry. Has he shown you his oliver?"

"His what?" I asked, thinking, He has the most beautiful hair: brown, wavy, and longer than I initially thought.

"His oliver."

"Oh God. Don't tell me. Another pervy—"

"Go on, ask him to see the oliver," he said. "He'll love you if you ask him."

"What is it?"

"You don't want to be surprised?" he teased.

Part of me did, but I shook my head.

"It's his silver tin of green olives," he whispered, so that the metal-shop dicks couldn't hear. "He keeps it in his pocket for martinis. 'Always keep your oliver on your person.' That's what he used to say. You're a junior?"

I nodded.

"I had him freshman year. He's toned it down since then. I think he's a less-happy drunk these days."

"Aren't we all," I said.

"Settle down there, Dorothy Parker." He held out his hand. "I'm Will Weston."

"Thea Galehouse," I said.

"I know." He smiled proudly.

"How do you know?"

"That yearbook picture of you, sleeping on the desk. Your name was in the caption. 'Thea takes a breather' or something stupid like that. Was that during a class? Or homeroom?"

"Homeroom, I think. I was tired."

"No shit. I could never sleep like that. In the middle of everyone. I wish I could. You have the same hair still. Like wet grass stuck to your face." He pushed a clump of loose hair into my cheek with his thumb as people started to stream back into the building. "Anyway, don't stress about Blake." Will took the steps two at a time, so I did too. "He skews it to the pretty ones."

We got inside the double doors and I faced him. "Do I look stressed out?"

"Little bit."

I hate offhand comments about my moods. My mother still makes them constantly. But the way he said it made me think, Maybe I *am* stressing out about stupid freaking metal shop.

"You know," Will said, "ever since I saw that picture of you, all schlumped out all over that desk, I've wanted to meet you. Do you like burgers?"

"Love 'em," I said.

"Have a burger with me, then."

He said it in the nicest way. It was one of the shining moments of my life. A total shock and yet right as rain.

The huge oil painting of peg-legged Peter Stuyvesant, our school's namesake, loomed over Will by the staircase. School, the place where we spent so much of our time, was so deathly dreary at that moment. It was like Will put it all—the gray walls pockmarked with painted-over thumbtack holes, the gummy stair railings that made your hands smell like spit—into relief. He glanced at a short girl in clogs walking by. She almost stopped to talk, then didn't. He looked back at me and I got the first jolt. The first java jolt. The first whiff of desire for his big, scary, manly-man body. And the desperation to be included in his thoughts. Me, Thea.

We made a plan to meet Friday.

I tried to think of some cool exit, but I ended up smiling and doing my weird secret-wave thing that my best friend, Vanessa, always makes fun of me for.

"Ask to see the oliver!" he called. I looked back at him. He stood there smiling at me, the sea of people jostling past him.

When I pointed Will out to Vanessa during lunch, he was standing outside between two parked cars, talking to an Asian guy in a ski jacket.

"I see what you mean, kind of," she said, twirling her long brown curls behind her shoulder.

"What do you mean, *kind of*?" I asked, annoyed at her.

"I like his little slump," she said, appeasing me, "like he can't hold up all that tall, like it's a real burden. Poor thing. He has a nice smile."

I stared down at the ripped, stepped-on backs of Vanessa's long jeans, afraid to look. "What's his deal?" I asked her.

"I don't know, he is so not a hipster, but I've seen him hang out with them. He almost has an anti-look, it's so nondescript. Midcentury Gap. White T-shirt–ville." She looked at me. "It's fine, though. Completely inoffensive."

"Do you think he looks like he's just met someone?"

"Someone meaning you?" Vanessa continued staring blatantly. "I think he went out with Judd Lieberman's sister."

"When?" I asked, the squeak of sneakers on the marble floor grating on my nerves.

"Last year," she said, putting her hand absently on my shoulder. "She graduated. Calm down."

I went to the library and found Amanda Lieberman in the yearbook. She was pretty in a neat, preppy way I wasn't: clean, shiny brown hair and wide, bony cheeks sort of like his. I was more blobby—cherubic, not chiseled. I kept my highlighted blond hair dirty because washing it made it limp. When it got too greasy, I sprinkled it with powder, like I read George Washington used to.

At home after school I fell asleep on our gray sectional and had a dream that Will and I were lying together on a car hood in the blazing sun in our underwear. It's funny how love is like the flu, how one minute you're fine and the next it digs in and takes over.

"Have you finished your homework?" Mom asked, rousing me out of my coma.

"Haven't started yet," I said. "I don't start till after five."

"Since when?" she asked, glancing at her Canal Street Chanel watch.

"Since always." I pried myself out of the split in the sectional.

"You'll never guess what just happened," she said, jamming the sleeves of her blazer up her arms.

7

"What?" I was sitting up now, braced.

"I think I just sold my first flat. The two-bedroom on Astor. Can you believe it? The client made an offer and the seller accepted. I just got the call." She waved her cell phone around, then combed her fingers into the front of my scalp, "lifting" my hair. "Would it kill you to wear your gorgeous hair down one day? It looks so grotty when it's in that godforsaken mess at the back of your head."

"Anyway, congratulations," I said, falling back onto the couch, taking in the whole picture of what she was wearing: a short black skirt that was possibly shorts, black tights and high-heeled boots that went up to her knees. It was her signature look: a Barneys version of Madonna's Danceteria phase.

"You wore that to the showing?" I asked.

"Got a problem with it, honey chile?" she asked, her working-class-and-proud-of-it English brogue morphing into a pathetic attempt at ghetto. She strutted into the kitchen, her wavy blond hair hitting her cheeks as she uncorked an open bottle of pinot grigio. "'Cause yo momma is some hot shit now, yo momma is yo real estate ho."

I rolled over onto my stomach. I needed sugar.

"They finally gave me my business cards today," she called. "Come see."

I stumbled into the kitchen and she handed one to me. Her fire-engine-red grin ate up the postage stamp–sized photo in the upper left, and in the middle, in royal-blue italics, were the words "*Fiona Galehouse, Sales Associate.*"

"*Galehouse?*" I asked, flabbergasted.

"It sounds nicer than Addison," she sniffed, dropping an ice cube into her glass. I slumped at the kitchen table. Only my mother would take her husband's surname once they'd finally *divorced*. "It has a better ring for sales." She avoided my

8

eyes and I realized the real reason for the switch: she wanted to distance herself from the whole tax-evasion thing. My mother had gotten into some kind of trouble when I was twelve and Fiona's, her nightclub, was winding down from its heyday. It had to do with taxes, and all I know is that Mom secretly blamed Dad for it, for not being "aggressive enough," even though it was never really clear to me that he'd had anything to do with it. He worked at an investment bank and never spent time at Fiona's, or with us, for that matter. It didn't help that the tax thing coincided with the summer Dad stopped drinking. Everyone was weirdly on edge that summer—Mom screaming on the phone all day, Dad coming home from work with five bottles of Clamato—but then after making such a huge deal about getting Dad to quit drinking, Mom went and divorced him anyway.

After they did the intervention on him and Dad went away to rehab, Mom realized that she was pissed as hell that it took Dad's *boss* to get him to stop, when she'd been pleading with him for years. She'd tried leaving—I remember trekking out in the middle of the night many times with my hamster and staying at her friend Maryanne's—but we always ended up coming back to the same routine: Mom in the bedroom with her plate of cheese and crackers, her phone and the TV, Dad in his leather swivel chair in the living room, ignoring us, with his headphones and piles of paper. They had an uncanny habit of never being in the same room together. But when the almighty Bill Mindorff told Dad he'd get the ax if he didn't sober up, only *then* did he take it seriously. Bill Mindorff. I'd never met him, but the picture of him in my head was crystal clear: red tie with little blue polka dots, white shirt, feet up on his desk, wielding his untold powers over Dad.

"Apparently we don't factor in nearly as importantly as the

possibility of not becoming a bloody managing director," Mom had said one night while Dad was away "drying out." I'd dabbed my pinky into the tub of her cold cream and swirled it around on my forehead, wondering how Dad could love his job more than us. But the fact that he was gone for all but maybe five hours on the weekends meant it must be true.

"I've got some beautiful asparagus for dinner," Mom said, wiping her hands on the blue-flowered dish towel. "It's after five. Start your homework."

"I met a guy," I said, fishing a rice cake out of its plastic pack.

"Ooh," she said, downing a sip of wine.

"He's a senior. His name's Will Weston."

"Is he cute?"

"Beyond."

"Well, well, well, I'm really pleased, Thea," she said unconvincingly, wiping her lipstick off the rim of her glass. "I'm not surprised. You're a knockout." She smiled at me and I studied the crescents of her red-rimmed brown eyes, eyes that looked like she could be crying even when she smiled, as if even though she was smiling, she was never, for a second, forgetting how screwed up the world was. I wondered if anyone thought she was an addict. My mother was a vegetarian who drank wheatgrass shots and herb tinctures and did yoga every day, but she still had red-rimmed druggie eyes. She banged her glass loudly on the slate countertop. "You could have anyone you want. Just take your hair out of that hive."

2.

The week crawled by until Will and I went for burgers that Friday, four days after the fire drill. The restaurant was in the basement of a garment industry building with fake wood paneling and head shots of soap actors. There were a few suits at the bar and that was it.

"She's beautiful, my friend." A guy with a bow tie cupped my elbow as I caught a glimpse in the mirror of my too-yellow, flat hair, which Mom had made me wear down. "Where do you want to sit? You have the place to yourselves."

"He doesn't say that about just anyone," Will said as we headed to the back of the room. I looked at the empty booths, awash in red-webbed candlelight. The last thing I wanted to do was eat. I was dying for a drink but didn't want to get carded, so I ordered a Diet Coke. Will got a beer. He clinked my glass, still on the table.

"Glad you agreed to dine with me." He swallowed with a quick jerk of his head, like he was swallowing an aspirin. He leaned forward, his wide, square shoulders pointing at me through his wrinkled button-down. "So tell me about you," he said. "Where do you live?"

"I live in Chelsea with my mom," I answered. I was having trouble figuring out which eye to look into. Looking into the left one, the one that worked, felt too focused, too intense. It made me feel like I was ignoring the right one, but looking into the right seemed wrong, since I didn't think he could see out of it. I pushed the paper off my straw, deciding to just get it over with. "So can I ask you . . ."

"The left one." He smiled assuredly. "You're good. Most

people skirt around it for years. Just ignore the right one. Pretend it's not there."

"Okay." I sipped, catching some lemon pulp, trying not to make lemon lips. "Were you born with your eyes that way?"

He shook his head, sucking in his cheeks to quickly down the beer he'd just swigged. "I looked up into a tree when I was three and an acorn popped me in the eye."

"Did it hurt?"

He shrugged, smiled, didn't answer.

"So where are you going next year?" I asked, focusing on the left side of his face.

"Columbia," he said. "Got in early. I hope it's less of a waste of time than this place."

"Well, you get to stay in New York. That's a plus."

"That's right," he said. "Close to home. I'm a city boy. A New York boy."

He explained that his dad was a financial analyst who did consulting with big banks. "He works two days a year," Will said. "The rest of the time he walks up and down Broadway. He's a big walker. He goes to the movies a lot. He's seen everything." I told him that my own father worked endlessly, was consumed by his job, and had very little personality to show for it. Will had two brothers. He got along with Johnny, the younger one, but not Roy, the older.

"What about your mom?" I asked.

"Mom's got a degree in public health management, whatever that is." He sighed. "Yet she spends all of her time baking desserts no one eats and puttering. How many times can you leaf through a twenty-year-old *National Geographic,* I ask you?" He shook his head in wonderment. "You got any siblings?"

"No," I responded, worrying about my hair.

He snatched a French fry off my plate. "That was a test," he said. "Good sharing. You passed with flying colors. How are you with attention? Do you need someone's undivided attention all the time or are you more of an independent-spirit only-child type?"

"Independent-spirit only child. Type."

"Good. Actually, now that you tell me that, I see it. You have a lonely way about you."

"I'm not lonely," I protested. "My mom's home all the time."

"That doesn't count," he said dismissively. "All the time?"

"Yep."

"Is she okay?" He leaned back. "I know what you're going to say. Depends what you mean by okay, right? Does she work?"

"She used to. She used to own a club."

"What kind of club?"

"A club club." I shrugged. "Fiona's."

"No way," he said, his left eye widening. "Did you ever go?"

"Only when it was closed. It scared me when I was little. The guys dancing in cages, you know, half-naked, dog collars . . . she sold it when I was twelve."

He bit off giant bites of his burger, dipping what he had left in a pile of mustard. He said he didn't like ketchup. Only mustard. My mom drowns everything in ketchup, including Chinese food.

"Didn't she . . ." He paused, examined his bun. "This is awkward. Didn't she get, like, busted for tax evasion or extortion or something like that?"

"She took a plea," I answered quickly.

"A plea?"

"Some kind of plea-bargain thing that let her off," I said, dousing my fries with more salt. "You can tell I so enjoy talking about this, right?"

"Sorry." He grinned, his good eye lasering into me. "What's she doing now?"

"Watching *Days of Our Lives,*" I said. "Moisturizing."

"What about Dad?"

"They're divorced," I said.

He looked at me pensively. "Did you take it hard? How old were you?"

"I was thirteen. Of course I took it hard, although I never saw him." I slid my empty, wet glass around on the table. "Doesn't everybody?"

"Don't deflect. Some people are waiting for it, or expecting it."

"I wasn't expecting it," I said.

"So your mom sold Fiona's and then right after, went about getting a divorce?"

"Sort of makes your head spin, doesn't it?" I chirped.

He peeled at his beer label. "Does it make you not want to get married?"

The room blurred behind him into chunks of brown and red light. "I do want to get married," I said.

"Awwww." He pretended to swoon.

"Walked right into that one, didn't I?"

He reached for my hand and patted it.

"Boys," I sneered. "Anyway, now that they're finally divorced, she's decided she wants Dad's name. How weird is that? She was always Fiona Addison, now she's Fiona Galehouse."

"Okayyy." He smiled.

"Hopefully it's just on her business card."

"So she *is* working."

"Yeah, sort of," I said. "She's started selling real estate. Apartments. She's always made a big deal about working. 'You never want to be financially dependent on anyone,' she tells me that all the time. 'It's the most important thing. Financial independence. If you don't make your own way, you'll have no choices in life.' When I was little, I had no idea what she was talking about. Whenever she said 'choices,' I always pictured parting my hair on the left, then shaking it out and parting it on the right. To this day, when I hear the word *choices,* I think of parting my hair."

He sat very still as he listened, which made me worry that I'd been rambling. After a moment he cleared his throat dramatically. "So Thea," he said, looking at me sideways. "You seeing anyone?"

"Who, me?" I asked, my tongue feeling as though it had quadrupled in size.

He looked down at his plate, then up again, waiting.

"I'm not seeing anyone at the moment," I said. "What is that, anyway? Seeing someone?" I made a peekaboo gesture. "I see you!"

He waved for the bill. The bow-tie guy threw the billfold across the room like a Frisbee, and Will caught it and folded in money.

"Thank you," I said. I wondered if his family watched the Oscars together. And if he'd ever seen his parents naked.

We navigated the dark stairs up and out into the empty street. The sidewalks were streaked with black ice, and the howling February wind shot up and down the street. Will put my arm through his and we walked hunched into the cold like old people. He told me about his favorite building, which we were nowhere near.

"Did you know that if you work in the Seagram Building, you can only have your shades all the way up, all the way down or exactly in the middle?" he asked.

"That's assuming you have a window office."

"I'm going to assume that," he said emphatically. "I'm an optimist. You have to be an optimist in life. No one told me that, by the way." The wind screamed at his face, making his eyes water. "Shiver me timbers."

"I feel like I've seen shades in that building that were five-eighths of the way down," I said as we both stopped to find our gloves.

"That would be hard to believe, Thea."

"Well, I think I have," I said. "Actually, I'm sure of it now. I have."

"Well, why don't we go verify that?"

"We're twenty blocks away."

"It'll be worth the trip. Let's make it interesting. If there is one shade not in its rightful place—high, medium or low—it's five dollars. For you."

"Okay, deal."

"All right, then," he said, straightening up with purpose. "We'll be there in no time."

It felt like we were crossing Antarctica. I had no hat and my ears burned. We barely said a word, it was so cold, and I didn't want to complain. When we got to the Seagram Building, we went up the steps and stood in the middle of the plaza.

"There, I see one," I said. "The shades are three-quarters down. Six floors up, four from the left. We have to stand back a little."

"Jeez, you're right," he said, surprised. "How did this happen?"

"It must be busted." I held out my hand as he fished for the five.

"I appreciate that deep respect for order, I must say," he said, slapping it into my hand. "Philip Johnson, he liked things in their place."

We stood there for a long time, freezing our asses off. It was so beautiful—the ceilings on every floor were illuminated, rich, deep blocks of orange. All those squares, hovering over all the private conversations about God knows what that I would never know about, all I would never know. Will was looking up at the top of the building, pensive and still, a smile frozen on his face. Finally he turned to me and I knew what he was going to do, so I stood still and waited, letting the fantastic terror of those tiny milliseconds crawl through me as his cold face came to mine. Everything that had been moving around us—the revolving door pouring out late-night stragglers, the Poland Spring truck plowing its way through the avenue traffic—everything seemed to come to a halt, as if we were all in a weird game of freeze dance. I felt incredibly grown up and hoisted out of my life, kissing him in his black coat, a shock of black in the orange haze. He stood back, slowly stamping his feet as I cupped my ears and blew into my gloves.

"It was Mies van der Rohe," I said. "He was the guy who designed it."

"Really?" he asked, not minding being corrected. "Well, maybe Johnson helped."

We got a cab back to my house and he walked me to my door.

"Want to meet my mom?" I asked nervously, hoping she was wearing something other than that dumb yoga tank with the stick figure of the guy doing a sun salutation.

"Not tonight." He winked, taking my hands.

More kisses in our dim, carpeted hallway, quiet except for the echoing wind in the elevator shaft. Who were his friends? I wondered. Why me? Did he like tall, thin girls? Because I was tall but not exactly thin, and I wasn't sure he'd realized that yet. We kissed and kissed, that new kissing you could do forever. I wondered how long my turn with him would last.

3.

"I want to make this," I said as I sat on Vanessa's bed in her large, powder-blue bedroom. I handed her an old photo I'd found of me standing on the beach on Charter Island in a red, white and blue bikini.

"Look at you!" Vanessa said, examining it. "What a cutie. How old were you?"

"Sixish," I said, peering at it next to her.

"You look like you have a big boat sponge or, like, a gigantic maxi-pad under your crotch," she said, and she was right. The bikini bottom sagged in the crotch because the suit was made of crocheted wool. When it was wet, it would stay cold on my skin and never, ever dry. I remembered it being incredibly itchy, but there was something about it I absolutely loved, and looking at the picture reminded me of how much I loved it.

"My grandmother made it for me," I said. "She made blankets mostly, in hideous mustard tones, but she made the bikini, too. I wish she'd made more." I grabbed the photo out of Vanessa's hands. "I remember her taking that picture so clearly. We were on the beach on Charter and it was really early in the morning. We were hiding from my parents after some giant brawl in the middle of the night, after Dad got bombed and called Mom a shit-hair."

Vanessa burst out laughing. "What the hell is a shit-hair?" she asked, reaching over me to a yellow apple on her desk. "Are they dumber than shit-heads? Meaner? Ted, man, he's got a way with words. Thank God he quit the hooch. Now we just need to find him a together young lady." She bit into the apple, spinning it around between her thumb and index finger. "I'm officially off Snickers. I think I'm turning diabetic."

"Do you think I could find a pattern for the bikini?" I asked, tapping the photo.

"I can't imagine who would publish a pattern for something like that," she said, pulling an old canvas tote out of her closet.

"Well, I can," I said. "People are weird."

"Why don't you start with a scarf and see how it goes?"

"I don't want to do a scarf."

"I don't wanna," Vanessa whined. Her black bra strap burrowed into her shoulder and she shoved it to the side. Vanessa had big, beautiful boobs. No points, just circles. "Now, if I'm going to show you, you cannot get frustrated." I sat up against the wall and she moved next to me, pressing a gray, metal crochet hook into my hand. It was thin and cold and I liked the way it felt.

"I won't, I promise," I said.

She fished around in the bag and pulled out a large, messy pile of dark purple yarn. Then she yanked a line off it and took the hook from me. "The first thing you've got to do is cast on, which is basically a series of little knots, also known as chains. Repeat after me . . . *chains*." She did the first two, then moved my fingers around the hook until I got it.

"Do about thirty for a scarf. You want it long and skinny, right?" Her head knocked against mine while she watched, and I could feel her breath on my hands. "Tell me about last night. What's he like? Is he all Arthur Miller–tortured or is he normal?" She lifted my index finger and bent it, like it was a piece of Play-Doh, farther down the hook.

"Vanessa, I like him so much it's freaking me out," I said, clutching the loop that hung precariously from the hook.

"Be specific," Vanessa implored. "What was the place like?"

"Dark and steak-housey, and sort of desolate and empty."

"Sounds *awful*," she said, holding my elbow out as I tried another chain.

"He's a little weird," I admitted.

"How?"

"Well, his family sounds pretty out there. His dad works two days a year and spends the rest of the time going to movies, and his mother's got a degree in public health management, whatever that is, but he says she spends all of her time baking and leafing through old magazines."

"Weird!" Vanessa exclaimed, intrigued.

I remembered to bring the yarn around from the back of the hook, thinking of Will's face, his body, his stillness. "I feel sick," I said. "Is he going to call me?"

"Don't go rexy on me," she said, turning the hook toward my chest.

"I won't."

"Or bulimic. You better not." She took another bite of her apple and chewed loudly. "He'll call. Then you'll 'bandon me for the boy. Perfect, you're getting it. Do a few more and then we'll start the first row." She dropped her apple on the bed, where it made a wet stain on her quilt, and fished in the bag for another hook, this one with a square of flecked beige hanging off it.

"Ooh, what's that?" I asked enviously.

"I just started it." She spread the chains across the hook proudly. "It's going to be a sweater."

"How come you get to do a sweater and all's I get to do is this crap scarf?"

"God, Thea, you're *so* impatient." She rolled her eyes dramatically.

"Do you think when I'm done with this boring eighties scarf, I'll be able to do the bikini?" I asked.

"Let's jump off that bridge when we get to it," she said with a sigh.

4.

By the end of March of my junior year, I had a life-ruining B average. I'd finished the first semester in December with a B-plus, not great compared to everyone else but good enough for me and, more importantly, good enough for Dad.

Dad was forever dreaming up ways in which I could be improved. That was the secret to our relationship. It's what kept him interested.

I went to a "specialized high school" for math and science geeks, but I hated math and was terrible at it. If Dad hadn't quizzed me for a year with those little flash cards held up to his chin, I never would have gotten in. Even though I always majorly screwed up in math, I was usually able to offset it with As or A-pluses in English and history and dumb, extraneous classes like metal shop. But by the end of March of my junior year, I had a B-plus in biochemistry, a C-plus in geometry, a measly B in English and a B-plus in history. I was screwed.

The problem was, I'd stopped doing homework. Will was a second-semester senior and had none, so it became too hard to face mine. I didn't want to do homework. I wanted to be with him. We took long walks after school to the East Village for French fries, or to a café between our place and Dad's, where we drank hot chocolate and lounged for hours on the black velvet couch in the back. The homework was always there, the obscure stress of not doing it getting louder and louder as the afternoons wore on.

When the March grades came in, Mom called Dad and he cornered me at one of our Wednesday-night dinners.

"Look, Thea, you need to try harder," he said, yanking his tie loose. "You're a junior. This is your most important year, for Christ's sake. The grades at the end of this semester are crucial. This is it, kiddo, you know that. You've got to get it back up to at least a B-plus. At *least*! I don't know what's going on—Mom says you've got some new boyfriend. Maybe you're going through something, but you've got to try harder."

"I *am* trying," I squealed, pissed that Mom had told him about Will.

"What's the situation with the tutors?" he asked, curling his hands into problem-solving fists.

"I'm going to Binder for biochem and geometry."

"He does both?"

"Mmm-hmmm."

"How often do you go?"

"Once a week. We do an hour on each."

"That's it?" he demanded, shoving his glasses up the bridge of his thin, narrow nose.

"That's *enough*." I thought of Mr. Binder sitting at his dining room table in his boiling hot apartment, waiting for me in his yellow undershirt. How my elbows would get sore from leaning on his lace tablecloth. If Will, science-fair-finalist Will, found out I had a tutor, I thought, he would realize what a dumbass I truly was and that would be it. Game over. I had a fantasy of going to some progressive private school where my homework would be to read *Madame Bovary* and to create and perform an interpretive dance based on it. But Dad believed in public education. "If you don't go, who will?" he said. He actually believed that if he sent his daughter to public school, other investment bankers would follow.

"Well, I'll say it once again, this semester is crucial, Thea," he said, pausing with his hands in the air.

"I know, I know," I said, watching him chew. He always looked like he was grinding his teeth rather than eating.

"So what's your first choice these days?" Dad asked, taking a roll from the basket in front of us.

"I don't know," I said, relieved he'd changed the subject but annoyed at his lame, forced switch to the aspirational, his fallback. "I'm thinking it might be good to stay in New York."

"What about Wesleyan?" Dad had gone to Wesleyan. We both knew it was rapidly becoming a pipe dream, given my plummeting grades, but he liked to dream.

"I'm a New Yorker. A city girl. I think I'd get bored."

"Hardly," he said.

"NYU's still within my reach if I do well on the SATs. And I'd be close to home."

He threw salt from the shaker onto his roll in jerky bursts, as though the salt weren't coming out.

"What's wrong with that?" I asked.

"Nothing," he said. "Let's get cracking on the grades so we have some options, shall we?"

"'Let's'? I believe it's 'You get cracking, Thea.' Last I checked, you've been out of school for, like, decades?"

He took a deep breath, as though trying to suppress some deep, white-collar rage he felt toward me and my lack of ambition. "You know, Mommy never finished school," he said.

"Yeah, but who cares? She ran her own business."

"I think she suffered for it," he said. "She's savvy but undisciplined. That, in my mind, is a result of not having a good, solid education. I don't want you traveling down that route."

"None of her friends in Gloucester went to college. If you're smart and creative, it's a waste of time."

"Not exactly," he said, his left eye twitching slightly, as if he were imparting some secret knowledge he wasn't supposed to. During moments like those, hearing his tight, confined sentences and comparing them to Mom's loud rush of words, I wondered how they ever got together in the first place.

I sat back, tossing my napkin onto my plate, knowing how much Dad hated seeing dirty napkins on plates. "I should get home," I said. "I have tons of homework."

"Let's get you home, then," Dad said, wincing at the napkin or me, I couldn't tell.

5.

Mom went to a real estate conference over a long weekend in May. I was supposed to stay at Dad's, but I'd neglected to mention to her that Dad was going to be at a banking conference in Bermuda, and they didn't bother checking with each other anymore.

"Who is it?" I asked, even though the doorman had already told me on the intercom.

"It's the plumber," Will answered in a low monotone. "I've come to fix the sink." He jumped just a little when I opened the door, and it occurred to me that he was nervous too.

It was weird having a boy in our white, fluffy-kitten apartment. Mom rarely had any men over. Alex, her married, veiny-templed boyfriend, occasionally. But Alex was so wimpy, slithering into her room like it was a hole in the wall, like a mouse fleeing danger. Will was different. A foreign mass our house had to reconcile itself with. We sat down on the living room couch and he picked up Mom's long strand of wooden beads, spinning them around on his finger.

"This place is cool." He smiled, looking around. "It's exactly how I pictured it. Took you long enough to invite me."

"I've invited you before," I protested, mashing my knees together to make my legs look thinner.

"Just that one time," Will said. "When I walked you upstairs, the first night we went out. After that, nothing. What I can't figure out is whether you're scared to have *me* meet her or to have *her* meet me." He leaned toward me and batted his eyes.

"Need I remind you that I've yet to meet your parents?"

25

"You will, sometime soon," he said. "Not that that's anything to look forward to. Anyway, your mom has nice taste. Minimal, for lack of a more imaginative word. My parents are stuck in Shakerville. When people come over, they're like, 'Dude, you Amish?'"

"Maybe they like to keep it simple," I said.

"Nah, they're just too depressed to figure anything else out. To change anything. They're big wallowers."

"But you," I said perkily, "you're not depressed. You're an optimist."

"That's right," he said, sticking his thumbs under his armpits, mock-proudly. "I said that on our first date, didn't I?"

I nodded, pulling my hair out of its messy knot, subconsciously channeling my mother and trying to "lift" the front.

Will stretched, reaching his hands behind his head. "So what do you and Mom eat for dinner?"

"Salad in summer, stir-fry in winter," I said, pulling my T-shirt down over the lower bit of my stomach as I leaned back next to him. "That's pretty much the way it works around here. She's a vegetarian."

He took my hand and slowly waved it around with his. "Rembrandt's was closed this week because of a flood," he said, referring to the restaurant his parents went to every night for dinner. "They almost couldn't cope. Dad made us breakfast last night. Ham and cheese omelets and a head of iceberg with salsa. Real lettuce scares him. He came home at five last night. I couldn't believe it. Usually he's home after seven. He likes us to think he's coming home from a long day at the office, but everyone knows he's actually been at the Israeli market buying cashews."

"He really works only two days a year?" I asked, looking

at the brown, braided belt around his impossibly narrow waist, which only reminded me of my never-ending, visceral need for underbaked chocolate cookies.

"Yes, and he wouldn't have it any other way. He's not exactly a people person."

"He must be very smart," I said.

His left eye darted around my face quizzically. "I don't think you have to be that smart to get a job like that."

I didn't say anything. Even after three months of being together, there was something so intimidating about him.

"Anyway, this is too friendly, what we're doing," he said, his gaze fixed on the black and white photos of me and Mom across the room. "I don't want to be friends right now."

"You don't?" I asked, feeling my stomach flip.

"I do want to be your friend—who wouldn't want to be your friend." He said it fast as a statement, not a question, putting his hand, which was hot and shaking just a little, on my knee. "But right now I want to jump on you. And if we keep talking, I'm worried it will be too late."

We looked at each other for this crazy, scary moment that seemed to stretch on and on as the white living room grew gray and hazy behind him. He pushed me backward on the couch and got on top of me, kissing my face, then my mouth, our bodies matching up in a straight line, all the way down. He was heavy, almost too heavy, but I felt safe and enclosed as he undid my jeans with his confident, searching hand. He did whatever it was that he did to me and I felt the couch somehow drop away, and it was like for a few seconds I entered some alternate universe where everything was humming and buzzing and not really real.

It's not like I was a novice. I had two boyfriends before

Will. First was Bo Brown, the summer after seventh grade. We fooled around a lot. Never anything past second, but he basically had his hands and his mouth all over my boobs all summer. I never got tired of it. We swam out to the rocks that led into the Charter Island harbor once and Bo did his thing, his spit, metallic-tasting from his braces, washing over me with the salt water. It must have been the weekend, because Dad was there. I remember seeing his big, bald head from the water, shining in the sun. He was up on a ladder, painting something on the side of the house.

"Thea Galehouse, for Christ's sake, are you aware that there's a riptide?" he yelled at the house, not at me, which made him look deranged. "It could have swept you right out. Jesus!" I hoped he'd seen us.

Michael Cunningham was the second. I was fifteen and he said he was nineteen, but it turned out he was actually twenty-four. I met him hitting tennis balls against the backboard in the park across the street from our apartment. But he was a stoner, and after a while it started to freak me out. There's smoking pot and there's smoking pot. Mom got it way before I did, after meeting him for a split second in our lobby.

"Tell me it's just marijuana," she said.

"Huh?" I asked.

"What's he on?"

I shook my head. Too dumb to play dumb.

"I'd rather you didn't spend time with him. Irrelevant, I realize, but don't do drugs with him. Come to me if you want to get high."

But the stuff with Bo and Michael had been nothing like *this*. I get it now, I kept thinking as I lay underneath Will, I get it. After a while I felt a wet spot by my hip.

"I told you, I'm a class act," he said, embarrassed. "Sorry."

I nudged him to my side and we lay like that forever, in a little astrodome of lips and rough, salty skin amid the fading Friday-afternoon light.

"Galehouse Rock," he said, running his finger along my hairline. "G-Rock. Your eyes are always open. Every time I open my eyes, your eyes are open."

"Like bug-eyed?" I asked. "Like I'm a meth addict?"

"No, you freak." He laughed, prying my eye wider with his thumb and index finger. "You're just taking it all in. You don't look like you have a lot of judgment going on in there. I like it."

"I judge," I said.

"I know you judge yourself. I'm going to bet you give yourself the business. Anyone who has Fiona Galehouse for a mother can't help but be a little cracked."

"Thanks," I said.

"I mean it as a compliment," he said, bumping his nose against mine. "You're welcome."

We ate hummus and carrots, drank Mom's white wine and talked, finally falling asleep on the rug under the coffee table. We woke up Saturday and fooled around all day, did everything but, then did it for the first time Sunday. We were going to do it, then we weren't, and then we finally did, right before he was about to leave.

"You don't want to wait a little longer?" he asked, sliding a condom on dexterously with one hand. It was clear to me he'd done it before.

"Nope," I answered.

"Big of me to ask, though, right?"

It was a big deal, but not in the way I expected. I was

expecting to be transformed into someone I felt like I was supposed to know, but hadn't met yet—the ten-years-older version of me. I'd imagined her hiding behind a midnight-blue velvet curtain, and I thought that when I finally had sex, the curtain would go up and there she would be—the new me, and the *old* me, that little girl digging her short fingernails into an orange on a January night, she would disappear forever. But she was still there, with her goofy secret wave and all.

After we did it, I took a picture of Will lying in between two of my bears. They lay in the same position, the three of them naked with my pink flannel sheet covering their chests, each with their left arms sticking out stiffly at their sides. I lined up their heads in the frame and got on top of Will.

"You know," I said, framing the shot, "when I was little and I went to work with Mom and saw that guy in the cage at Fiona's, his giant penis scared the crap out of me. It was covered by his green leotard, but it was, like, you could see the outline of it, which was almost scarier than the real thing. But yours is different. It's friendly looking. Pretend you're sleeping."

Will closed his eyes, trying not to smile. "Do you think the bears have feelings?"

"Of course," I said. "I know they love *you,* for one thing. They just have a hard time showing it."

I heard heels clonking down the hall and froze. "I'm home." Mom peered into the room. The clock on my desk said six-thirty. The last time I'd looked it was two o'clock. I was straddling Will on top of the covers and thanked God I'd thrown on a tank top and my underwear. "I see you're having a cozy time of it."

Will stared up at the ceiling, frozen like the bears.

"How was the conference?" I asked, not looking at her.

She moved farther down the hall to her room without answering. We got a grip, threw on some clothes and crept toward the kitchen. Will was right on some level: I hadn't had him over because I wasn't sure Mom would like him. You had to prove yourself first, have a story of intense personal suffering to be worthwhile in her eyes.

"Why is everyone so stupid today?" she said, crashing into the kitchen counter with some plastic shopping bags. "That damned Rolf." To an outsider she would definitely look slightly mad, with her red eyes and smudged fire-engine-red lipstick.

"What'd he do?" I asked, relieved that the focus was off us and our sexual misadventures.

"He's just a tosser," she said simply. "That thing I needed to go out Friday morning before I left is still there. Such an attitude. I wish they'd fire him." She looked pointedly at Will. "Hi."

"Mom, this is Will," I said.

"Hello, Will." She held out her hand.

"How do you do," he said, shaking it.

"Very well, thank you," she said, an amused smirk sneaking across her face at his formality. She turned away and pulled toilet paper and toothpaste out of the bags.

"What's going on?" I asked as nonchalantly as possible.

"Sort of a rubbish weekend," she muttered, twisting the plastic bag into a knot and throwing it into the cabinet under the sink. "Had an unpleasant meeting with Don Trainer. I've known this man for twenty-five years. But he's a bridge burner, which you should never be in that business." She peeled waxy paper away from a hunk of dark yellow cheese. "Will, would you like to try some Old Amsterdam?"

31

"I'd love some, thanks."

She scraped a thin slice. "I shouldn't share this, it's too good," she fake whispered.

"I appreciate it, Fiona," he said. I looked at Mom. She didn't seem to mind the first name.

"I thought you said you didn't want to work with that guy," I said.

"I didn't but he called again, and you know."

"Mom."

"What?"

"Lose the losers in your life."

"Don't I know it." She winked at Will, chewing.

"You're right, this is very good," he said. He got up and went to the fridge and pulled out a can of Diet Coke, which he cracked open and drank. Again, Mom didn't bat an eye.

"You keep saying you want to pursue the real estate thing, so why don't you partner up with someone you actually like?" I asked.

"I don't know, Thee." She sighed, leaning toward the kitchen counter. "I don't know."

Will stayed for dinner; he helped Mom by chopping up broccoli and dumping it into the pot when she said, "Okay, now."

"I like him," she said when we were on her bed later that night. "He's gorgeous, Thea, you didn't tell me."

"Yes, I did," I said. I was sitting next to her on the bed with the purple mess of yarn Vanessa had given me to crochet the scarf. It had been sitting in a sad pile on my radiator for months, but for some reason that night I was determined to untangle it and roll it up into a neat ball, even though I had many, many unread pages of biochemistry sitting on my desk.

"What's that?" she asked, as though I had a dead mouse on my lap.

"Just some yarn Vanessa gave me," I said.

"Anyway, he's gorgeous in that truly American way," she said, fishing for the TV remote, which was buried under a pile of magazines and notes to herself. "Like someone is pointing a blower at him, keeping him awake and bushy-tailed. He's got no pretension. He's an old soul."

I rolled my eyes, leading the end strand of the yarn through a series of snarls and pulling.

"What?" she asked. "I'm not saying it lightly. He has a maturity about him."

"When you say 'old soul,' it cheapens it."

"Oh, well." She scowled. "Terribly sorry to cheapen it. What's wrong with his eye?"

"You mean, how it wanders?" I asked, rolling what I'd untangled into a small, kitten-sized ball. "He looked up at an acorn tree when he was little. Isn't that cute?"

"He can get it fixed," she said, muting the TV. "He's quite funny, actually. He'll seem sort of serious, but then he breaks into that lovely grin, quite at the drop. Which is nice. You don't want anyone too heavy, Thea. That's for sure. I was always going for the darkish ones. Like Daddy. But dark is actually boring, lo and behold. Anyway, Will is welcome anytime. You can tell him I said that."

"You're not mad at me?" I asked.

"I'm not mad," she said. "A little jealous, maybe—"

"Mother!" I said, dreading what was coming next. I don't like talking about sex. I don't bond over it. My mother has always provided me with far too many details. About how Bruce, her orange-tanned, social-worker ex-boyfriend, nibbled his way up her thighs until he found her spot and brought her off, or how one of the backers of Fiona's who she ended up screwing had a penis that curved like a scimitar. Mom was purposefully graphic because, she said, she didn't want me to be a victim.

"I'm kidding," she said, laughing. "That was tacky. Sorry. Just don't do anything stupid. Should we put you on the pill?"

"I don't know," I said. The pill was for older, more mature people who were serious about sex. "Yeah, maybe. Please don't tell Dad."

"Oh God, why would I do that?" she said, starting to read the program guide on the screen. "He'd just blame me. You're seventeen, for God's sake. It's none of his business."

By the time I untangled the last bunch of knots, I had a nice ball of yarn the size of a tennis ball. I squeezed it, letting little images from the amazing, perfect weekend with Will drift by. The way he slept in a fetal position with his leg curled up around my waist reminded me of the framed *Rolling Stone* cover on the wall in Mom's bathroom where John Lennon is lying curled up around Yoko Ono. I took the crochet hook and stabbed it into the ball. It looked like a piece of sculpture or artwork, full of weight and purpose. When I pulled the hook out, it brought a couple of strands of yarn with it and I thought, That's my heart right now—stabbed by a blunt object, with little bits of heart mush oozing out. That's my heart. My heart is hooked.

6.

All spring, I expected Will to graduate and that would be that. He would realize how silly this thing with me was, given the sea of women about to become available to him in September. So June took on a Lifetime-television-for-women quality, like soon Will would . . . die tragically of leukemia.

But we didn't break up. When school ended, we got summer jobs, me at Mom's friend Ella's shop on Lexington Avenue, he at a law firm, and we'd meet every day for hot dogs in Central Park, sweaty and irritable.

We drove to Charter Island one weekend in July and made it to the station by 8:05 to pick up Dad, who'd caught a train at Grand Central after work. I saw the train pull up and there he was, his head in the window, looking down at some "important documents." I thought of Mom and her fits of rage as they were splitting up. "Tosser marches off to rehab the second Bill Mindorff raises a red flag, but we don't count for rubbish."

Was it true? If it was true, why didn't he try to change? To shift his priorities around a little bit? It seemed stubborn and selfish of him not to try, and look where it got him: facing backward on a train on a Friday night, his shoes stuck to old newspapers, another summer closing in on him.

"I can't understand why anyone would want to endure I-95 when there's that perfectly nice Metro-North," Dad said as he got into the car, carrying stale train air with him. "You must be Will." They shook hands and I saw it right away in his eyes: this was the reason his daughter wouldn't be going to Wesleyan.

"Nice to meet you, Ted," said Will. Dad glared at Will.

I knew he was put out by the first name. I wished he would relax and not sit so straight in his seat, his wide head like a cement block in front of me.

"We had decent luck on the way up, not much traffic, thank God," Will said as we pulled out of the parking lot.

"I have a car, but it sits in the garage by my apartment most of the time," Dad responded.

"What kind of car do you drive?" Will asked in an overly chummy way.

"An eighty-four Aston Martin."

"Oh man, I would love to see that."

"A fellow at work sold it to me when he took a job in capital markets in London," Dad said placidly.

"So I hear you're a banker," Will said, stopping a little too short at a red light. "What area are you in?"

"It has to do with risk," Dad said vaguely, as if Will couldn't handle a complete definition.

"Is that why you're in it?" Will asked.

I squirmed in the backseat. The question was sassy and Dad ignored it.

"Did you two have dinner?" Dad asked.

"We did," I said. We'd stopped at McDonald's on the way up, and the car still smelled like heat-blasted strawberry milk shakes. "We were starving. Sorry."

There were whitecaps on the water that glowed under the moon as we drove toward the house. We parked on the gravel and I led Will to the guest room, where he dropped his bag and swung old tennis racquets and picked up books from the stacks on the table. I was glad Dad was still upstairs when Will went to the kitchen and opened cabinets. The snack cabinet was packed with family-sized bags of chips and Goldfish that Dad kept around in case people came over for a sand-wich or drinks. I wondered if Will thought it was weird that a grown man who lived in a house by himself had giant bags of junk food in his closet. I was always wondering what Will thought. He took an old metal pinwheel off a shelf in the li-brary and went out to the porch to watch it spin. I sat down next to him on the damp wicker couch and before long, Dad came out in jeans and a brand-new Harvard Business School sweatshirt.

"So, nice to have you up here." He nodded and raised his Coke to us ceremoniously before he placed it deliberately onto a coaster, then pulled the legs of his jeans up and lowered him-self to his chair.

Will leaned forward on the couch next to me. "This is a beautiful spot, Ted. It must have been wonderful to grow up here." I looked around. It was what you would call a casual house. Sailing trophies were strewn around on shelves, and a rack of croquet mallets jutted out into the living room. But that was my grandmother. Not Dad. Dad was so uptight, so stiff and ill at ease, I wondered how he could have any friends. I could tell that Dad thought Will was out of line, calling him Ted again. I could almost see him squirming and seething in his chair. He sat with his knees together, as though he were hold-ing in pee, gripping his glass on the table next to him.

"Thea doesn't come up as much as she used to," he said. "This is a treat."

"What are you talking about?" I said. "I was here last weekend."

"We've got to get you up on skis," he said, turning to Will. "We took her out last weekend and it's the damnedest thing. She just can't stand up."

"You rev the engine too much," I said, making a fist and turning it. "You've got to go lighter. You jerk me around. Literally."

"She's never gotten up," he said to Will, ignoring me. "I can't figure it out. Her feet are exactly where they should be, her legs—"

"Dad, hello? What did I just say? It's too much of a jolt."

"No one else . . . the Hendricksons didn't seem to have any problem with it. I think it has more to do with your stance. You lean over too far."

"Well, how about I lean back next time and you pull the throttle to half where you were pulling it." I remembered floating sickly in the water, hanging on and wanting to let go, anticipating the smack down. Everyone on the boat turned to the water, watching me, except Dad, his head turned away, hand gripping the throttle.

"We'll get you up one of these days," he said. "By golly, we're going to make it happen!"

Why had he brought this up out of nowhere? I heard Jim, the caretaker, come in through the kitchen door and start to get Dad's dinner ready. Jim had looked after the house for my grandmother, and after she died, Dad kept him on and the job somehow evolved into shopping and cooking for him on the weekends. The house looked more formal, fancier, than it actually was. Dad sighed and closed his eyes in forced relaxation, then glanced at Will.

"How'd you like to go fishing tomorrow morning?"

"I'd love it," Will answered, overly enthused. "What time?"

Dad got up and walked over to the tide chart hanging on a pillar.

"The optimum is three hours or so before dead high," he said. "So, five or six."

"Ouch," said Will.

Dad looked at Will like he'd said a word he didn't understand.

"What the hell." Will slapped his legs. "I'm game. Morning air. Good for the brain." He broke into a wide, jovial grin. He looked slightly ignited, a little too hungry, next to me in the dim light.

"All right, then," Dad said. "We have a taker."

Dad had never once asked me to go fishing. Sailing, yes, but fishing was a man's thing. This infuriated me—how he could complain that I didn't spend enough time with him, then spend the day devising new ways to get away from me when I was actually there.

"Let's go for a walk," I said to Will.

"Sure," he said.

Dad stood up. "I'll tap on your door at around quarter of tomorrow," he said.

"Would that be quarter of five or quarter of six?" Will asked.

"Six," Dad said. "Let's sleep in a little." He winked as if he'd just said something very sly. I cringed. What a nerd. "You two have a nice walk," he said, and started for the dining room. Will and I went out and found his sandals on the front porch. We headed down the street, and through a crack in the hedges I could see Jim lighting two tall, white candles and pouring water into a crystal glass. Dad tucked his napkin into his sweatshirt collar, lord of the manor, commencing his meal.

My bare heels banged against the pavement, and our shadows grew taller and thinner under a lone streetlamp.

"How glad are you that you're not a fifty-year-old divorced investment banker with no life?" I said.

"*So* glad," Will said, looking back toward the dining room window. "Who's that guy waiting on him?"

"It's just Jim," I said. "He's been around forever. He helps Dad out on the weekends."

"Nice," Will said, his expression hard to read underneath the dim yellow streetlamp.

7.

They went fishing the next morning for three hours while I sat on the porch eating Grape Nuts, worrying Will would catch something and show Dad up, or not catch anything at all and feel like a failure. He ended up catching one lonely snapper, which he threw back.

I watched Jim go into the kitchen that night with moving brown-paper bags, remembering how Mom would run screaming from the kitchen when she saw those bags. Eventually she would boycott lobster night altogether.

I pulled out some old green-glass salad plates shaped like crescents.

"I'd wash them," Jim said sheepishly. He filled the big black pot with water.

When the water was boiling, Jim squeezed the tops of the lobsters' heads, which he said deadened the pain, then threw them in. Will came downstairs and smiled, his back to the pot, when he heard the lobsters hissing.

The wind had died down, so we ate outside on the porch while Jim cleaned up the kitchen. Dad focused on his food, and we would have eaten in complete silence if Will hadn't started talking.

"Did you spend a lot of time here when you were a kid, Thea?" Will asked me, his lips glistening with butter and salad dressing.

"We would come up for a week or two in the summer," I said, "but most of the time I went to day camp in the Bronx. Mom didn't like it here."

"Fiona was not one for island life," Dad said as the claw he was cracking fell into the butter. "This island, anyway."

"That's hard to imagine," Will said. "It's beautiful here. It's one of the most beautiful spots I've ever seen."

Dad stared at his plate, chewing, avoiding Will's eyes. I begged him in my head to at least acknowledge the compliment.

"When Thea was little, she used to think lobsters were monsters," he said. "She'd see the bags and run outside, all the way out to the end of the bluff. Remember, you wouldn't come in until they turned red?"

"Well, it was hard to watch Mom freak out and not think something terrible was happening."

"Thea was also afraid of rain." Dad rose suddenly, scraping his chair, and went to the pillar in the corner. "See what I did here? I haven't shown you, have I? I moved them."

"Moved what?" I asked.

"Your height measurements."

I got up and went over, followed by Will.

He turned on a lamp. "I marked it all up on a tape, so I think it's still pretty accurate." I looked at the markings, immediately remembering the sensation of a pencil being leveled on top of my head: the first when I was around a year old, then every few months after that, the gaps ranging from incremental to gaping, depending how much time passed in between. The original markings had been done in different-colored pens, and Mom had done some of the early ones, so the handwriting looked different from year to year, depending on which one of them wrote it. But now the markings were uniformly etched in black graphite, Dad's script as neat and tight as a calligrapher's.

"Why did you move them over here?" I asked.

"The chairs kept smacking against the pillar by the table, so when the porch was finally painted last fall, I transferred them over here, out of harm's way," Dad said. "It's a wonder you ever grew at all, given how much you hated vegetables. Do you remember how crazy we used to get?"

I nodded, remembering the nauseating stench of corn-on-the-cob steam escaping from a jiggling lid. Nana, of course, blamed my mother and her lack of discipline in raising me.

"But now look at you," he said. "A broccoli fanatic. And salad. Salad was the first thing you started to come around on, if I remember correctly. Salad with little cherry tomatoes."

He looked me up and down, arms stiffly at his sides, and it was like I could read his mind: she needs to lose a few pounds. After the divorce I'd become Mom's property and therefore vaguely distasteful to him.

"Let's eat," he said, steering us back to the table.

"So where do you get the lobsters?" Will asked. "Do you guys have a trap out there?" He elbowed toward the water.

"No, it's illegal now, you need a license. Thea, why are we eating salad off ashtrays?"

"What?" I asked. "I thought they were salad plates."

"These were Nana's and they're actually ashtrays," Dad said, picking up his plate and holding it at his chest. "This gives you an indication of how much they used to smoke. They would lay these out all over the house during cocktail parties."

"They really do look like plates," Will mused. "Were you ever a smoker, Ted?"

Dad nodded, mashing his napkin across his mouth. "Two packs a day at one point. I'd somehow resisted temptation all through college. I raced crew and played lacrosse, so I took that very seriously. But when I met Thea's mother, actually, that's when I took it up."

"Right, all her fault," I chimed in.

"I'm not saying that, Thea," he said, looking at me pointedly. "No one to blame but myself on that front." He pushed his bowl of empty lobster shells away from him, toward the glass-enclosed candle in the middle of the table. "I think I got caught up in all the headiness of it, you know, the parties, the scene, all that. They all smoked."

"What brand?" I asked. I pictured him slouched in his chair in the living room, drunk.

"Camel Lights, whatever was around. Anyway, needless to say, I hope you don't fall down that little rabbit hole," he said, rattling his glass of ice and draining it of water. "Nicotine addiction is no prize. It's been, what . . . almost a decade? And still, I'd kill for a cigarette."

"Really?" I laughed.

"Oh, absolutely," he said, smiling and shaking his head. "Absolutely. It never really went away for me. And sometimes at work . . ." His voice trailed off.

"What about a drink?" I blurted, surprising myself. His drinking was more of a taboo subject for me than sex. To bring it up was not just embarrassing but dangerous. I still had pervasive, floating fears that he'd start again. And somewhere in my head I believed that if he started again, it would do him in. Whether it was true or not, that's what I believed.

"That too," he said, his face stiffening, closing up. He watched Will's reaction, gauging how much I'd told him.

"I could see how they'd go hand in hand," Will said.

Dad nodded, chuckled skittishly. "Not too clearly, I hope."

"How did you stop?" Will asked.

"The same way I stopped drinking," he said quickly. "I put my mind to it." He leaned back in his chair and crossed his leg.

"Was it hard?" Will asked, wide-eyed, encouraging. I could hear it in his voice. He was digging for color, but I knew he wouldn't get any. "Did you have, like, withdrawal symptoms?"

"With the drinking I did, sure," he said. "The smokes were more of a habit. But like any smoker, I guess, a beloved one."

"What do you miss most?" Will asked.

"What, about smoking?"

"Or the drinking, or both."

Dad arched his eyebrows skeptically. "You're extremely interested. . . ."

"I just mean a successful guy like you, you know, you had these . . . demons that you conquered, so to speak." Will sat back and crossed his legs, jiggling his foot on his thigh. "The partying, you know, you and Fiona, boozing it up, getting high, it seems very glamorous from where I'm sitting."

Dad looked at Will carefully. It was definitely crossing the line into too-personal territory and we all knew it, but for some reason Dad talked. "I wouldn't say I miss anything about it. It's more that I miss my youth, and the requisite reckless-ness. I'm in my late forties. I'm human. I feel old."

"You're not old," Will said.

"I'm not young." He let out a forced, theatrical sigh. "You know what's funny? I miss being married. It's funny how I associate smoking with marriage."

"You miss being married?" I asked.

"Of course I do. Does that surprise you?"

"Uh, yeah," I answered in my best teenager voice. Mom once told me men were like dumb little pups, sitting in a window waiting for a home, any home.

"Well, it shouldn't." He smiled. "Enough about me and my checkered past. Who wants dessert? I think Jim picked up a Fruits of the Farm pie."

Jim appeared silently in the kitchen doorway. I wondered what he'd heard.

"Jim, were you able to get your hands on anything at Chelmsfords?" Dad asked conspiratorially.

"I got lucky," Jim answered.

"Music to my ears," Dad said, rubbing his hands together as Jim brought out the pie and set it in front of him. "Who wants a slice? Food. Pie. That's my downfall now. Who?"

8.

Mom stood by my door with a pair of jeans under her arm and her white sunglasses on top of her head. "What in God's name are you doing?" she asked.

"Crocheting," I said, gathering the ball of purple yarn farther up my lap. "Vanessa taught me."

"God, you're giving me chills," she said. "You are single-handedly conjuring the horror of Evelyn Galehouse," she murmured, meaning Dad's mother, my grandmother. "The way her fingers twitched when she made those awful blankets! She would always *appear* to be so engrossed, but every time I looked, I caught her glaring at me, like the evil little witch she was. Anyway, how can you even look at heavy yarn like that in this heat?"

"It's August, Mom," I said. "It's hot outside. Deal with it."

"What's wrong with you?" she asked, rolling the jeans into a little bun.

"Nothing." I gripped the loop I'd just done tightly with my finger. "Will's moving his stuff up to Columbia today."

"Well, we knew the day would come," she said matter-of-factly. "Honestly, Thee, do not get so wrapped up in this. You have the rest of your life to need a man to be happy."

"I'm not wrapped up."

"Good. Do you have anything for Josephine?" she said, referring to the tailor who worked at the dry cleaners downstairs.

I shook my head. My phone buzzed and Mom jumped. She hated loud, sudden noises and looked at me like the phone ringing was somehow my fault.

"G-Rock, money-love," Will whispered as Mom waved and left. "Wanna come up here and check it out? Help me unpack all my bongs?"

"Okay," I said, squeezing the ball of yarn and smiling from ear to ear. I thought it would be weeks or months until an invitation came. "Do you need anything?"

When I got out of the subway at 116th Street, there were plantains at the vegetable stand on the corner instead of bananas, and the plantains spoke to me. They said: We dare you to succeed in our strange new world. We dare you to try to hold on to him.

The street outside the main building was a sea of cars with lampshades, stuffed animals and stereo speakers on their roofs. A girl ran by in a tennis skirt with a purple boa around her neck.

"Mom, wait!" she shrieked. "I have the keys!"

I walked through two stone pillars into a grand, imposing courtyard and had a flash that I was in some other part of the world—one of those piazzas in Florence, where I'd sucked face with some now-almost-faceless boy—and that I'd be leaving soon, getting on a plane or something. I went into the building, up the stairs and around a corner with a bulletin board displaying ads for used couches and rides. There was a note card tacked to it: "To whoever made a grilled cheese in the lounge toaster 4/23 . . . clean it out, asshole!" I wanted to stare at that board for every clue of what life would be like for him, but I continued down the carpeted hallway, which smelled of cigarettes and Doritos. I passed a huge, plastic black cat with a skinny neck and a pointy snout. It was almost as tall as me, its creepy, imperious eyes following me as I stopped at room 208.

Will's door was ajar and a tall man gazed at me with a sandwich perched at his mouth. I smiled at him and then registered the woman sitting on the bed reading. She didn't look up. A wave of something close to panic overtook me. Will had neglected to mention his parents would be there.

"G-House Rock!" Will yelped, stepping down from a grimy wooden desk chair. He hugged me with a mix of enthusiasm and awkwardness, turning me around by the shoulders to face his parents. "Thee, this is my mom and dad, Phil and Lynne Weston. Guys! This is Thea!"

"Pleasure to meet you," Mr. Weston said, crumbs dangling from his lips. His handshake was surprisingly limp. Mrs. Weston crossed her arms and didn't stand up. Her dark hair was pulled back in a messy ponytail, with little bullets of unruly strands sticking out at the sides. She looked at me with her spooky gray eyes and heavy, arched eyebrows, which somehow had the ability to angle down at me even though I towered over her as she sat on the bed. She and that creepy plastic cat in the hallway automatically morphed into the same person in my head.

"Hello, Thea," she finally said. She had a switch on–switch off smile that zipped across her face, almost like a tic, then disappeared.

"This is my special fwend you've heard so much about," Will said in an off-putting baby voice. On the desk there was a fish tank with two coral reefs and a fake Campbell's soup can propped in the corner of it. A green fish with rainbow-colored gills swam around in a plastic bag inside the tank.

"I didn't know you had fish," I said.

"Not fish," Will said, holding up the plastic bag. "A fish. Ricky, meet G-Rock."

He turned to his father. "Did you remember to throw in the extension cords?"

Mr. Weston nodded blankly at Will. "I should go check the car," he said. He turned to me and I noticed little lakes of long-ago stains on the navy-blue polo shirt that stretched across his belly. "Will is under the impression that double parking is now allowed under some new citywide ordinance," he said, winking at me. "Do you find his laissez-faire attitude toward life as refreshing as we do, Thea?"

I shrugged like a dumb teenager, cursing my cutoffs and

wishing I'd been somehow better equipped for meeting them. I felt blond and fat and didn't know where to stand.

Mrs. Weston picked up a framed poster of a big tree with violins hanging off it like Christmas ornaments. It was for a music festival in the Berkshires in 1969.

"Where do you want this, sweetheart?" she asked, standing to face the dingy, cinder-blocked wall as Mr. Weston almost tripped over a laundry basket stuffed with hangers on his way out.

"I'll do it later, Mom." Will looked at the digital clock that had been plugged in but was still sitting on top of an opened box. "We should go to this reception thing . . . it's already started. Dad, just meet us there, it's down the hall." I saw Mrs. Weston look away as Will put his arm around me, and I had a moment to take in what she was wearing: a white tank top under a too-big, untucked denim shirt.

"Will you be my l'il date, G-Rock?" Will asked, batting his eyes at me.

A large tray of white and orange cheese cubes was the only splash of color in the drab, olive-hued lounge. About thirty kids stood around, some forming triangles with their parents. A guy with short, black hair and a sweater tied around his neck stepped toward us.

"Excuse me, I saw you across the hall from my room," he said. "You're the other lucky one." Mrs. Weston, Will and I stared at him blankly.

"Oh," Will said, "the singles, you mean?" He rubbed his hand through his hair. "Yeah, that was a break, I guess. I tend to be lucky in things that involve sweepstakes."

"My name's Olivier, nice to meet you." He shook Will's hand.

"I'm Will, and this is my mom, and my girlfriend, Thea Galehouse."

Olivier nodded, assessing me with his French eyes. "Listen," he said to Will, "I've asked some people from the hall over for a little thing tonight. I hope you can swing by." He looked and sounded like he couldn't care less if Will came. I dubbed him "Sweaterboy" in my head. So far college seemed like an endless series of "little things" where people stood around avoiding each other. After some more small talk Olivier cleared his throat. "I'm just off the plane from Paris this morning, so I'm starting to fade. Time for a catnap." He nodded again and sort of bowed to Mrs. Weston, whose smile switched on and off as he walked away.

"So, Thea, you're a senior now, is that right?" Mrs. Weston nibbled on a cube of cheese and bored into me with her gray eyes, which looked somehow icier now that she was standing by a window. "What are your plans? How is Thea Galehouse going to set the world on fire?"

"Good question," I said, belching out a stiff, truncated laugh. "Haven't quite tackled that one." I looked around the room at all the tall, tanned kids oozing summer relaxation in their new olive-hued lounge, and felt suddenly overwhelmed. How was I going to face senior year without Will? Take the SATs? Apply to colleges? Write essays? How was I going to do any of it? Dad's face flashed in front of me. His intense, steely scrutiny, demanding results and performance. How was I supposed to be a normal high school student when I had this rope pulling me here? It wasn't fair that Will had gotten away to this place, to his own room with the plastic cat in the hall and Sweaterboy across the way, while I still had this mountain to climb.

Mrs. Weston must have read something on my face

because she paused, orange cheese cube in midair, and said gravely and urgently, "Be positive, Thea."

I nodded, seething at her new age–claptrap comment. Be positive. Could two words in the English language be more meaningless?

"Frankly, I think your generation has it made," she said, folding her arms. "Mine was still scatterbrained. Too many mixed messages from our mothers." She tapped her bony temple with her fingertip. "Anyway, Thea, I wish you every success. We need strong women like you out there, forging ahead with great things." Will looked at me, wide-eyed, as if to say, Don't mind her, she's crazy.

Mr. Weston appeared next to Mrs. Weston and cleared his throat. "There's an officer circling the cars downstairs. Lynne, I think we should make ourselves scarce." He seemed to always have the same smiling expression on his face, as though he were cracking deeply ironic personal jokes to himself all the time. He pulled his glasses off and rubbed them with his shirt as he turned to Will. "You all set?"

"Yep," Will answered, giving his father a hug with half his body and patting his back.

Mrs. Weston turned to me and held her hand out formally. "Goodbye, Thea," she said pointedly, and I understood the gesture right away: she believed she was saying goodbye to me forever.

They ambled side by side through the swinging doors as Will started to reach for a toothpick to pick up a cube of cheese. He glanced at me and retracted.

"You could have told me they'd be here," I said.

"I didn't tell you?" he asked. He reached again and this time popped a cube into his mouth. "Sorry."

"Your mother hates me."

"What are you talking about?" Will rolled his eyes and stuck the toothpick in the side of his mouth. "She wouldn't know how to hate you. What was all that about setting the world on fire, or whatever she said? She's a repressed bra burner, stuck in the seventies."

"Did you hear her tell me to be positive?" I asked, realizing that other people in the room were tentatively striking up conversations with their hall mates. I felt like I was holding Will back. He looked around quickly at everyone, then leaned toward me.

"I must have you. Now. Let's blow." He chucked his toothpick into a grimy, black wastepaper bin and we pushed through the swinging doors.

Back in his room, Will lifted the vinyl-upholstered bolster running along the side of his bed and gestured to the shelves underneath. "You can put your exfoliators and night creams and whatnot in there," he said, grabbing my ass. He pushed me down on the bed, angling my body away from a bag of opened fish-tank gravel as a warm rush accosted my stomach. It never ceased to amaze me how quickly sex worked.

"Nice intro to your bad boy," I said. Usually he played around with me down there before the main attraction. "Don't mind me, I'll just lie here."

"Sorry, I'm feeling very . . . focused," he said, thrusting.

"You like fucking me in your new room?" I whispered.

"God, yes," he said. There was the sound of footsteps running down the hall and I felt that letting-go, almost sick feeling, our backs growing sweaty on his bare, unmade mattress.

We lingered in what felt like timelessness afterward as the room got darker, listening to the constant stream of noise out in the hall. The bad thoughts started crowding back in. *Be positive*. Schmee schmositive.

"Have I mentioned that your mother hates me?" I asked.

"She doesn't hate you," Will said, running his fingers along my boobs. "She's just an odd bird. They're in their own little rabbit world." When the room was pitch-black, I got up and felt around for my sneakers.

"Do you really have to go?" he asked, pulling my hand.

I nodded and kissed him, turning on a light. I wanted to stay, but my heart was already aching at the thought of leaving and I wanted to get it over with.

"Good night, G-Rock, Rocker-G, Special Sauce." He stood up, naked, his distracted, disgruntled expression reminding me of Dad's whenever I left at the end of a weekend. Like he didn't want me to go, but at the same time his head was already somewhere else.

part two

9.

As a special parting gift from Stuyvesant—a final act of cruelty—
I was awarded zero-period gym my senior year, which meant
I had to be in the girls' locker room by quarter of eight each
ever-darkening morning. After school Vanessa and I had SAT
prep on Twenty-Third Street, and then we'd go for coffee and
anxiously bark vocabulary words at each other while doing
our other homework.

I got home late one night in October and heard Mom's TV.
I was in a phase where I'd decided to stop worrying about her.
She'd passed the real estate test and she had two new listings,
so she had stuff to keep her busy. I was glad she was awake, in
bed with a hunk of white, runny cheese, her latest obsession.

"How was the class?" She held a cracker out at me, still
looking at the TV.

"I'm totally fried," I said. "It's too much. I can't wait till it's
over."

Mom said nothing and went back to her cheese. Her bed
was overgrown with mail and dry cleaning hangers. I made my
way to it, using the flashing TV light to navigate.

She was watching a movie where two kids were getting
married, and they didn't want a big wedding but their parents
did. It was a movie from the fifties. I could tell because the girl
character started every sentence with "Why," as in "Why, I
wouldn't dream of going to the picnic without you."

The guy on TV was yelling. "Maybe we should forget the
whole darn thing!" he said. I turned and leaned my head
against her leg. Her duvet smelled like nail polish remover.

"Why can't you be more like them?" Mom asked, her head
gesturing up at the screen.

"What are you talking about?" I asked.

"They're just so polite and . . . obedient. They respect their parents."

"I respect my parents," I said, although I could hear my own mocking tone of voice.

"Right," she said. She'd cast the cheese onto the pillow next to her and was patting Pond's onto her face. My mother had a penchant for cheap drugstore beauty products. "That rental car company is still breathing down my back. Honestly, Thea, I got another bill from them today. It's been months since that little episode."

"Really?" I asked sheepishly.

"Yes, still," she said. "We gave you our hard-earned money to go and be on your own and study in another country, and what did you do?" she asked. "You took that money and paraded around the continent doing God knows what." She set the Pond's jar down on her chest and yanked the tie on her robe.

"God, we've been through that so many times already," I said. "Can't we laugh about it yet? Can't it be a story that we have now that we like to pull out of our hats from time to time at parties?"

"Don't be flip, Thea," Mom snapped. "There is absolutely nothing amusing about that episode and there never will be, to me or to Daddy. You could have been in a much more serious accident, or gotten raped or murdered, and we might never have found you."

They'd given me three thousand dollars for a work-study program in London, where I was supposed to take some "new math" course at UCL (Dad's thing) and a design class at Central St. Martins (my thing). I stayed at Mom's older sister's in

Fulham and got a job at a café. But by the beginning of August I was getting really bored. Vanessa was doing an exchange student thing, living with a family outside of Venice, so two weeks before the classes ended, I quit my job, told my aunt, who was clueless, that I was going to visit a friend, and I met up with Vanessa in Italy. I had a thousand euros from the café job and from what Dad had given me, and Vanessa had more, so we took off. I'm not sure why, but I felt like I deserved to do what I wanted, and what I wanted was to go with Vanessa to Portofino and then up to the top of the Matterhorn in Switzerland, to watch the sun rise, and then to Ireland or Scotland, if we had money left, to check out all the beautiful yarn. I love yarn, especially raw, prickly yarn straight off a lamb, in rich, dark colors. It was the best two weeks. We were the dirty Americans. We got drunk and found cute guys everywhere, made out with them in cafés, behind crowded market stalls, in smelly bathrooms. We slept in hostels or in two-star hotels, or sometimes in the train station, on our bags. We'd wake up sweaty and hungover and change our minds about where to go next and find some cheese and bread and stay another day. I'd called Mom and lied, lied, lied, saying I was still in London. I knew she'd never check in with her sister because they didn't get along—Dad had actually been the one to call her and arrange my visit. We would have gotten away with it if I hadn't sideswiped someone in our rented car in Galway, on our way back to Dublin, right at the end. It was the first time I'd used a credit card the whole trip, and I thought I'd be home in time to intercept the bill. But when I returned the car, the rental company called my mother, the primary cardholder, to get her insurance information. After that it was a shit show.

"Such callous disregard, Thea," Dad had said, the pain of

deception knitted into his thin, gray brows. "I'm deeply, deeply, disappointed." Well, so am I, I remember thinking. I'm disappointed that you couldn't figure out a way to stick it out together so I wouldn't have to pack my stupid rolling Swiss Army suitcase every weekend like a traveling monkey and waste my allowance on cab fare to your stupid house by the river—far, far away from any subway, when I'd rather just stay put at Mom's.

"I would think twice before you ever pull a stunt like that again," Mom said, slapping the lid on the Pond's jar.

"Actually, there's this arts program at Edinburgh next summer that I wanted to talk to you about," I said.

She muted the TV and glared at me.

"I'm kidding," I said. The phone rang in my room and I rolled off her bed.

"Don't stay on long," she called. "I can hear you, you know."

"College is so boring," Will said when I answered. "They're all next door. I can hear them."

"Are they eating pineapple pizza?"

"Yeah, that's right, and friggin' taco sandwiches. Hell, I just want to go to sleep. With you. I wish we could be together all the time. I wish you could live in my drawer. I wish I could uncork you from a bottle whenever I wanted. God, I just miss you, Thee."

I breathed in his voice, little pinpricks moving across my chest, as though my heart were waking up from falling asleep.

"Imagine we're really old and you die and everyone sees me trudging up and down First Avenue with my boots undone," he said. "They'd say, 'Poor Vic.'"

"You changed your name?"

"Yeah, I changed my name to Vic, thinking it would make me feel better."

"But it doesn't," I said.

"No, it does not," he said indignantly. "But they all say, 'Poor old Vic, lost the love of his life,' and the other widowers bring me Ovaltine and doughnuts, which I can't eat because I'm so bereft. And they ask me out."

"The widowers? You've gone gay?" I watched puffs of cottony smoke billow from a tower outside my window, thinking, White looks so strange in the dark.

"No, I mean widows," Will said. "The ladies. I take one out a few times, but soon enough, wouldn't you know it, she starts to bug the shit out of me."

"Let me guess, she gets on you about exercising."

"Right. 'Fitness first,' she cackles over and over, like a parrot, so I break up with her because she just reminds me that I don't care about fitness anymore because you're not there. At night I'd lie in my little single bed, remembering G-Rock, my flower girl. Your green eyes that catch fire when you're in the sun and the way your face automatically points to the sky when you laugh. I'd look out my window, at the little sliver of moon and I'd say, 'Damn you, moon, give me back my girl.' I'd curse, then I'd beg, then I'd curse, then I'd beg, all night, every night, till I finally died too."

"Wow," I said.

"Sad, right?"

"So sad."

"Well, maybe it'll end happier than that," he said. "Maybe you won't die and I won't die and we'll live happily ever after forever. We'd be the first people to live forever."

"That'd be nice," I said. I stretched my legs to a cool part of the mattress and pictured us living in a tiny, gold-wallpapered apartment in Paris on the Seine, next to that famous bookstore. How great and weird would it be if we stayed together forever, I thought. High school sweethearts. How great and weird.

10.

"I can't take it," my friend Jill said as she squeezed a slimy lemon onto a wedge of washed-out-looking honeydew. We were cutting fourth period at a coffee shop near school on a brisk morning just before Thanksgiving break. Jill's mother raised Pomeranians and sold them at cut rates. I used to see the handwritten ad at a deli near my house. A sketch of a pug-nosed dog inside a lopsided heart. There were something like twelve Pomeranians living in Jill's apartment, and Jill's mother made her walk the bigger ones every night before she went to bed.

"She makes me carry these tiny wads of tinfoil, which aren't big enough to pick up the poo," she continued. "Then, when they get their periods, they walk around in public in little doggie diapers. People stare at me on the street. I hate her." As I pictured twelve diapered Pomeranians dancing at Jill's feet, a cold, sinking feeling rushed through me. Where was *my* period? I quickly calculated the dates in my head and realized I was a few days—maybe even a week—late. How could it be? I was a sophisticated, sexually active teenager on the pill. But then I remembered the Friday night a few weeks earlier, when

I'd told Mom I was staying at Vanessa's and instead I'd stayed at Will's. I hadn't brought my stuff with me. I'd told myself not to worry and to just forget it and had done a good job of it, until then.

I obsessed over whether or not to test when I got to Dad's apartment that afternoon. Mom was away at a spa in France, and I didn't think I could handle all those days in a row with Dad if the results were positive, so I decided to wait, wishing the weekend were already over. Will was leaving with his family to spend Thanksgiving at his aunt's in New Jersey, and Vanessa was going upstate somewhere. Dad and I were having Thanksgiving dinner at home. A trader who worked for him was coming with his wife.

I went into my bedroom, found my crochet hook and yarn and curled up on Dad's stiff canvas couch, grateful for a tactile distraction. I'd kept the project by my bed at home and I picked it up sometimes when I was on the phone late at night with Will, but after a while it hurt to crochet and hold the phone in my neck, and the phone always won, which meant I never got very far. But I liked having it by my bed, marking time, waiting to be finished.

Dad's apartment was silent except for the noise from my grandmother's antique clock on his desk. I looked up at the slats of dark wood, the old warehouse ceiling that was Dad's favorite thing about the apartment. Sitting there reminded me of all the nights I used to stay up late, reading his old photography books, waiting for him to come home so I could say goodnight and go to bed. He'd been in that apartment on West Twelfth Street a while, two years maybe, and it was so much better than the dump on Twenty-Third Street he went to right after he moved out. Nothing was more depressing than that.

The elevator buttons were the really old kind that lit up when you touched them, but they were so dirty and disgusting I'd only touch them with my elbow, which was hard when I had a coat on. A never-ending hallway with grassy, dentist-office wallpaper led to his scuffed-up metal door. He'd open it on Friday nights, his living room a murky brown hole behind him, and hug me and my knapsack with some strange kind of desperation, like he was drowning.

He came home that night at around seven, his phone jammed to his ear. "A Maserati's a fine car, as long as you drive it in a straight line." He chuckled. "That's right. Well, enjoy. Don't do anything I wouldn't do." He took off his coat and smiled at me, slipping his shoes under the chair in the foyer. "How was school? Any homework?" He kissed me on the forehead and headed toward his bedroom. He did that all the time—asked a question and walked away or asked a question and looked down and read something. It drove Mom crazy. I try to look at it as some form of adult attention disorder. It could hurt your feelings if you let it.

"It's Wednesday night," I called after him.

He came out of his room, still in his suit pants and a brand-new white undershirt. His undershirts and socks and towels always looked brand-spanking-new. It was a complete mystery to me. He either bought new ones all the time or it was some secret of Rula's, our longtime housekeeper who Mom and Dad shared after they split. It was his one fashion statement. "Why not get it over with, that way you'll have the whole weekend free in front of you."

"Uh-huh," I said, unwinding some more yarn from the ball.

"What are you doing?"

"Crocheting," I said.

"Crocheting what?" He went toward the cluster of plants in the corner, arranged as precisely as a landscaped garden, and stood over each with his brass watering can.

"A scarf, it's just practice. I just learned."

"No kidding," he said, looking up at the sculpted bust of the headless, armless woman in the corner. He'd bought it at an antique show, and whenever I looked at it, I wondered if Dad secretly hated women. "I'm all for hobbies where you're actually making something. People don't make things any-more. But start your homework soon, okay? How's it going? Any tests this week?"

I told him I got a B-plus on a geometry quiz I'd taken that Monday.

"Where does that leave you?" he asked, setting the water-ing can down and balling his hands into fists at his sides. "Where does that leave your average?"

"I'm in good shape, don't worry."

"You're sticking with that idiotic plan of yours?" he blurted, his metal eyeglass frames catching the light as he flinched in disgust. I'd applied early decision to NYU, which had effectively snuffed out his dreams of my attending Wes-leyan for good.

"My idiotic plan?" I asked, stopping what I was doing to glare at him. He was completely incapable of editing himself. It was like thoughts came into his head and he would vomit them out without thinking about how the other person might react. Mom said he had Asperger's syndrome, that it just hadn't been diagnosed.

"I'm sorry," he said flatly, plucking a dead leaf off the rubber tree plant he'd had forever. "I'm just really, really disappointed."

"NYU is a great school and it's the perfect fit for me," I said, borrowing lingo from Ms. Weiss, my college counselor at school. "If they ding me, then I'll apply everywhere else. It's a waste of time, pursuing other schools right now."

"Well, I couldn't disagree more," he said, tossing the dead leaf angrily into the wastebasket by his leather chair. "You did yourself a huge disservice, not leaving your options open." He sat down in his leather swivel chair and started opening mail, the sharp sound of ripping envelopes cutting through the thick silence. I focused intently on my hook, torn between explaining to him, calmly and coolly, how carefully I'd thought about applying to NYU, and telling him to go screw himself for being his usual jackass self.

I looked at the photograph of *Mixed Nuts,* his beloved sonar racing boat, on the bookshelf. Ever since I was a tiny thing, Dad had found countless ways to demean me via sailing. When I was four, he took me out on his boat and tried to teach me how to read the wind. "It's there, Thea, you have to pay attention," he said again and again, flailing his arms in frustration. "Pay attention." But the wind was completely lost to me. I couldn't see it, only the menacing August jellyfish dotting the water and our big, brown shingled house gone all Shrinky-Dink from afar. When I started sailing lessons, he bet me I couldn't get to the nun in the harbor a half a mile from our house, so of course I had to try. I got to the nun easily, but getting back took hours. Every so often, Dad would emerge on the lawn and watch with binoculars, as passively as if he were watching TV. I sailed the boat to the end of the bluff, my hands blistering from gripping the lines, then diagonally back toward the house, over and over, telling myself I was making progress.

"Why couldn't you get in the dinghy and help me?" I asked when I finally made it in, freezing from my still-wet suit yet burning with rage.

He lowered the paper he was reading and looked up at me, as if he'd just realized where I'd been. "You're going to have to get in a whole lot quicker than that, kiddo, if you ever want to race with me."

That's how life was with him, I thought, seething as he crumpled up paper and tossed it into his basket. My potential was the only interesting thing about me. If there was something to be achieved—winning a sailing race, getting into Stuyvesant, getting a high grade—count on Dad to swoop in, demanding dedication and results. Otherwise, I wasn't worth his time.

I went to the kitchen and looked in the fridge for something for dinner. There was Old Amsterdam Gouda wrapped in wax paper in the drawer, just like at Mom's. I made grilled cheese sandwiches with an overripe tomato and we had them on our laps in the living room. He ate his while I squeezed mine and tore it apart, feeling sick from imagined pregnancy symptoms. Part of me was afraid he'd be able to discern my potential problem just by looking at me, and I got a shiver down my spine at the thought of him finding out.

"So when is the turkey coming?" I asked.

"Tomorrow morning, between nine and eleven," he answered, not looking up from his paper.

"Do you think they'll drown it in rosemary bushels again?" I asked. Thanksgiving always came from some herb-crazy caterer uptown, which we joked about every year.

"I don't know, Thea," he said lifelessly. He could go

forever without talking. When I was younger, I'd sit in the living room with him, and the silence compared to Mom's chatting actually confused me. But that night I could tell he wasn't talking because he was still pissed off about college. I picked up the empty plate from his lap and went to my room for the rest of the night.

11.

"I wish the weekend weren't over," Will said on the phone Sunday night. "Four days without you. Sucky."

"I know," I said, telling myself I wouldn't mention the potential problem until I knew for sure what the deal was. "I'm so sick of Dad, I can't wait to get out of here."

"Uh-oh, what happened?"

"Nothing specific," I said. "Wait, that's not true. Let's see, I spent Thanksgiving morning making these hors d'oeuvre–y things he likes, or at least I thought he liked."

"What did you make?"

"Devils on horseback," I said. "Mom made them for parties all the time when I was little and he would devour them." I remembered hearing her heels clomping restlessly around the kitchen as she filled the hors d'oeuvre tray with olives and toothpicks. Mom was always really animated when she threw parties. When it was just me and Dad, she was bored. "But when Dad's guests came on Thanksgiving, I put the hors d'oeuvres out and he wouldn't touch them. The pudgy trader guy and his wife ate all of them. When I mentioned that Dad used to eat entire plates of them when Mom made them, he glared at me as though I'd insulted him. 'Well, that was then, Thea.' I swear I can't win with him. You're lucky your parents are still together."

"My dad says divorce is overrated," Will said.

"He's right!" I said.

"Yeah, but it sort of sounds like he's considered it as an option." He laughed. "Parents."

"Parents," I said.

"What else?" he asked. "Did I mention I wish you were here?"

I threw the blankets off and sat up. "Will, I'm scared," I said, immediately wishing I'd waited. "I think I might be pregnant."

"What? We've been on the phone this whole time and you don't say anything until now?"

"I wasn't going to say anything until I took a test."

"You're on the pill!"

"I know, but it can still happen. Remember when I stayed up there a few weeks ago? I skipped it that day," I said.

"That was one pill!" he said.

"Well, I'm probably just late," I said, remembering that Vanessa's cousin had done the same thing—skipped one pill— and gotten pregnant. There was a long silence. A door slammed on his end.

"I almost wish you hadn't told me. How am I going to sleep?"

"Sorry," I snapped. "Don't worry. You don't have anything to worry about."

"What's that supposed to mean?"

"I mean, I'll take care of it. It's not your problem."

"It's not my problem? Of course it is."

"Well, it's not even a problem yet. I'm just a little worried."

"In a way it'd be cool," he said.

"What would?"

"Having it," he said.

I heard Dad walk by my door on the way to his bedroom and turn out the light. "What do you mean?" I whispered.

"I don't know. I know we can't. It's just nice to think about. A little green-eyed G-Rock baby, rockin' the bridge."

"It's late," I said, lying down and pulling the covers back up. I looked at the ceiling and found the streaks of light shining in from the building across the street. They formed a distorted face across the beams—eyes, nose and straight, mean mouth. She looked like a mean queen.

"Call me tomorrow," he said. "It's going to be okay, okay?"

12.

I waited until Monday morning to take the test at school, a weird place to do it, but I thought taking it there would make it less likely to come out positive. I was wrong.

Debbie Marshall was on the phone with her mother outside the stall as I was waiting to look at the stick. The volume was so high I could hear both sides of the conversation. She was telling her mother how all the seniors liked her, and how she was the only freshman invited to the holiday dance. I saw the lines the same moment Debbie's mom cackled that the only reason they liked Debbie was because of her "big booty butt."

I stepped out of the stall and breathed the cold air coming through the crack in the window. All I could think was, Where would it sleep? My room at Mom's was tiny. Dad had carved it out of the living room when I was two and they'd decided I should have my own room. It was hard getting me to sleep in there at first. "Daddy had to come in a hundred and fifty times the first few nights to put you back in bed," Mom had said. "It was our fault for keeping you in our room for so long. We were hippies about that one particular thing." My room didn't have real windows, just a couple of glass blocks along the curved side of the wall to let in light from the living room. Babies needed windows. Air.

It would be easier in Vanessa's room, I thought. She had a deep closet you could fit a crib into, if you took off the sliding doors. I had a closet at Dad's but not in my room at home. Just an armoire. Mom had made this stripy pattern all over it with a comb when the paint was wet. There was the armoire and my bed, which took up the whole wall on one side. My desk stuck out along the wall across from it. I had to walk sideways in between my desk and my bed because the pile of clothes on my chair would fall off if I walked straight. I thought, We could build a loft bed, where I'm on top, and the baby's in a little crib underneath. That's the only way it could fit. Or we could not build a loft bed and I could get an abortion.

I left the bathroom to find Vanessa. She was in homeroom and I wasn't supposed to go in there. Mr. Scarpinato eyed me like I was going to start an insurrection.

"It's an emergency," I whispered, and for some reason he let me pull her into the corner.

"What?" she asked.

"I'm pregnant."

"No!" she said, her smile catching me off guard. It made me smile too.

"Yes."

"Have you told him?"

"Not yet."

"Okay, well, do that, and we'll figure out the rest." She looked out the window, thinking. "We can find out who Jamie's doctor was." Jamie was her cousin in New Jersey who'd had an abortion a year earlier. "I'll call her."

I ran my finger along the radiator dust, picturing Jamie, her red hair falling off the sides of a doctor's table, her freckly, pointy knees sticking up in the air. I looked at Vanessa, who was watching me with her arms folded. "What the hell?" I said, shaking my head at her.

"Don't worry," she said, grasping my shoulders. People were staring at us. "We'll figure it out."

Mr. Scarpinato cleared his throat, pulled a piece of chalk out of his brown polyester pants and started writing on the blackboard for his next class.

I went back to the bathroom to call Will.

"So, yeah," I said.

"No way," he said. "What do we do?" Any trace of wistfulness in his voice from the night before had vanished.

"We're finding a doctor."

"Well, I'll go with you."

"No," I blurted. "It's okay. Vanessa's going to come." I knew right away I had to keep him out of it. In the back of my head I worried that any shared downer experience would be dangerous for us, and I couldn't have that. I hung up, stuck my phone in my jeans pocket and stared at myself in the bathroom mirror, the new me.

13.

I sped out of Dad's house that night like it was any other night and I'd just spent the weekend there instead of ten days. I'd told Will, and now I had to tell Mom.

"See you Wednesday?" I called from the door.

"See you Wednesday," Dad answered from his leather chair in the living room, where he was surrounded by piles of paper he'd dragged home. Mom used to pick up his briefcase and call him "the brick salesman." I could tell he was hoping for a little more departure fanfare—a hug, for example—but I wasn't up to it.

Mom was unpacking when I got home.

"So how was it?" I sat on the love seat next to her bed.

"We had a great time," she said. "It's a beautiful area. We'll go when you're old enough to drink."

She threw me a couple of blouses, catching my eyes for the first time. "Can you throw those in the dry cleaning? How are you? How was Daddy's?"

"Okay."

"I love Beryl," she said. "She's a bit over the top and socially ambitious, the complete opposite of me. But she's good on trips."

"You met people."

"We met people, no one earth-shattering, other single type-As, mostly from New York."

She circled the bed, arranging piles, pouring shoes out of bags, not yet ready to stop moving. I knew I was about to catapult her back here, home, where she didn't really want to be.

"I don't know why I brought these." She licked her thumb and wiped a smudge off a strappy grape sandal.

"Mom, something's happened."

"Oh no," she said, putting the sandal to her chest.

"Don't worry. No one died. I'm not sick."

"Then what?"

"I'm pregnant."

"What?" She walked around the bed, dragging a scarf that had attached itself to her leg. She stood over me, inspecting.

My silence must have confirmed it. "Jesus!" she said. "Since when?"

"Mom, wait," I said, not sure what I was asking her to wait for. "I took the test this morning."

"It's Will?"

"Yes, it's Will. Who do you think?" I started crying.

"How could he—you're on the pill, for Christ's sake. Do you bother taking it?"

"Stop yelling."

"I'm not yelling." She grabbed the scarf that was stuck on her leg and hurled it across the bed, and it fell on the floor. "I don't understand, Thea. Why do I bother? Why did I bother getting you that gynecologist's appointment?"

"Look, it happened," I said, picking up the scarf. "Now I have to deal with it. It's no one's fault."

"Did you take your pills?"

74

"Yes!"

"All the time?" she asked, her eyes ablaze.

"Yes!" I lied. Why couldn't it be Will who had to remember to take it? I was so *bad* at it.

"Vanessa knows a doctor," I said. She pushed the overflowing suitcase aside and sat down, facing me, fists in her lap. "She says he's very good."

"Have you called him?" The crease in between her eyebrows was deep, deep, deep.

"Not yet," I said. "I wanted to tell you first."

"I'll ask around and find you someone tomorrow," she said, rubbing her temples. "The timing is really unfortunate, with all you have coming up. Honestly, Thea."

"It'll be okay." I rolled the numbered dials of her suitcase lock until they all hit zero. "I'm sorry," I said, because it seemed like the right thing to say.

14.

"The thing I figured out when I was doing it is that they're stupid the way video games are stupid," Will said, pushing the floppy SAT book up toward the edge of his bed. "The more you do them, the better you get. That's really the only trick. You just have to take, like, a million practice tests." Our elbows fell together on his flimsy mattress. 2320, I thought, over and over, as I watched Will's quick, confident face scanning the pages. He'd gotten a 2320 on his SATs. I imagined I felt a little flutter as I lay on my stomach. Mom had called to schedule "the procedure" with someone named Dr. Moore, but the appointment wasn't until later in December, when I was further along. In the meantime, I had the SATs to keep me distracted.

We went over a question about a motorcycle stuntman riding over the walls of a circular well.

"So if the radius of the well is five kilometers, the distance he travels is . . . ," Will said, his voice rising expectantly, like a preschool teacher's, trying to engage me. I wondered if stress could make you miscarry.

"I don't know, three and a half kilometers," I guessed. All I could think of was the economics homework still on my desk at home. It had taken me two hours that morning to do the supply schedule and to make the stupid line go straight up, and I hadn't even gotten to the supply curve. We were only a couple of months into the semester, only a couple of months of watching Mr. Goff's skinny, Levi'ed ass tottering on the edge of his desk while he took that same bag of pretzels out of his desk drawer every day to demonstrate the endless stream of economic principles, principles that slipped from my grasp almost as quickly as they piled up. I shut the SAT book suddenly, folding some of the thin pages over. "I'm tired."

"Let's take a nap, then." Will slid his finger through the folded pages, laying them flat, then dumped the book on the floor. He smiled with his face inches from mine and closed his eyes.

"I'm sorry you have to, you know, go through this with the other stuff going on," he said, rubbing my temple. "Not exactly great timing, is it?"

I shook my head, my eyes welling up.

"Not exactly looking forward to it, are we?"

"What, the SATs or the abortion?" I asked.

"Both, I guess." He sighed. "I'm sorry."

"It's okay."

"You can totally do this, Thee," he said urgently. "You're much smarter than you think you are."

"This is you trying to cheer me up," I said, sulking.

"I mean it. You're weird."

"I'm not weird."

"Oh, let's see," he said, drumming his chin with his fingers. "You memorized your eye doctor's vision chart. That's weird. You like saggy, dead trees, that's weird, and your peach-pit collection? That row of fossilized little pits on your windowsill?" He reached for my hand. "That's really weird, G-Rock, I hate to tell you. But weird equals smart, at least in my book." He curled his leg over me. "You just have to test your ass off over the next couple of weeks."

I stared at the wall. He'd finally hung the Tanglewood poster up, and slats of bent light from the trashed Venetian blind zigzagged across the floating, fuchsia violins. 2320. Stick with it. I fell asleep with my head burrowed in Will's neck and woke up to him kissing me twenty minutes later. Screw econ, I thought. Screw everything. Still half-asleep, I got his jeans down to his knees, pinning his legs together, and started going down on him as he splayed his arms out across the bed, like he was making an angel in the snow.

"You didn't have to do that, you know," he said as he walked me to the subway. "But it was nice that you did."

"I don't *have* to do anything," I said, squeezing his waist. We were going down Broadway, and a transvestite with neon-blue hair glanced at us as we went by. Her eyes dismissed us, as though we were dull white-bread kids, which was completely opposed to how I actually felt. I felt like I was roiling. In love to the point of roiling. I thought of the crochet hook plunged into the ball of yarn on my radiator at home. I was still hooked.

Will stopped in the middle of the street we were crossing and kissed me. We stood there on a wide, white crosswalk strip until cars honked. He pressed his forehead against mine, a straightforward, matter-of-fact lust on his face, piercing through the dusk, and still didn't move. "I love you."

"I love you too," I said.

"I said it first." He smiled. "I win."

We walked the rest of the way to the subway without a word. A guy outside a pizza parlor was whistling and shouting at a brown van moving down the street. Everything moved, bendy buses, skinny dogs on leashes, bike messengers in army jackets whipping around corners. The city had an evening glow, an anticipation, which would normally depress me a little, make me feel like I was missing something, but I didn't feel that way then.

"Sayonara, milady." He grabbed my hands and rubbed his lips across my knuckles. "Take a test tonight. For me, okay?" I didn't want to go but I also did. I wanted to pore over this weird new feeling, trust. I trusted him.

"Uh-huh," I mumbled.

"Uh-huh," he repeated. "You've still got a week before the big day, so test your brains out. I'll call you later to see how you did."

15.

I took the SATs on a Saturday morning at a dank-smelling vocational school near my house. The test room had rows of puke-yellow chairs with holes in the back that made them look like lifesavers. A week later, on the morning of "the procedure," Mom sat on my bed, pulling a feather out of my comforter. "Do you want me to come? Because I will if you want me to," she said. It sounded almost like a threat.

"It's okay, Vanessa's meeting me," I lied. For some reason I'd gotten it in my head that it would be easier to go alone, to just go alone without anyone feeling sorry for me or worrying about me. I'd have to fudge the exit—someone was supposed to take me home—but I'd figure some way out of it.

"Okay," she said. She seemed both hurt and relieved. She pressed her red fingernails up against her eyebrow, fanning it out. "Call me if you need anything, okay? I know this probably feels hard, but you're doing the right thing." She patted my leg and stood up.

I put on sweats, thinking, If it really hurts, they'll be easy to get back on when it's time to go home. I tasted rotten orange peels in the back of my mouth on the subway. Was that a pregnancy symptom? I looked at a woman in front of me wearing a thick, bulky cardigan that disguised her shape and thought of something my friend David told me: that there were hundreds of people in New York City walking around with guns, you just couldn't see them. It might be the same with newly pregnant women like me who aren't showing yet, I thought. Little secret pocket dolls, hiding from you.

The office was packed with rows of women sandwiched

between fake birds-of-paradise. I took a seat and pulled out my yarn, thinking my scarf-in-progress could stand in as a security blanket. My hands were shaky and I pulled at the yarn like a skittish kitten. A door swung open and I spotted three empty cots in a row. They reminded me of giving blood with Vanessa in the basement of school freshman year. I remembered sitting next to her, both of us squeezing the red balls, racing to fill up our bags. Then we ate four-packs of Fig Newtons and drank apple juice while the nurse had us recline for twenty minutes. Vanessa said the apple juice looked like urine.

A redhead in a flowered pajama top and a name tag that said *Annie Kay* walked by. The young-looking woman across from me in a khaki pantsuit burped. I focused on my yarn, embarrassed for her. I looked up again and she was staring at the wall, clearly worried. I thought of Mom's sister, Pat, who'd had a hysterectomy when she was thirty, and I began to wonder why the fuck I'd come alone. Annie Kay stepped into the doorway and called my name into the room, like we were all there for an audition and it was my turn to read.

"Do you have someone here with you to take you home?" she asked me, scanning the seats around me.

"Yes," I lied. "She's downstairs getting a magazine." I wondered if I was making a big mistake but thought I could always call Vanessa and have her come get me if I was dying from the pain or out of it. Annie Kay made a motion to follow her down the hall and I hoped that was the end of it.

Dr. Moore was the kind of person you'd want to get an abortion from. Blond hair cut very straight above her shoulders, and skin that clearly got frequent, maybe compulsively so, peels. She stepped quietly into the room, followed by a nurse, and everything immediately grew very serious.

"Thea Galehouse," she said, looking at her chart. "So, you think you're about eight weeks along, correct?"

"Something like that."

"We'll just take a quick look." She asked me to scooch down the table and picked up the phallic-looking magic wand. It was dark in the room and the screen illuminated her face, making it bright blue. She stared at the screen for a long time, then took the mouse and moved it around, clicking and clicking.

"Okay," she said, letting out her breath. Something was printing out. "Eight, nine weeks looks about right. I'll be back in a minute and we'll start."

She and the nurse left. I sat up on my elbows and pulled the screen toward me without thinking. A circle inside a larger gray circle, frozen on the screen. The littler circle was shaped like a comma that you could color in, or a cartoon bubble for voices.

I looked away from the screen and looked back again, and when I looked back, I got scared. For some reason I thought of Sam Negroponte, the artist guy who died across the hall in our building. I bugged Mom until she fessed up that he'd hanged himself. He was dead in his apartment for almost a week. I was in fourth grade, and when I got off the elevator one day, the smell crept into some part of my brain that registered exactly what it was without needing words. You're not ready for this, my brain said. Not ready to know this smell and what it is or what it means.

The same thing happened when I looked back at the screen. Not ready. I'd just take a little more time. I got off the table and threw on my clothes like you'd imagine putting your clothes on in the middle of the night if your building's on fire.

As fast as you can, thinking and not thinking at the same time. I sped down the narrow, empty hallway and ducked past the receptionist, who was deep in discussion with a woman at the counter about her insurance co-payment. No one noticed me leaving, and it struck me how easy it was to become invisible when you needed to.

I walked outside, gathering my down vest around me to fend off the December wind. Someone had discarded a perfectly healthy-looking pine tree on the corner. Christmas was still a couple of weeks away. I imagined some perfectionist Upper East Side housewife throwing it out because it was too short or something and immediately connected the unwanted tree, with its wide, wet stump, to whatever was growing inside me. I got a smoothie on Seventy-Second Street and sat on a hard stool in front of the window for an hour. Then I went home. Mom was at the dining room table paying bills when I walked through the door. She asked how it was. I told her Dr. Moore was very competent and professional, that it hardly hurt, that Vanessa was a huge help, that I was glad it was done.

"Anything for insurance?" she asked.

"They're mailing."

"You don't feel crampy?"

"No," I said, making a mental note to complain later. "Not yet."

"I bought a big thing of Advil," she said. "You can take more than the bottle says. Take some the second you feel anything." I started for the kitchen, but she was swinging an envelope between her second and third fingers like a little white flag. "Something came for you this morning." She smiled.

"No way," I said. "You opened it?"

"I'm sorry, I couldn't stand it, and I wanted to prepare for bad news in case there was some. But you're in. Early decision."

I grabbed the envelope. "New York University" in purple letters in the top left corner. My SAT scores had been online for a couple of weeks, but I'd been too afraid to look. I rubbed my thumb along the mangled edge where Mom had opened it and felt an almost dizzying surge of relief and pride: I'd done it. I thought about all the nights with that freaking SAT phone book on my lap, the desperate hope that I could somehow absorb the contents via osmosis. All the Saturdays I'd spent that fall staring at the backs of plastic red chairs at the Princeton Review, missing Will and desperate to be with him instead of there. I'd done it. Maybe all the stressing over econ and calc had somehow been enough to maintain a B-plus average. Maybe stressing was as effective as working, because I definitely did more stressing than working. But it had all somehow come together.

"Well done, you clever girl, as my mum used to say to me once in a blue moon," Mom said, standing up and coming toward me. "You pulled it off and now my baby is flying the coop at last. But you'll be a stone's throw away. I'm getting the best of both worlds. I can hardly believe it." She stood up and walked over to me with her arms extended, and I saw myself in our flecked mirror above the stereo console as she hugged me: a smiling, rooty blond girl with a thorny secret.

16.

I kept my laptop screen tilted away from my bedroom door. It was January—a month since my un-abortion—and I jumped every time the radiator in my room clanked, thinking it was Mom coming home from dinner. No, I did not want to become a member of Babylove.com, I just wanted to quickly see what it looked like. I signed in as a guest, and the Web page asked for the conception date. I didn't know for sure but guessed it must have been sometime in late September, after Will moved up to Columbia, since he'd been away with his family before that. It took me to a page that said my twelve-week-old baby was two inches long and developing reflexes. The page said, "Click here to see what your baby looks like."

I'd called Dr. Moore's office the afternoon I got home from the un-abortion in December, afraid they'd call me and Mom would answer. They'd asked me if I wanted to reschedule, and I'd made another appointment for the following Friday. I gave them my cell phone number and asked them to call that, not my house, to remind me. When Friday came, I'd left school early, without saying anything to Vanessa. I'd gotten a 6 train to Moore's office on the Upper East Side, but as the train flew past Eighth Street, then Fourteenth, I started to feel sick, the collar of my down jacket choking me. I focused on the lawyer advertisements plastered up and down the train, but I felt dizzy, like if I took my eyes off the subway ads, the rest of the world would go black. So I got off at Forty-Second Street and grabbed a shuttle to the West Side. I thought if I could just tell Will how sick and scared I felt, he'd understand and know what to do. I got on a 1 train uptown and when I got to Will's hall, I spotted him in the lounge, sitting at a card table doing a million-piece puzzle with a red-haired girl. I paused to spy for a moment but didn't get the sense that there was anything going on with her. As I moved toward them, I realized the puzzle was all white. Every single tiny piece.

"G-Rock!" He looked surprised but happy to see me. "It's the Beatles' White Album," he said, maneuvering me onto his lap. "Melanie and I have committed to finishing it by Sunday. Right, Melanie?"

Melanie nodded and we smiled at each other. The air around her smelled like cigarettes.

"You're going to help us, right?" he said, nuzzling my neck, sending a delicious chill through me that for a lovely moment overpowered everything else. "We neeeeed you."

So I ended up staying and doing the puzzle, thinking we'd go off to his room and I would tell him everything, that I hadn't had the abortion yet and that I didn't know what to do. But we didn't go to his room. He seemed so happy that night—so unlike the lovelorn soul he was on the phone with me, complaining about how it was too loud in his dorm and how there were too many people around and how maybe this place wasn't for him. It sounds lame considering what was going on, but I didn't want to spoil it. Or maybe I just wanted to escape it too. Someone turned on the TV and then a stereo blared out of a room near the lounge, and someone brought in some beer, and Will smoked pot with a guy in a purple rugby shirt, and we did the puzzle and talked with whoever came through, until it got late and I told him I had to get home, and he walked me downstairs and got me a cab.

I clicked on the tab to see what my baby looked like. Someone had done a line drawing of an enormous head on top of a small tadpole-like body. Big, wide-set black eyes and holes for ears. So, this was my baby, I thought. How had someone drawn it? Had they studied a printout of an ultrasound or was it something else, where the baby wasn't alive anymore? Not ready, I said to myself. Not yet. I pushed away the thought that I was almost three months pregnant, that the tiny person inside me was now larger than a quarter, and as I heard Mom's keys in the door, I felt a strange, visceral urge to defy the hopelessness of it all.

17.

I had to ask Ms. Jedel for a recommendation to get into an English seminar at NYU. I'd sent the application in, but the recommendation was way late. When would I ask her? At the end of the day or the beginning? Which day was the best day to ask for something like this? Friday? Inside the classroom or outside? What would I say? *"Ms. Jedel, I know I haven't been doing so terrifically, but I wondered if you would consider . . ."*

Ms. Jedel had a very formal demeanor, and she wore tailored pencil skirts and navy patent-leather pumps, which made her stand out even more next to the bedraggled male teachers in jeans and sneakers. When I had her freshman year, she stood at the blackboard, holding the chalk in her fingers like a cigarette. "If you cannot spell *separate,* you are not up to par," she would say. I'd imagine her going home at night to her apartment with a single paper grocery bag nestled in her arms—

dinner for one—and I imagined her pushing her glasses daintily up her nose as she undressed next to the closet door. I always pictured her wearing a beautiful cream silk slip under her skirt and blouse, and imagined her getting undressed down to that, then padding off to the kitchen to ladle her take-out risotto onto a white plate and eating it sitting down with a tall glass of water. In some weird way, she gave me hope that my adulthood would be elegant.

"Ms. Jedel, I have a big favor to ask you. . . ."

Then senior year something happened. I took her film class and she discussed *Dog Day Afternoon* and *Raging Bull*, in her same skirts and pumps, and she was too far removed from real life. She was a nerd. And a spinster. I ended up getting a B-plus for the fall semester.

"Ms. Jedel, believe it or not, after my less-than-stellar performance so far in the film class, I'm actually thinking of majoring in film. I know, I know, but this year has been hard for me. I'm deeply in love, and now I'm with child, actually. Could you cut me a break, Ms. Jedel? Could you?"

I endlessly put off asking her, until I finally got up the nerve on February twelfth, my eighteenth birthday. I thought that asking her on my birthday, even though she didn't know it was my birthday, would somehow mean she'd say yes. I was wrong.

Vanessa was waiting outside in the hall.

"What'd she say?"

"I can't believe it," I said. "She turned me down."

"No!" she said, her eyes widening. "So obnoxious. I'm sorry, Thee. I can't believe it. Come with me later and we'll do birthday ice cream, and you can help me buy tennis sneakers. I'll cheer you up."

"Okay," I said, thinking, This birthday is turning out to be complete rubbish, as Mom would say. Mom had asked me if I wanted a party, but my last big birthday, my sweet sixteen, took place at Dad's squash club with too many kids I didn't know smoking pot on the dark empty courts. I just wanted this one to come and go.

I went with Vanessa after school to buy tennis sneakers on Thirty-Fourth Street. She'd picked the last semester of our senior year to join the tennis team. I was jealous because I knew she'd be good at it and probably get really skinny, whereas I was a depressed slob, getting fatter by the second, coming home from school every day and crashing onto the couch like a plane.

A mop-topped boy brought out a stack of boxes and popped the lid off the first one.

He bent down and took the heel of her foot.

"How's Fiona?" Vanessa asked. "Still howling at the moon?"

"She's okay," I said. "She just sold her second apartment, so she's all excited. Maybe the real estate thing will be her . . . thing."

"That's so great. She's found her calling, I know it." She looked at the white leather lace-ups that made her already narrow foot look even narrower. "What do you think?" She twisted her ankle around. "You're coming to my first match, right?" She grinned and gathered her long brown curls into two ponytails on either side of her head. "Promise margarine?"

I nodded, trying to conjure up watching a game on the shiny new aluminum bleachers in Battery Park. My favorite sunglasses had split in two at the nose when I had sat on them the summer before. They were still on my dresser, sitting, sitting, sitting, as if one day I'd magically take them into the kitchen and Scotch tape them perfectly together. Why couldn't I just throw shit *out*?

"Ness, I'm really fucked up," I said, a shelf of misery forming in my throat.

"What is it, babe?" she asked, taking the sneaker off and gripping it. "You still thinking about the you-know-what?"

"I would be," I said, staring at the stack of boxes. "If I'd *had* the you-know-what."

She froze. "What do you mean?"

"At the appointment, I don't know, I freaked out," I said. "I hopped off the table."

"Thea, that was way over a month ago—why didn't you tell me?"

"I don't know," I said. I honestly didn't. "I'm going back. I just had a little moment that day. I'm going back."

"Aren't you running out of time?"

"There's still time," I said. "It's not too late." The boy returned and paused in front of us with another box, which he set on the floor by Vanessa's feet.

"I'm going to take these, thanks," she said, pointing to the sneakers and quickly getting her boots back on. We went to the counter and Vanessa pulled out a crumpled wad of twenties. I didn't know what she was thinking; she'd gone mute. I'd been sort of coasting with this fuzzy problem in the back of my mind for weeks, but the look on her face—she looked like she'd seen a ghost—brought it raging to the front.

We got outside and the tide of people on Thirty-Fourth Street coaxed us toward Seventh Avenue.

"Will doesn't know, does he?" she finally asked. "You have to tell him."

"I'm going to tell him. It's so hard to find the right time."

"There won't be a right time, Thea, it doesn't exist. Just get it over with."

"I know." We got to the corner and waited at the light.

"Thea, do you really think you and Will are going to go off and, like, just blow off college and get sucky jobs and live on love in some prairie town, with a baby?" she asked. "What's going on? What's going on in your head?"

"I—I don't know," I stammered. "Maybe part of me thinks that. I can't help it. What's wrong with me?"

"If you decide to go ahead and have it, I'll shut my mouth, but right now it seems like a bad idea." She held her knapsack, with its prickly pink rubber key chain dangling off it, in front of my face, as if to prove a point. "We're really young, in case you haven't noticed."

"How different would it be if we were, like, twenty-four?" I asked.

"That's still young!" she exclaimed. "But at least you'd have a college degree. You'd have a shot."

"Is college really necessary anymore?"

She shook her head. "What are you talking about?"

"I don't know, is it?" I shrugged.

"I don't know what to say, Thee," she said, brushing her hand across my stomach. "Jesus, babe, what a moosh you are. You can't let go of anything, can you?"

18.

I got it into my stupid head to tell Will at Dad's Pave the Way benefit a few days later. I didn't know what I'd say or how I'd say it, but I thought a gorgeous candlelit ballroom would help romanticize the whole thing and make him see things my way, even though I wasn't sure what my way was. I'd found an old forest-green suede tunic of Mom's and dressed it up with long beads and a black chain belt that hid my stomach and showed off my arms.

"That is so Fiona," Vanessa said when I tried it on for her that afternoon. "I'm so having a visual of Fiona with her bangs and her huge black leather bag, walking around in that a few years ago. God, she has the best clothes."

"It's okay, right?" I asked, tugging at the sides and cinching the chain belt around the narrowest part of my waist, which at that point was up around my rib cage. I looked up and caught Vanessa staring up at my bulging stomach.

"What?" I asked.

"Nothing," she said, still staring. "You haven't told him yet, have you?"

"No," I said. "Check out my scarf." I gestured to the balled-up crochet project still on my bedside table. "It's coming out lopsided. What am I doing wrong?"

She looked at me long and hard and I braced myself for a lecture. She'd been silent on the subject and I, of course, never brought it up, so it was hard to know what she was thinking. She just rolled over and grabbed the scarf while I quickly pulled the dress over my shoulders.

I was the first one to arrive at the hotel that night. I was watching a guy in the lobby jewelry shop take coral necklaces out of the window boxes when Will slid through the revolving door, eyes darting around. He spotted me and walked across the lobby.

"Hey." He gave me a nervous kiss. "You look great."

"So do you," I said. "You okay?"

"I'm fine," he said, looking at me like I was crazy. "Why wouldn't I be?"

"Why are you answering my question with a question?" I said.

"What, does that bother you?"

"Does it bother me?" I asked.

"Does it bother you?" he repeated.

"Shut up."

"No, you shut up," he said.

"No, you."

Dad came up the steps behind us. I was sure he'd heard Will tell me to shut up.

"Hello, kids," Dad said. His tux was blacker than Will's. I'd thought black was black, one shade. "Good to see you again, Will." Will missed a beat before shaking Dad's outstretched hand.

"You too, Ted."

"Where's Elizabeth?" Dad's eyes started darting around the room like Will's, and I thought maybe it was a survival thing men did when they were nervous. Elizabeth Ransom was Dad's friend from growing up on Charter Island. I didn't think they'd ever done it, but I wasn't positive.

I shook my head. "We just got here."

I wished Will would say "Thanks for inviting me," or "What does Pave the Way do, exactly, Mr. Galehouse?" But he just stood there, his tux accentuating the broadness of his shoulders.

"Are you speaking tonight?" I asked Dad, putting my arm through Will's.

"Naw, no," Dad grumbled. He waved to an older couple, lowering his head as they walked by. "Harry's speaking. I don't do it unless there's a gun at my head."

Will smiled appreciatively.

Elizabeth blew in. "Sorry, sorry, sorry," she called from across the lobby. "I've just had the afternoon from hell. Corky chewed up the Pearsons' baby ball. I had to stop at Mary Arnold and have one messengered over, of all things."

"Do us all a favor, Lizzie, lose the yippy little sausage," Dad said, kissing her on both cheeks.

"Nevah," she cackled.

Elizabeth was a decorator and had gotten Dad his living room furniture. Big brown leather stuff with buttons, and a couple of stripy-wood end tables that struck me as very him: unadventurously tasteful, directly linked to the great outdoors. He wouldn't let her do anything else with his apartment. He said she was too expensive.

"How are we all this lovely evening?" she asked, gathering her diaphanous wrap around her, and before anyone could answer, said, "Shall we mingle with the masses?"

Dad put his hand on the small of Elizabeth's back and guided her to the elevators, alerting me to the fact that Elizabeth's ass was half the size of mine. The ballroom upstairs was a patchwork of sumptuous black fabric—chiffon, gabardine, taffeta—all swishing around over the gaudy, Saudi-palace carpet. Will and I were the youngest ones there. I hoped we stuck out in only a cool, sexy way.

"Can I get everyone drinks?" Will asked, his voice fading into the din.

"Champagne?" I asked Dad. "C'mon, one glass."

"One glass," Dad said. "Lizzie?"

"White wine, please. Emma!" she called to a woman a few heads away. "That wasn't your show—Diane's? Where the lights fell down on the stage?"

Emma shook her head solemnly.

"Thank God!" Elizabeth yelled, a little softer but with exaggerated emphasis. "I read that and thought, Oh my God, I hope that wasn't her show."

If she'd said "I hope that wasn't Emma's show," instead of "her show," it would have come out sounding nicer. Elizabeth reminded me of Mom a little, the way you couldn't always tell whether she was on your side or not.

Will stepped over to the bar a few feet away. I heard him say "Can I get a white wine . . ." and saw Dad wince. He was always on me to say "May I please have" instead of "Can I get." "It's vulgar, Thea," he'd say. "The kids who work for me say it all the time too. Their breakfast orders in the morning make my head hurt. 'Can I get an egg and cheese?' You all need to be reprogrammed. It's basic English." At least I did it too, and people at work. Not just Will.

Will came back with Dad's seltzer with lime and Elizabeth's wine, then my champagne and a beer for himself, which he drank out of the bottle. The four of us stood in an awkward huddle.

"Teddy tells me you're at Columbia," Elizabeth said to Will.

"Yeah." Will nodded uncomfortably. I saw Dad look away.

"That's a wonderful school. My nephew just finished up there."

Will swigged his beer.

"So who are we sitting with?" I asked, molding my cocktail napkin around the base of my flute. "Work people?"

"Mostly, yes, and some friends of Harry's," Dad said.

A woman wearing a polka-dot dress and green glasses was talking near me. "Bruno, my youngest, loves the ladies," she said, her tall husband nodding in agreement. "He likes to escort them down the steps of his preschool and bid them good afternoon."

We found our table, close to the stage. Elizabeth put her tiny handbag, shaped like a turtle and covered in rhinestones, next to Dad's chair, and another couple quickly parked themselves on his other side. The other free seats were across the table, so any further Dad-Will bonding wasn't in the cards. We spent the night talking to a pale, pudgy Australian guy who worked for Dad. "I love this city," he kept saying, as though trying to convince himself. "I love the Upper West Side."

Mostly we snuck out into the atrium for drinks, our first trip right after the salads. We ducked behind a big pillar decorated with fake orange lilies, our buzzes escalating at the same time in a whirling rush.

He leaned toward me and winked. "You are the fairest of them all, milady. Ma'am. Your Honor."

"Gee, thanks," I said, fluttering my eyelids. I kissed him, noticing how every angle of his body inspired a crazy-making, lustful lurch inside me. I wanted to step into him. Just get in him and live in there. I leaned against the pillar, cold against my bare back.

"You know, I love you so much," Will whispered, brushing his lips across mine just like he did when we had sex. Even then I knew that chances were, I loved him more. Will was drunk. It reminded me of when I was younger and Dad had scrawled the words *I love you more than you can dream* on the back of a picture of me in our living room one night when he was bombed out of his mind. I'd come home from school and found it, next to an ashtray filled with butts, the table sticky with beer from the previous night's all-nighter. I had crossed it out, making deep, pissed-off Bic-pen indentations into the cardboard. I remember thinking he could only bring himself to love me when he was shit-faced.

Still, I loved hearing Will say he loved me, over and over.

"Will, I have to tell you something," I said.

"What," he said, kissing my neck and pulling the chain around my waist.

"I'm still pregnant. I didn't go through with it, that day I was supposed to. I couldn't."

He looked at me and his body seemed to lurch backward in slow motion.

"I didn't mean to hide it," I said. "It's hard for me to explain."

"Jesus Christ," he said. I tried to find a trace of something I could recognize, in his eyes, in his expression, but his face reflected back only the worst—that I'd done something very wrong by not telling him.

Someone had made an announcement I didn't hear and everyone started to file back into the dining room.

"I'm out of here," Will said. He started for the elevators, then kicked open the fire-exit door and let it slam behind him before I had a chance to call his name.

19.

The tangle of Mom's belts hung off my desk chair when I woke up the next morning. A couple of them were on the floor. Mom loves her clothes and preserves them fastidiously in her closet like museum pieces. My first thought was actually to get up, roll the belts and put them on my desk before she saw them like that. Then I remembered the previous night and wondered if I could just close my eyes again and have everything end right there. I felt like someone had run a bulldozer over my body and wondered how I was ever going to get out of bed, get clothes on, deal with Mom in the kitchen and get out the door to school. I remembered Dad's face when I went back into the dining room and told him that Will had gotten sick and that I was going to take him home. He'd sat back and laid his dessert fork down as if he were trying not to wake someone, even though the room was ringing with the sound of silverware through the drone of voices. "Okay," he'd said flatly, taking a sip from his sweaty water glass, and I could read his thoughts like a news feed running across his face: Here we go again, Thea's up to her old tricks—she's drunk and her boyfriend's drunk and she's let me down once again. I'll let her go before she embarrasses me any further.

I told Mom that the party was fun and that Will loved my dress and that I was late for zero period, slathering some peanut butter on a piece of toast I knew I would throw into the junk-mail can in the lobby.

I somehow made it to school, to my spot on the floor in zero-period gym as Mr. Boone paced and talked about muscle recovery.

"When you work a muscle group to its maximum capacity, they need a period of time to reoxygenate," Mr. Boone said, weaving around us like we were cones on a road.

The reality that I wouldn't ever again lie in Will's bed at Columbia and see that Nerf basketball hoop hanging off his door, that I wouldn't get to touch his hair, flatten it out along the back of his neck, was starting to hit home. I realized I understood what the expression "hot tears" meant. There were so many of them going down my face, I gave up wiping them away. Wiping called attention to them. I didn't feel like dying. I felt dead already. Will hadn't abandoned just me, but also the beautiful, mysterious thing growing inside me that we had made together. I remember watching the track team come panting through the big metal doors from their run and having the feeling that the level of pain I was experiencing was way more than I bargained for. It was pain I didn't know existed. Mr. Boone passed by my spot and looked straight at me for a moment, and it was almost like he knew *why* I was crying, but he did a stand-up job of pretending nothing was wrong. I wondered over and over why I'd done what I'd done and what I was going to do next.

But then later, as I went outside for lunch, there was Will. He stood in the middle of the sidewalk with his arms folded across his chest. It was freezing cold and it reminded me of the first day I met him. He was standing by himself then, too.

"I'm so hungover." Will smiled, shaking his head. "Staying up all night didn't help."

"Do you want to go somewhere?" I asked. I saw Vanessa walking toward us in her maroon down jacket, but she saw my face and turned and went around the corner. I hadn't even told her yet about the night before.

"Tell me what you were thinking, Thea," he said.

"I-it was just . . . avoidance," I stammered. "I was avoiding it. I thought I'd go back when I was ready."

"You were scared," he said.

"I was scared," I repeated. "I *am* scared."

"What are you scared of?"

"I'm scared of doing it, I'm scared of not doing it," I said, looking down at my knapsack slumped at my feet on the curb. "I don't know what to do."

"What are you more scared of?"

"Getting an abortion," I said. "I don't know why."

"Shit, Thea," he said, setting his hands rigidly on his hips. "I wish you'd just told me. You could have told me you were screwed up about it. We could have talked about it. What did you think I'd do?"

"It's lame, I know," I said. "It's like I couldn't do anything. Except let another day pass. In a weird way, I know it's pathetic and awful, but I liked that it was getting bigger."

He looked at me, his good eye boring into mine. "You actually want to go through with this," he said slowly. "You want to bring a baby into the world. A child."

I love the sound of your voice, I thought. Your voice is my drug. All I'll ever need. "It's you, you know, how could I not?" I said, barely getting the words out. "It's you."

More staring. A gust of wind blew our hair up.

"What are you thinking?" I asked.

"I'm thinking, holy shit." Mr. Plumb, a history teacher, walked up to us, eyeing Will in his big, black down parka.

"Well, if it isn't . . . ," Mr. Plumb said, not finishing the sentence.

"Hello, Mr. Plumb." Will mustered a quick smile.

"The girl's reeled you back here, eh?" Mr. Plumb smiled, his crazy eyes bulging out of their sockets. "Where you at now?"

99

"Columbia," Will answered.

"Very nice, very nice," Mr. Plumb said, slapping Will on the back. "Well, I'm going to get a slice. Be a good boy, now."

"I will," Will muttered.

"All I can think is, Why not," I said. "Do you know what I mean?"

"No." He sighed, running his thumb over my palm. "But I can try, I guess."

"You can't do it just because you love me," I said.

"There's no other reason, Thea, sorry."

We both turned to stare at the big double doors at the top of the steps, watching as kids streamed into the street, chatty and enervated in the gray midday light. I wondered how close Will was to walking away.

"My parents are going to freak out," he said quietly.

"What do you think they'll do?" I asked, not sure what direction he was going in yet.

"Hell if I know." We looked at each other and hugged, and I imagined us in one of those telling soap-opera hugs, with him frowning behind me without me realizing.

20.

I thanked the bartender for the ginger ale, envisioning the straight, sharp lines across Dad's forehead. I wondered how he might come between us. What he could say or do to change Will's mind.

"I *knew* you wouldn't go through with it," Vanessa had

said when I'd told her that morning at breakfast that I'd decided to keep the baby. She stirred the streaky cream in her coffee as the words poured out of her. "I don't know why, but I feel like it's meant to be this way. I didn't want to say anything, I know it'll be tough, but if anyone can do it, you can. You're a *pioneer*. You make the rules. How did Fiona take it?"

"She's not speaking to me," I said, amazed at how Vanessa had so swiftly changed her tune to support mode without blinking an eye.

"Shocker," Vanessa said, squeezing my hand. "Typical Fiona, so constructive. Don't let it get to you. She'll come around."

Now Will came in and sat at the bar without taking off his coat. "So I told them," he said, breathing fast. "They're pissed, but weirdly, I think they get it. Deep down, they're closet hippies. I told you that. This is normal to them on some level. They want to meet with your parents." He flagged the bartender and mouthed the word "Heineken" after he'd gotten his attention.

"Okay," I said. "What else did they say?"

"They said that if it's what I want, they can't really stop me. But I know my dad was this close to having a stroke. My future up in smoke, all that." I tried to read Will's face, unable to tell if he felt that way too. "But I have to hand it to him. They may have some ulterior thing cooking. I have no idea."

"Like what?" I asked, feeling sweaty and sick at the prospect of Dad walking into the restaurant at any moment.

"Like hiring our dry cleaner who's also a hit man to off you?" he said, pulling out his wallet.

"You think?" I asked, folding down my straw.

"I don't know, I don't think so, but we can't be positive." He smiled tightly and took a big swig of his Heineken. "Just be extra careful."

"C'mon," I said. "What else did they say, really?"

"That they'd talk to my aunt Florence, try and work something out with us living in her apartment while she's teaching in Africa. Florence doesn't want to sublet to anyone she doesn't know, so we may have a leg up in that sense. They actually wondered why they hadn't thought of it earlier, since it would be cheaper for me to live there than to board at Columbia, because of the rent control. They want me to stay in school. They said they'll do *anything* they can to help as long as I stay in school."

"Do you think they hate me?" I asked, realizing how juvenile the question was.

"They didn't say." He rolled his eyes.

Some Italian ballad bellowed out of the jukebox speakers. The whole normal world went on around us.

"Mom asked about your parents," he said, his eyes scanning the bar nervously up and down.

"What about them?" I asked, tugging on the arm of his coat to pull it off.

"Like whether they approve and whether they'll contribute."

"Oh," I said.

"Then my father got to how much." He stood up and got his coat off, looking around for a place to hang it up.

"How much what?" I asked.

"How much 'everyone,' by which he meant your dad, was going to contribute. I'm not sure if they think he's going to foot the whole thing, but they might." *Foot the whole thing.* It came out casually and awkwardly at the same time. I wondered if Will thought that too.

"We'll work it out," I said quickly.

"Well, they should meet." He glanced up at the muted news on the TV. "Does your father have any conception of time?" Will asked, incredulous, pulling his phone out to look at its digital clock. "It's quarter of. How is he not here yet?"

"Sorry, he's completely anal about everything else." I looked at Will's profile against the blue lights from the window. He looked jittery and scared. I was just grateful that he cared about any of it, that he was in the restaurant with me and that he wasn't making me get an abortion or dodging me.

"What the hell is he going to do?" He shook his head. "What do you think?"

"It'll be okay. Just follow my lead. Let me talk."

Dad appeared at the front of the bar, a navy-blue cashmere scarf neatly crossed around his neck.

"Waiting long?" he said, moving toward us. This was how he apologized. Fleshy splats of spring rain disappeared into his trench coat.

"Not too long," I said.

"Good." He kissed me and flagged the host. "I didn't know you'd be joining us, Will," he said, his chin rooting around in the air, which meant his feelings were hurt that I didn't ask him first if Will could come. He kissed me and his cheek was cold, and he smelled like his office. Like black glass and paper.

We sat and Dad hid behind his menu, pulling at his eyebrows, changing lanes in his head. Will and I dove into the bread basket, keeping busy.

"So Dad, we actually have something pretty big that we

want to talk with you about," I said. I poured olive oil onto a plate and put it in the middle of the table for us all to dip the bread into, a loving cup.

Dad took off his coat and hung it around his chair. "What?" he asked, looking at me quizzically. "Did I do something wrong the other night?"

"What? At the benefit?" I asked. "No, why would you think that?"

"You two left sort of abruptly," he said.

"Oh, sorry about that," I said, looking at Will, who was studying the menu. "No, you were in the middle and everything."

"What, then?" he asked, lifting his water glass and sipping. "What's wrong?"

"Nothing's wrong." Will leaned forward, jamming his hands under his bum.

"Don't freak out, okay?" I said, smiling as though I had a terrific surprise.

"Why would I freak out?" Dad asked.

"Because," I said. The waitress drifted over in her black sneakers with red laces, then retreated when I said, "I'm pregnant."

"Wh-who," he stuttered.

"I am," I said, looking at Will. "We are."

He stared at me, glass in hand, frozen.

"We're going to have a baby," I said. "In July."

"Thea, I don't understand." He sat back in a way that made me feel contagious.

"It wasn't intentional," said Will. "But I guess you could say it is now."

I expected anger or disgust, but not death. Dad looked like someone had just died.

"How pregnant are you?" he whispered.

"About four months. Dad, I know it's a lot, but we're figuring it out. We're making plans."

"Please God," he whispered.

"It's not a please-God situation." I laughed. "I know it wasn't exactly in anyone's plan, and I know it's going to be tricky, but it feels like the right thing." I felt like I was talking to an old man. Will and I stared at each other, wide-eyed. I looked over the top of Dad's head, toward the lights above the bar, letting them pin in and blur out.

"I'm sorry, no. That's quite enough." He stood up, pulled some bills out of his wallet, even though we hadn't yet ordered, and grabbed his coat off his chair, then stalked toward the door. We sat there paralyzed, our empty white plates shining at us.

"Quite enough," I said. "Jesus."

"He's clearly not a fan of mine," Will said.

"It's not you," I snapped.

"He couldn't even look at me."

"I was not expecting that," I said. "It was like he didn't even see us."

"Only his broken dreams." Will downed his beer, shaking his head. "What now?"

Outside the window, people were walking home from work with briefcases and bags from the Food Emporium. I thought about a cab ride I had taken with Dad once. An old Jennifer Lopez song had been on the radio, and at the end of the song Dad had said, "There's a place in this world for Jennifer Lopez." He'd said it matter-of-factly, with no derision. That's how I'd imagined him being about the baby. That he'd figure out a place for it. That or better. I'd fantasized that Dad would see it as something unique to me, like parents see certain gifts or talents in their children. That he'd see it as something I was somehow destined for. But that was how *I* saw it, I realized. Not him.

"He's going to call Mom," I said. "I should go home."

I raced home, unlocked the door and went straight to the bathroom, turning the tub water on. I got in and when I turned off the water, I could hear the defensive quality in Mom's voice as she talked to him on the phone. Except now it was more like a schtick. Like Alice and Ralph Cramden, black-and-white and gritty and muted. Firecrackers shooting onto garbage cans and sputtering off.

"She told me last night," Mom said, not caring if I heard. "She said she wants to have it, the same thing she told you. It's a crusade, Ted, she's clearly on a crusade. . . . For Christ's sake, of course I have . . . unequivocally. . . . My daughter's fallen pregnant . . . you think I'm swinging from the rafters? . . . You'd think if she'd learned one thing from me, it's independence. . . . Most of the time she's going to the bloody opposite . . . so this is perfect. . . . Stop it . . . if you act for one second like this is my fault . . . one second, Ted . . . I mean it . . . She's got it all *mapped out,* Ted, for God's sake. . . ."

I heard a pause and then she said, "Fine, so come and talk to her about it. . . . No, tonight . . . tomorrow's no good." She hung up and called from her bed.

"Daddy's coming over."

"Now?" I yelled. "It's almost ten."

"Now. Get out of the tub."

I put on sweats instead of a nightgown and opened the door to my tall father and his runny nose. He glared at me and headed for the living room, pausing by the dining room table. It had been years since he'd been to our apartment. The table was littered with change and receipts and shopping bags with tissue paper hanging out. A chair had a stack with my folded laundry on it from when Rula had been there. I hadn't yet brought it to my room.

"Do you have some water?" he asked. He looked as though his thoughts had hardened into slabs of granite.

I went to get him water as Mom came out of her room in her bathrobe and sat on the ottoman, the Nivea on her calves smelling up the room. Dad sat on the couch, still in his coat. I sat in the white armchair, dragging it a little to face them as a wave of thick, intractable loneliness crawled over me.

"I'm disappointed you didn't feel like you could come to us before this point," he began. "What prevented you from having a conversation with one, or both of us, at the very least?"

"I found her a doctor, Ted," Mom said, throwing her arms up. "As far as I knew, it was taken care of weeks ago!"

"Is that true?" he asked me.

I nodded, feeling guilty for not including him in that chapter.

"I want to just clarify something." He leaned forward on his elbows, his fingertips touching. "And it's delicate, so I'll just ask it. . . . An abortion is . . . no longer an option. Is that correct?"

"I could probably find someone if I tried, but I don't want one."

"Then, Thea, we have to seriously consider adoption."

"No," I said, picking at the seam of the chair.

"You're bringing a human being into the world," Dad said. "That alone is enough for an eighteen-year-old. That would be an accomplishment."

107

"Not happening," I said, probably too quickly. I looked down and saw that I'd ripped the seam and put my hand over it. Mom didn't notice because she wasn't looking at me. She stared straight ahead, her face expressionless. She'd already given up on me. Dad looked at her for help, and for a minute I thought it had switched to Dad and me against her.

"What is it about adoption you're opposed to?" he asked.

"I don't know," I said. "But I know I couldn't do it."

"You have to do better than that," Dad said.

"I just . . . This baby is already mine, I can't explain it," I said. "I can't imagine giving it to someone else."

"Well, I've clearly lost the plot, Thea," Mom sniffed, pressing her crossed arms to her rib cage. "Exactly how do you plan to keep it? To support it?"

I stared at the glass bowl on the coffee table. Dad had used it as an ashtray when I was younger. It had little bubbles on the bottom, and I remembered I used to picture the bubbles rising to the top of the ashtray and popping.

"I guess I'm hoping you can help us," I said, the room humming with silence as I realized, for the first time, what I was asking. What I was asking of everyone. How I was crowding up their lives with this mysterious, massive thing.

"I know it's a lot to ask," I said. "I know."

Mom turned her head toward the window, her face a tight ball of disgust.

"Maybe whatever we do, we could treat it as some kind of five-year loan or something," I said. "Or ten years. We think we've got a place to live. Will's aunt Florence is teaching in Africa for two years and may sublet her apartment to us."

"Where?" Dad asked sharply.

"It's in the Village, it's a big studio, I haven't seen it, but it's a rent-controlled apartment, so it's like nine hundred dollars a month or something like that."

"So when you say you've got a place to live, you mean you've got a place to live that we have to pay for," Mom practically spat.

"I'll get a job if you want," I said, pulling my knees up to my chest.

"Good luck with that," she said. "No one will hire you if they know you're pregnant."

"You want to keep it." Dad sighed. It was like he'd fallen behind and had to review the basic facts. It was like I was with Mr. Binder, my tutor.

"I want to keep it," I repeated.

"Thea, forgive me if I'm having trouble envisioning you as ready to take on the burden of raising another human being," Dad said. He stood up and paced between the couch and Mom's pink birdcage-as-artwork in the corner. "It was just a couple of summers ago that you were not even capable of handling *yourself* in a responsible manner."

"Not that again," I said. "Look, I know, I was a bad, bad girl. I get it. But this is not the same thing at all."

"Tell me this, then," Mom said, the dark roots on top of her head coming into full view as she looked down at her cuticles. "What, exactly, has changed? You've gone and screwed us over again, have you not?"

Dad sat down and cleared his throat. "Thea, I'm going to say this once. Ever since you were born, I've dreamed of you going to college. You can roll your eyes all you want, but I've dreamed of it."

"Why?" I said. "Why is it so important?"

"Because when it's the right fit, it affords you the rare

opportunity to learn things about yourself. On your own, without anyone . . . interfering."

"It's not like I'll never go."

"You'd have a child," he said, pulling off the scarf around his neck. "You'd be distracted, not to mention burdened. It wouldn't be the same."

"He dragged me to his reunion before you were born," Mom said, suddenly changing the tone of the conversation. "They kept calling him Tinny—why, I'll never know. They went out into the cornfields and tipped cows and left them there like that."

"You start to carve out your life," he said, ignoring her. "It's an exciting time. It's wonderful." His voice cracked.

"And it can all be yours," Mom said, imitating a game show host.

"I can go later," I said, trying to reassure him.

"Thea, this is beyond comprehension to me," he said, thrusting back on the couch, gripping his knees. "How are you going to live? Will's going to take care of you? Will's going to have your health and the health of the baby as his first priorities? Fiona?"

"That's the plan," said Mom.

"Well, I don't think moving in with Will is the solution."

Mom shook her head. "She's going to do what she wants, Ted. You're being a bit thick. If you'd been tuning in for the last year, you'd have realized that she's obsessed with him."

"I'm not obsessed with him, Mom," I said. "Will wants it this way too."

She looked at me for the first time since we sat down. "He wants it because *you* want it and you've managed to convince him it's the right thing to do. Don't think for a second he'd have come to it on his own."

110

"Okay, calm down, everyone," Dad said. "Fiona, we need to help her."

"She's had a ton of help, Ted. She's had nothing but help."

"Stop making it sound like I've turned on you," I said. "Like I'm turning on you and like I'm just some manipulative . . . slut. I'm just trying to figure out the best thing." I thought of Will and felt a sharp stab of fear—did he secretly hate me for wanting this? I hated Mom for making it sound so bad. I remembered Dad chasing Mom around the house when I was little, Dad yelling, "Come back here, you little minx." I remembered Mom half-naked with a hairbrush in her hand.

"Mom, what's a minx?" I'd asked.

"A minx is a devious little thing," she had yelled into the doorframe of my bedroom. "A vixen. A cunning little trollop." Her eyes had poured out something hard and feminine and she'd run off, but Dad had caught her under the armpit and led her away like a cartoon cop dragging a baddie into custody, Mom screaming and laughing, Dad slamming their bedroom door behind them.

"The best thing would be for you to grow up." Mom stood and headed to the kitchen, clearly sick of being my mother.

"Thea, there are hundreds of very good placement agencies," Dad continued. "Parents who would give anything for a child. You have no idea. I know of people, women at work who can't have children. People who are desperate to have families, who can't have babies by themselves. Thea, please, I'm begging you. Think about it. Take some time and really think about it."

"Give it up, Ted, she's already gone." Mom came back in, chewing a handful of pretzels. She thought this was all his fault.

"I'll think about it," I said.

"Oh, please, don't lie," said Mom.

Dad stood up. "Fiona!"

"What?" she screamed. "You think she's listening to a bloody word you're saying?"

"At least I'm trying," he said.

"Right, and you're really reaching her, Ted."

His eyes seemed to recede beneath his eyebrows. Was it anger or hatred, or both? I'd seen it on his face before, and I understood how there would be no turning back about someone after that. How no amount of talking or making up or whatever could undo it. He paused for a moment, shaking his head at me, then walked out, slamming the door.

"Yeah, that's it." Mom exhaled loudly, her mouth O-shaped, like she'd just finished a sprint and was catching her breath. "Useless coward."

21.

"What if it's a girl?" Vanessa turned to me while we were stopped at a red light on our way to Stash, a knitting store on Charlton Street. "I envy you."

"Yeah, you envy me," I said. "You envy the looks Mr. Kushman gives me throughout the entire forty minutes of calculus, like I'm all woman now."

"Ew!" she yelped.

"I think it's a boy," I said, changing the subject. I pictured a baby in a yellow undershirt that snapped under the crotch. A baby rolling around on the lawn, on the mildewed quilt that hung on a nail in our shed on Charter Island.

"I wonder what it will say to you, the boy," she said. "What will it say?"

"They don't talk right away," I said, holding her back against the curb as a taxi whizzed past us.

"Of course not," she said. "But imagine him saying, 'That skirt looks so nice on you,' or 'Don't wear that lipstick, Mommy,' or 'I'm tired, Mommy,' or 'I love you more than my Thomas trains, Mommy, I love you, I love you, I love you, Mommy.'" Vanessa's head bobbed and swayed like a belly dancer's. "Could you just?"

"Maybe I should turn the scarf into a blanket for it," I said.

"Or you can start something else for it."

"What do you think it would like?" I asked.

"It could use a lot of things—a blankie, some sockies, you name it, it could use it."

"It," we both said, doing our Madonna blinks at each other.

A cowbell jangled over our heads when Vanessa opened the door to the yarn store. A pale-faced woman in a tie-dyed thermal shirt looked up from her computer.

"Those bells are loud," she said dryly.

Vanessa strode across the white floor, her rubber biker boots clomping as loudly as rubber could. "Hi, we want to buy some yarn." She popped the gum she was chewing.

The woman got up slowly from her stool and walked around the desk, her faded black cargo skirt trailing threads from the hem.

"Are you starting something or do you need to replenish?" she asked, sticking a pencil behind her ear.

"Replenish," Vanessa said. "I'm making something for her baby. It's a secret." The woman arched her eyebrows at me, more in benign surprise than disapproval, and I felt what it was like to be pregnant, out in the open, for the first time. It still seemed like it was happening to someone else.

"How should we do this?" she asked Vanessa. "Do you want to whisper it to me?"

"It's okay, I'll go over here," I said, walking to the opposite corner and seeing the table of thin, glossy, hardback books. *Leona's Big Book of Caps. The World's Coolest Socks.* There was another woman sitting in an office in back with straight, reddish purple hair and severe bangs. She was knitting something tartan, and Jimi Hendrix was playing on her computer.

"Ella?" the woman in the cargo skirt called to her.

"Yes?" Ella called back, not looking up.

"Do we have any more skeins of Mongoose Forty-Four?"

"Skeins." Vanessa smirked at me from across the room. "I love that word."

Ella glanced at the ceiling in the office. "It's on order. I'd give it another month."

"Shit!" Vanessa pouted.

The woman looked over at me and whispered something to Vanessa.

"I know," Vanessa said. "I could do that." I looked away. The walls were lined with little box-shaped shelves filled with yarn, and by the window there was a big wooden spinning wheel with a crank that looked very old.

"I'm considering just showing you so you can have a part in this decision," Vanessa called, being overly serious. "I'm at a crossroads and may need to change tacks."

"Okay, so show me." I shrugged and walked over.

She pulled it out of her bag and held it up. It was the same beige yarn she had shown me the day she taught me to crochet in her room, only now it was half of a hat.

"I thought you were making a sweater," I said. That day in Vanessa's room seemed like a million, trillion years ago.

"I undid it. I thought it would be a cool baby hat. I'm going to make a tiny brim in front, so it's kind of trucker. Except now I need to do the top in a different color. I don't want to wait a month. What about a light green?" She swiveled the unfinished hat around on her fingers. "You don't like it."

"No," I said. It was hitting me hard at that moment that I would soon have a tiny infant who I would have to feed and change and be responsible for every second of every day for the rest of my life. The room went a little foggy. "It's cute. I love it."

Vanessa turned to the woman.

"So if I go with the green, how do I do it?"

"Just finish the row and switch." The woman blinked. "You pull the new color through the loop. You know how to do that, right?"

Vanessa nodded, but I could tell she was too proud to admit she didn't know how to do it.

"If you have a little yellow left, you could do the very top in a little gather, or you could do a little pom-pom. Up to you."

"Hmmmm, cunning," Vanessa said, stealing a glance at me. "But I don't think the baby will be the pom-pom type. Do you, Thee?"

"Hard to say," I said, watching the woman walk over to the green shelf. She was maybe ten years older than us, and she inhabited the room in the way that a place becomes a part of someone after they're in it for a long time. It was the same way Mom was at Fiona's. Like she owned it and it owned her, too. There was something about this woman, something funny.

That bell is loud. I looked back at the beige nubs of yarn on Vanessa's needle. There was a tiny hole near her hand.

"But we'll go with the green, right, Thee?" Vanessa asked. "I'll take a *skein* of the green, and then I've got to split. Have to get uptown for Miles's thing." She plunked a credit card down on the high Lucite counter. I reached into my jacket pocket for a tear-out from *Vogue* of a woman in a crocheted dress with a blue, yellow and green zigzag pattern. It was the kind of look I wanted for a new version of the crocheted bikini from the photo of me on the beach. I was still obsessed with making it, and I had that photo with me too.

Vanessa stuffed the new green yarn into her straw beach bag. "You coming?"

"I think I'll linger," I said.

"I'll call you later. Byeeee." She waved, clanging the cowbell on her way out.

It felt easier to approach the woman now that Vanessa was gone. I looked at the shelves again. Everything was arranged by color, and when you looked across the shelves, it was like looking at a very detailed rainbow spectrum, blue into teal into green into yellow, each color predictable yet surprising. I thought about zigzaggy sunburst patterns and interwoven squares in primary colors. Thinking about the crocheted bikinis made me feel like the world was opening a window into another world. I went up to the counter, where the woman was staring into her big flat-panel computer screen.

"Paper cutters, my new fixation," she said. She turned the screen to me and pointed to a white paper cutout of a woman with a huge skirt. "There are people out there who spend hours with, like, tiny razor blades, cutting these incredibly meticulous designs. It's just bizarre. But beautiful, right?"

I looked at the screen. The woman's skirt had hundreds of

swirls and what looked like little unicorns all over it. "Wow," I said. She was right, it was absolutely beautiful. And a little heartbreaking. All the painstaking, obsessive effort that went into it.

"So can I help you out with anything else?" she asked, eyeing the tear-out in my hand.

"Well, I had this idea and I was hoping you could help me find a pattern, or you know, some instructions."

I pulled out the bikini photo and handed it to her.

"Is that you?" she said, moving it closer and farther from her face.

"Yes, when I was younger, obviously. I was hoping you could help me find a pattern that, you know, looks like it."

"Hmmm . . . interesting." She studied the photo, fiddling with the green stone on the thin, black satin choker around her neck. "Was there elastic in the waist and leg?"

"Yes," I said, distinctly remembering the feeling of rubber bands against my skin.

"I guess you could lead some kind of elastic through when you were all done." She looked at me, considering. "Have you worked on other projects or will this be your first?"

"I've done a few things," I lied. "Though this seems like it will be more complicated."

"It will, but no biggie. I don't have a pattern, but it's pretty straightforward stuff. I could probably figure it out for you."

"Really?" I asked, trying not to sound too excited.

"Sure." She lifted the stone again and dropped it. "It'll take me a few days. I'll have to look at a pair of undies. What size are you? This is for you, I take it?"

"Medium," I said. "Normally, that is. Yes, it's for me—I'm not sure I was actually planning on *wearing* it. In my current state, and all."

"You just want to re-create it," she said. She continued studying the picture. I could tell she was intrigued by the situation: a practically adolescent pregnant girl clinging to a remnant of her troubled childhood. "Yours looks like it was more of a tube top, right? It might be nicer to do a halter."

"I love halters," I said.

She started sketching on her blotter. "How's this?"

I moved behind the counter. "Is the bottom a little skimpy?" I asked.

"You want it to go higher, toward the belly button?"

"Yeah, I think so." She kept drawing and it became clear to me. "I want it sort of big, like a pair of big, unsexy Carter's briefs."

"Cool." She nodded enthusiastically. "A little weird, but cool. You sound like me. I detest thongs. I find them aggressively disgusting."

"I just think they'd look cool sort of big and, you know, like you're covered up."

"Like Marilyn Monroe. Marilyn wore big undies and big bikinis. Cool!"

"Right, like Marilyn," I said, getting excited. "Everyone wore big cover-up bikinis in the fifties, right? That's what I want."

She drew a little more. "That better? You could even do a cute band across the top."

"No, I want to do zigzags." I fished the *Vogue* zigzag dress out of my wallet. "Like this."

"Ahhh. Sort of a seventies vibe."

"Well, not obviously seventies, right?" I asked.

"No, it'll depend on what colors you use." She flipped a paper clip on the blotter, which was framing a calendar that had Xs marked through the days, and notes written in script with a fuchsia highlighter. She'd doodled the word *Expo* over and over again in the margins. "I think it could look very cool. I'll work out a pattern. Can I hold on to the photo?"

"Sure."

"I won't lose it," she said, pressing it to her chest. "Promise."

"Wow, thanks. I'm so excited."

"My pleasure," she said, moving a bowl of Red Hots toward me. "That's what yarn-store ladies are for."

22.

The parents got together one night in May to discuss our future. I took it as a good sign that the Westons were willing to come downtown.

Will called while they were out. "Notice how they didn't invite us?" he said. "It's like we're little children they need to sort out."

I sat on the living room couch and pulled the purple yarn I'd crocheted into half of a scarf out of its scarf form. The woman at the yarn store had told me to use some scrap yarn to practice new stitches I'd need for the bikini. I was feeling cheap and I wanted to save money for the good stuff once I figured out how to do it. I loved that about crocheting—how yarn could transform into something else just by pulling the hook out and unraveling. When the yarn unraveled, it bent in this cool pattern, like long, crimped purple hair.

I leafed through the crochet magazine I'd bought that showed the new stitches and watched the clock, envisioning the four of them. Dad would spot Mr. Weston and walk over to him with his arms extended, the way he walks across the lawn to greet someone at a summer party, and then he'd grasp Mr. Weston's elbow as he shook his hand. He'd introduce Mom to the Westons, and for a moment, the formal introduction would soften her heavily bleached hair and her fire-engine-red lipstick, smudged around her lips in a way that was okay for a Saturday visit to art galleries but foreign and a little odd to people who had a basketball hoop in their living room.

I imagined them sitting at an outdoor café on lower Fifth Avenue, the May breeze billowing through Mom's pretty blond hair and Mrs. Weston's scraggly ponytail. How they'd order drinks and the Westons would wonder about Dad's choice of plain tonic with lime, but at the same time they'd notice his quiet, distinguished demeanor and understand that whatever battles he'd had were in his past, and they would respect him for overcoming them. Dad would smile at Mr. Weston's twinkly-eyed attempts to lighten the situation. He'd take out a legal pad to figure out our finances and Mr. Weston would make a joke about the pad, and Dad would laugh gruffly and say, "Well, I am a numbers guy." Mrs. Weston would watch Mom in her low V-neck, black jersey wrap sweater and wonder why she didn't try to dress like that every so often instead of in her usual baggy button-downs and jeans. She'd wonder where she could find clothes like that, stuff that was for every day but that also had a little edge. She'd be tempted to ask Mom, but decide to do it when they'd see each other again. Toward the end, they'd give each other knowing looks of resignation and talk about Will's and my endearing, exasperating habits, like how Will comes home from school and records basketball games that he never watches, and wastes Mr. Weston's DVR space, or how he leaves his socks balled up under the dining room table like little cow pies, or how I leave the caps off everything—toothpaste and especially medicine bottles—and how I'm going to have to be careful about that when the baby comes. "They're in for it," I imagined Mom saying as they put on their coats, and I pictured them giving each other knowing looks, behind which would be little flickers of joy and anticipation for their unborn grandchild, as if he or she were already in the restaurant with them, drawing them together into an intimate football huddle.

Mom walked through the door at ten on the dot.

"Hi," I said, rolling up from the couch.

"Were you sleeping?" she asked, undoing the belt of her coat.

"Uh-uh," I said. "How did it go?"

She threw her coat on a chair and went to the kitchen. I heard her unlock the dishwasher and start clattering stuff onto the counter.

I followed her and sat down at the table. "So how did it go?"

"One of these days you could empty the dishwasher."

"Sorry," I said. "What happened?"

"We talked." She tossed some forks into the tray, then picked up the small strainer she used to rinse berries and shook it dry.

"About?"

"Money, basically. We're each going to give you ten thousand dollars. You're going to keep separate bank accounts and be responsible for your own expenses. We'll see how far that goes. I hope they hold up their end."

"Wow, okay," I said, feeling suddenly like a helpless child.

121

"Like I said, we can treat it as a loan. We'll pay you back over time."

"I won't hold my breath," she said. "You won't exactly be employable, and Will's parents appear to be keen on him staying in school. Daddy is also hell-bent that you keep your spot at NYU until the time is right for you to go back." She shut the silverware drawer and turned around. "Honestly, I don't understand this country's obsession with education. Will should get a job, in my opinion."

"Well, thank you," I said, fingering the Bloomingdale's catalog on top of the stack of mail, too embarrassed to look at her. Money had a way of doing that.

"Other than that, we discussed our disappointment that you couldn't be persuaded," she said. "That took a while."

"Mom, I'm done. I'd always wonder. I know enough to know I couldn't live with not keeping it. Can we move on now?"

"Move on. My only daughter is wrecking her life. Move on."

"What did you think of Mrs. Weston?"

"What did I think?" She reached down to pull the plates out of the dishwasher. "What does it matter?"

"She's sort of bug-eyed, don't you think?" I thought about how so much of what I said came from rotten, anxious places. "She's more with it than she comes across, but she seems a little spacey, right?"

"I didn't notice."

"You were just together for two hours. You didn't notice anything?"

"Thea, don't." She shut the dishwasher with a neat click and dried her hands. "I know she wants more for Will, things that don't involve this crap." The way she drew out the word

122

crap, I felt like a trampy, knocked-up cretin with big buckteeth, wearing dirty, light-blue corduroys. "I sometimes wish you could just be me for a minute so you could understand how much this stinks."

"You know, what about just thinking about what *I* think is right for me?" I asked. "What's meaningful to me? It is my life, after all."

She turned around and faced me, one hand on her hip. "I forget who once said to me, 'Children are thankless,' but they were right. They were absolutely right." She pulled a Toblerone bar out of the butter door of the fridge and went to her room.

"I said thank you!" I yelled after her.

23.

The morning of graduation, the sky was a deep, sharp blue and the wind made the spouts of the Lincoln Center fountain bend in different directions like a frothy liquid compass. My purple polyester gown, striped with creases from the box, slithered against my now giant stomach. Vanessa took my hand and we skipped to the hall underneath the murals of dancers. I wished Will could have been there, but when I had asked Mom if I could invite him, she had given me a "Don't-even-think-about-it" look.

"I have no interest in celebrating your achievements with someone who's essentially destroyed your future," she'd said, and I had taken that as my cue to drop the subject.

The ceremony took two and a half hours, enough time for

four hundred kids to march across the stage and get their diplomas. Afterward, Stephen Bustello, a kid in my class everyone lusted after, stood on the granite ledge of the fountain and threw his cap in, and it floated on top of a spout before falling into the bubbles. The diamond stud in his ear caught the sun and reflected little dots of light onto someone's shoulder. I'll probably never see him again, I thought. I pictured him flying over the city like a superhero, laughing at all of us.

My parents and I went with Vanessa's parents and her brother, Miles, to a dark Greek restaurant with a big stone fireplace that had no fire in it because it was almost summer.

"Why there, why not someplace more fun?" Mom had asked.

"We want to go somewhere close by," I had said. It seemed important to have lunch near the actual event.

"Lincoln Center, yuck," she'd responded.

When Vanessa and I had graduated from junior high together, we'd had lunch at Tavern on the Green. Now when we sat down at the Greek restaurant, Vanessa's mother passed around pictures of twelve-year-old Vanessa and me sitting in tall brocade chairs, holding up glasses with ginger ale and cherries in them. We were the only ones at the table. My hair was too long and lemon yellow, and there was a blue ribbon hanging off the side of my head. I was grinning and looking sideways at Vanessa, and she was looking into the camera, her shoulders neat and narrow, her eyes smart with secrets.

"To the girls," Dad said. He sat across the round white table, next to Mr. March.

"To the girls," we all repeated.

"To the graduates," said Vanessa's dad. "The cream of the crop."

"All the best to both of you," Dad said. Mom fidgeted with her gold bangle bracelets and her vodka tonic and studied the people at other tables.

"To bravery," Vanessa's mom said. I knew she'd never wish my situation on Vanessa, but she winked at me.

"To stupidity, more like it," Mom muttered. No one else heard her. I slathered triangles of pita bread with olive oil and taramosalata and crumbled feta cheese, starving. The waiter brought plates of calamari and stuffed olives. Mr. March talked to Dad about how much our high school had changed since his father had gone there, when it was boys only.

"Constant brawls," Mr. March said. "He used to say it was like Rikers, I'm not kidding." Mr. March was skinny with a small potbelly and wore the same glasses Diane Keaton wore in *Annie Hall*. Dad chuckled politely, his index finger stretching his brow toward the ceiling. Dad injected something celebratory into the dim room. But he hardly said a word.

"I just want to lie on Thea's dock this summer," Vanessa said, stroking my cheek. "Kay?"

"Don't torture me, Vanessa, please," said Mrs. March. "We begged and borrowed to get you that thing at Nickelodeon."

"I knowww, but I just need a li'l breaky," she moaned.

"Breaky, I'll show ya breaky," Mr. March interjected, making a fist with his pudgy hand.

"What am I going to do without my Nessy around to rattle my chain?" Mrs. March mused at the menu, shaking her head. "Who's going to give me lousy pedicures?" She looked at my mother. "The first one to go, Fiona. My heart's about to snap."

Mom smiled empathically at Mrs. March and then her face faded behind a cloud. I realized she wanted *me* to go. I straightened my forks and had the weird sensation of being there in my body, sandwiched between Mom and Vanessa, but with the rest of me vaporizing out of the restaurant to a place where I existed completely alone with my thoughts and worried plans.

24.

I celebrated the first Monday of no school by going to Stash. The cowbell clanged and the woman behind the counter looked up as I entered. I was the only one in the store.

"So I think I figured it out," she said cheerfully, recognizing me right away. She pulled open a drawer, fished around and walked toward me with a piece of graph paper that had about twenty numbered instructions and a lot of capital-letter abbreviations. The photo of me in the bikini was paper-clipped to the top.

"What's that?" I asked, pointing to the letters *SC*.

"Single crochet," she said. "Which is mostly what this is, for tightness. Have you ever worked with a pattern before?"

"Actually, no, I've only done a scarf. Is it hard?"

"It's not hard," she said, and from the way she looked at me, I knew it would be. "It's just there are a few things you need to familiarize yourself with. If you have a minute, I could quickly go over it."

"That would be great," I said.

"You're lucky—I got nothing doing at the moment," she said. She went through the pattern abbreviations and got me started, casting on the first side with some practice yarn from a basket by the counter.

"It's basically a series of single crochets, joined together by chains and slip stitches," she said.

"Slip stitch?" I asked, staring at her blankly.

"I'll show you, don't worry."

"I'm glad the original was crocheted and not knitted," I said. "I've tried a few times to knit and I always screw up. I have these big ambitions with knitting and I can never follow through."

She smiled in an understanding way. "You just need someone to help you get started." She took my hook and checked it, then handed it back. "Crochet's a different game, maybe more fun, I sometimes think. More air. I'm a hard-core knitter, but crochet is airy. And it's more forgiving."

"You mean if you mess up," I said.

"If you mess up, and the flow, I don't know." She mimicked winding her fingers and an imaginary needle. "I'm obsessed with it all. Sometimes I think it borders on pathological." She sat back in the chair. "It makes everything better."

"How long have you had Stash?" I asked, spreading out the chains so I could see them better. "I'm Thea, by the way."

"I'm Carmen." She smiled. "Two years. It was my husband's idea. We were trying to get pregnant and I couldn't stop cleaning. I would go through, like, five bottles of 409 a week. So he was like, 'You have to stop cleaning.' He said I should open a shop."

"Well, it's a great place," I said.

"Thank you." She looked around contentedly and checked my hook again. "Okay, you did three of those, right? Now it's time to connect them with a slip stitch." She reached my hook across the three chains and pulled the yarn through. "It's basically just a connector stitch. No biggie. There, you got it. So when is your baby due?"

"In the summer," I said. "I'm moving in with my boy-friend."

"Are you in school?"

"I just graduated from high school."

"Wow," she said. "That's brave."

"What?" I asked.

"I don't know, having a baby barely out of high school."

"Well, we didn't exactly plan it. Our parents are still in freak-out mode."

"Yikes," she said. She looked at me like she wanted to ask a million questions, but instead she turned back to the pattern. "You're doing really well. You'll probably get stuck, make some mistakes, have some questions. Feel free to come back any-time. Come back anyway. I want to see how it turns out."

I stood up and thanked her, a little embarrassed by how much she'd helped me. She walked me to the door and saw me off, standing on the sidewalk with her arms folded, as though she were saying goodbye from her house. I started down the street, stopping at a light to jam the pattern into my bag, not knowing where to put the photo of me in the bikini so that it wouldn't get any more beaten up than it already was. I looked at my face in the photo; I had a sort of Mona Lisa half smile going, but even ten-plus years later, it was immedi-ately raw and decipherable. Me and my grandmother on the beach, after breakfast—toast and milk and orange juice, in side-by-side glasses. She was keeping me out of our house after another four a.m. blow-up.

"Why in the world would I want to go to Alan's with you?"

I remembered hearing Dad shout as I lay in bed. I'd crept to the top of the stairs and peeked. He was standing in the middle of the round woven rug, towering over Mom in a rocking chair. Then Mom stood up, my grandmother's dark green bathrobe draping at her feet. "If you don't like it, don't buy it," she'd said. "I can't imagine why they'd want us in the first place." She'd pretended to shake hands in the air, then turned and looked at her feet. "Uh, hi, uh-uh-uh, Alan, nice tacking out there, uh, today?" I didn't know what she was talking about, just that she was making fun of him. I focused on the big rusty fan in the corner of the upstairs hallway, feeling the silence in every pore, its terrible, inescapable vacuum. I wondered what it would be—one of the sailing trophies on the mantel? The TV? But this time, she struck first. He spat at her and gave her the infamously cryptic title of "Shit-Hair," and that was when she swung the storm lamp in an upward swoop, as though she were swinging a tennis racquet, slamming it at his ear. I remembered not needing to pretend to be asleep by the time the cops came, and after they left, Mom taking me upstairs to sleep in the guest room with the door locked.

"That's it, I promise," I remembered her whispering. I stared at the roses on her nightgown, which grew more and more detailed as light crept into the room. My eyes skipped from one rose to the next, and the white spaces in between them became the spaces between me and Mom and Dad, and I thought about how she wasn't scared of him, and it seemed stark, that fact. Something to be afraid of, maybe, in and of itself.

As I crossed the street, I caught a woman in a trench coat and heels glancing at my belly and then at my face. If she thought I was too young to be a baby mama, she didn't let on. I nudged the bikini photo into the chest pocket of my jean jacket, where it would be safe, as it started to rain.

part three

25.

I packed CDs, no shrieking ballads by women with angry, suffering voices. This was my new life; I was done with those. I took the salad spinner Mom didn't use. She used to pull the string too hard, making the top fly off, then gasp like someone had snuck up on her. I took a rusty peeler instead of the good one with the thick plastic grip, an old nail kit Mom didn't use anymore and washed-out gray bath towels with strings hanging off that she wouldn't miss. I packed and thought about how being with Will might be like chess, how you can play at that first level, a level that's hard but not too hard, and how getting to the next level would require the kind of concentration and willpower that you might not have, but that you wouldn't know whether you had it or not unless you tried.

I jammed my makeup into Dad's old Virgin Airlines travel case made of spongy fake leather. I took five to seven of each thing, underwear, short- and long-sleeved shirts, things I could wear pregnant and not pregnant. I left my turtlenecks—they reminded me too much of school.

Mom was in her room as I dragged my big duffel down the hall.

"So goodbye." She sighed, tossing a catalog to the side of her bed. "This is so utterly bizarre, this situation, I'm honestly at a loss."

"I love you," I said, which sounded weird; we never said I love you to each other. I looked at the white brick wall I'd gazed at from Mom's bed my entire life, and thought, This *is* utterly bizarre: I'm moving out. "I'll call you later."

* * *

Will opened the door to Florence's apartment. "Welcome to the pleasure dome," he said, walking backward with his arms extended. I followed him down the long hallway lined with posters by the cartoonist who hid the *Ninas*, into an airy, white room with high ceilings. There were two tall windows on one wall with multiple lead-pane squares, and a wood-paneled kitchen along the opposite wall. A sagging mohair sofa bed lined the window, and a leather armchair that looked as though a cat had had its way with it for decades sat across from it. A black upright piano with yellowing keys sat in front of the far window, and a narrow, thin-legged coffee table stood in the middle of the room. A very beat-up Oriental carpet covered almost the entire floor, bathing everything in a faded-pink glow. I loved it.

"How was the first night?" I asked, dropping my bag.

"The cars sound angry because of the cobblestone, but you get used to it," he said. "You sleep like the dead anyway."

It was hot. There was an air conditioner hanging out the corner window.

"Does that work?" I asked.

"I've spent the last two hours getting it out of the closet and screwing it into the window," Will said. "She had it wedged into the lower shelf of the bedroom closet. It was a nightmare. We need to go out for some of that insulation tape stuff that goes between the window and the unit."

"Unit?" I asked, smirking at his wonky word choice. I took his waist and pulled him down to the prickly, mohair sofa bed with me, and we had slow, side-by-side afternoon sex, throwing the cushions off to make room for my huge body.

At four o'clock I unzipped my duffel.

"Let's go for a walk," he said. He lay naked on the couch, combing through the wisps of hair under his arm.

"I want to unpack."

"Let's do it later. I have to make room first." He waved at the lone tall maple dresser with brass handles. All the drawers were open, his stuff hanging out.

We went out into the breezy June heat. There was no hiding my stomach anymore. I let it just hang out, feeling the ache in the small of my back. Will took my hand and we walked that way for a couple of blocks, but before long we were too sweaty and dropped hands.

We spotted a hardware store on West Twelfth and went in. The entryway was so narrow we had to turn sideways to get past the line at the register. I almost caught my belly on a rack of plastic key rings as Will chuckled from behind me. "Choo choo," he said. I shot him a dirty look. "What?" he asked, trying not to smile.

Will got into an involved discussion with an older hardware guy about how to properly seal in the air conditioner while I studied the back wall of seed packs, somehow comforted by the fact that there were so many of them, so many different kinds of things people would consider growing. I looked at Will and the guy, facing each other, their arms folded in manly collaboration. I picked up a roll of thick white rope wrapped in an orange sleeve and tried to imagine crocheting with it. The rope reminded me of the bumper ties on Dad's boat. Being in the hardware store felt like a whole new life. Will bought a thing of thick rubber siding and we stepped outside into the heat, which was visibly rising from the street, even at five o'clock. When we crossed the street, there was a guy outside selling ices from a sidewalk freezer. Will got two scoops of chocolate and I got a scoop of rainbow. I looked at the incredibly familiar Gino's sign that I felt like I'd seen in the window of every pizza store since I was born. Will handed me my ice and dropped a bit of cherry onto my stomach. He pushed a napkin into my T-shirt and looked up at me.

"I know everyone in the world was once inside someone else's belly," he said, licking. "I realize that and everything, but it still doesn't take away from the fact that it's just the weirdest concept imaginable."

"I know," I said.

We walked into a mattress store just as we finished sucking the last juicy bits from the soggy paper.

"We could ditch the couch and get a real bed," he said. "Florence wouldn't mind."

"What, you're just going to plop her old one out onto the street?" I asked. He hopped on a bed in the back and did all the stupid things people do on a mattress in public. Then he rolled onto his hip and whispered, "Come," caressing the mattress seductively. I lay down.

"Can my princess feel the pea?" He pushed my head back on the plastic pillow and kissed me as I heard a salesman clear his throat.

We went home and ordered Chinese, eating it on Florence's flowered plastic plates. There was no dishwasher, so we stood next to each other, me washing, him drying and doing the bump with me. After that we opened the sofa bed, throwing the stiff cushions into the crack in the corner.

I took the bikini pattern and the skein of lemon-yellow practice yarn I'd bought at Carmen's out of the paper bag as Will turned on the TV. Everything felt weird and new, but having a project helped. I studied the pattern for a while, then realized that before I started, I had to wind the yarn into a ball.

The skein was basically a big circle of yarn that would get too unraveled and messy if I just pulled from it. It had to be wound into a ball first. Carmen had a contraption clamped to a table in her store that wound skeins of yarn into balls, and she'd asked me if I'd wanted her to wind it for me. As I started to wind the skein around two fingers, I wished I'd taken her up on it. The yarn kept sticking to the rest of the skein whenever I tugged at it. Then I had an idea. I got up and went to the foot of the bed.

"Outta my way." Will craned his neck to see the TV. He was sprawled across the bed, licking the melted remains of a Reese's Peanut Butter Cup off his fingers.

"I need to borrow your feet," I said, looping the circle of yarn around his bare, outstretched feet. "Keep them flexed, okay?" I stood to the side of the TV and started winding. It went much faster with his feet.

"This is a huge help," I said, interrupting his *Law & Order* stupor.

"What are you doing?"

"I'm winding this yarn into a ball so I can crochet a bikini."

"A bikini?" he asked, not looking away from the TV.

"A bikini," I said. "I had a crocheted bikini when I was little that I'm trying to remake, sort of."

"What, so you can run around like G-House Rock, pregnant bikini-monster?"

"No, jerk," I said. "I'm not going to wear it now, don't worry. But thanks a lot."

After a while he let his left foot go slack. I pushed it against my leg to flex it again. A commercial came on and Will watched the yarn as it came up from each end of the loop. "Why are you spending money on stuff that you're not going to wear?" he asked.

"It didn't cost much," I said, guiltily remembering the thirty-buck receipt. "Who made you money cop?"

"I'm not money cop," he said. "But we've got to watch it. You don't even have a job."

"I'm eight months pregnant. We've already talked about this. I'll get a job when the baby's old enough to go to day care." I yanked the yarn, accidentally catching it on his toe.

"Ow!" he said. He pulled his foot out from under the loop. "This is stupid. I'm not doing it. Let's just go to bed. You're tired and I have to get up early."

"Fine," I said. I took the remaining loop off Will's foot and shoved it back into the bag along with the ball I'd started. He turned off the TV and reached over to the floor lamp next to the bed.

"Thanks for your help, by the way." I lay on my side in Florence's old sofa bed, feeling as though my head were lower than the rest of my body. Will didn't answer. Our first night together, I thought miserably. The lights from outside made shapes on the ceiling that, put together, looked a little like the mean queen from Dad's house, the evil, frowning stepmother queen, who followed me wherever I went.

26.

Will left the next morning for his job at the law firm—the same job he'd had the summer before—without speaking to me after the stupid fight. I pulled out the bikini pattern and the ball of yellow yarn and started in, ready to apply myself. "Chain four, join into a ring with a slip stitch." Easy. But then it told me to single crochet three times into the center of the ring and there was a problem: I couldn't find the ring. Carmen said it would be obvious, where the ring was, because it would look like a hole. But I poked at it and separated the stitches and I could not find it. I crocheted three times into the center of what I thought was the ring, only to realize it wasn't. A few rounds of that and I realized I was screwed, unable to start the bikini I was dying to start.

"Damn it!" I yelled. I hurled the yarn, furious at it, wanting it away from me. It landed on the rug by the coffee table as the buzzer rang. Mom and Vanessa were coming over for a makeshift shower-breakfast, which was really just an excuse to see our new place.

They arrived together, not on purpose, throwing their coats on Florence's accordion rack in the hallway. Mom plunked a Babies "R" Us shopping bag onto the coffee table and pulled what looked like a stereo receiver out of a box inside it.

"What's that?" I asked.

"It's a pump," she said. Vanessa and I looked dumbly at her.

"Tell me you know what a breast pump is." The black box was connected by clear thin tubes to a pair of baby bottles with suction cups on top. She plugged it into the wall, but nothing happened.

"I don't think that outlet works," I said.

"Of course it doesn't," she grumbled as I glanced nervously at Vanessa, whose brilliant idea it had been to get together that morning. "Is there one that does?"

"The other side of the couch," I said.

Mom lifted the black box and plopped it onto the far end of the coffee table so that the cord could reach the outlet. A whining whirr came and went in waves. She held up the suction cups with the tubes dangling to the floor.

"Annie had one of these," she said. Annie was one of the managers at Fiona's. She'd had her daughter, Tamsin, when she was forty-six. "You attach these little cups to your nips and it leaves your hands free to drink coffee and open your mail. Come here."

She reached over to the armchair where I was sitting and lifted up my shirt.

"Don't!" Vanessa cried. "You'll make her go into labor! I read that in her book. Nipple stimulation can bring on contractions."

"Why are *you* reading *her* pregnancy book?" Mom glared at Vanessa. "You don't have anything better to do?"

"What, it's fun." Vanessa crossed her legs, embarrassed, and pushed the plate of chocolate croissants she'd brought toward Mom.

"Anyway, after the first month Annie stopped nursing altogether and just pumped." She took a sip from the latte in her paper cup and looked at me pointedly. "She said it saved her booby dolls."

"I'll remember that, Mom," I said. "But I'm not as obsessed with my booby dolls as you are." If my mother weighed 130 pounds or under, she liked to wear her Steven Sprouse polyester button-downs from the seventies that she'd bought at a flea market in London. She said she couldn't wear them if she went over 130 because the fabric would stretch across her chest and stomach in between the buttons and she hated the way that looked. I knew what she meant, but I thought it looked trampy in a good way. When she wore the shirts, her boobs were her booby dolls, her friends, as in, "My booby dolls and I are going to Healthy Bagel." But when she felt fat, she'd lie in bed and watch them fall off to either side, her chin burrowed into her collarbone, scrutinizing. Then they were her "craven globes." "Fie on thee, craven globes," she'd say. When I was little, I thought she'd said, "Pie on thee." I thought it meant Dad had made his chocolate-chip pecan pie, which he did sometimes when he was hungover.

"So it's nice here, right?" I asked Vanessa, afraid to look at Mom. "It's a great deal. We're paying her rent, and she's on rent control. It was perfect for her because she didn't want to sublet to anyone she didn't know and she didn't have any takers in the two months she's been away. We lucked out."

"I love it," Vanessa said quickly. "It has a cool, Village-y artist vibe. Is she an artist? I love the windows."

"She's a sculptor," I said. "And she makes jewelry. And now she's teaching in Africa."

"Where the hell is it going to sleep?" Mom asked, shaking her head in dismay. "The closet?"

"The baby doesn't need anything at first," I said, lifting the wrapped box Vanessa had brought out of the bag. "Anyway, we can't afford anything else."

"Please," said Mom. "No poor-unwed-teenager thing. Please. We're avoiding that like the bubonic plague. Remember."

Vanessa chuckled, which eked a hint of a smile out of Mom. I watched Mom as she cut one of the croissants in half, and I was grateful that she'd at least made an effort to bury her disappointment in me and come over.

"Vanessa, when do you leave for school?" Mom asked.

"End of August." Vanessa sighed. "We're going to Maine for two weeks after Nickelodeon ends, then we're back for, like, a night, and then I go." She made a sad face at me.

My phone flashed. I reached for it on the side table and saw a text from Will. "Sry I wuz a jrk last nite. I luv u."

I shook Vanessa's box, relieved and happy about Will's apology. "Clothes," I said.

She rocked mischievously back and forth on the couch. "Open it."

It was a stuffed dog with calico patches all over it and lopsided men's ties for ears.

"Isn't he cool?" she asked, hopping in her seat. "I thought it was the cutest thing."

I smiled, thinking about all of the stuff we still needed—a crib, a baby tub, those onesie suits that covered their feet. All of a sudden it seemed totally pathetic, my shower—Mom shifting around on the couch as though it had nits on it, my teenage best friend who didn't know any better than to buy me an ugly stuffed dog.

"It's very sweet," I said. "He or she will love it."

"When are you going to find out the gender, for God's sake?" Mom asked. "It's so creepy–new agey not to find out right away these days."

"We want it to be a surprise," I said.

"It's a surprise no matter when you find out," Mom said impatiently.

"Well, I should go. It's ten-thirty." Vanessa stood up, hiking her wrinkled linen pants over her hips.

"You're skinny," I said.

"Are you kidding?" she said. "Anyone looks skinny to you right now." She patted my belly and kissed my mother on each cheek. "Bye, Fiona."

"Call me later," I said.

She nodded and slung her big fake white-leopard-skin bag over her shoulder. "It's great, Thee, really. I wish I were living here."

The door banged loudly, the metal of the old locks jangling with it. Mom pressed her finger on the plate, retrieving fallen croissant flakes. For the first time in my life with her, there was a heavy and awkward silence.

I looked at my blinking phone again. Another message from Will. I hadn't answered the first one. "Helu? You forgive me, yes?" I quickly texted him back. "Y. I luv u." I tossed the phone where Vanessa had been sitting, feeling grown up and proud of us for maneuvering through our fight so gracefully.

"You know, I've been thinking," Mom said slowly. "About that stuff with Dad. That night, when he came over."

"Oh." I shrugged. I wondered why she was bringing it up out of nowhere.

"It must seem like we've always hated each other, he and I."

"I know you don't hate him," I said.

"That's not what I was going to say." She recrossed her legs and I watched her small, round knees move underneath her black pants and wondered how it was that I had such big knees, such big bones. "He's waiting for this to blow up too," she said. "It's all we can do. It's hard. For both of us, in our different ways, it's hard."

"It might not, you know," I said. "Blow up."

She looked at me as though she were considering something. Music from a car radio drifted in. I had a weird urge to tell her that her life with Dad had not been a waste. That she hadn't wasted her life, that she'd been living a full life then, with its long, loud red nights at Fiona's and its siren voices and everyone's love problems and drama. That her having me and raising me hadn't been a waste of time either.

"Thanks for coming," I said. The visit was sliding away from me, but I felt unready for her to leave. I wondered how sometimes my mother could feel so familiar—the smell of her room, the way she tapped her brush against the sink before she turned on the hair dryer—and yet how I could still have such an unclear picture of her. How I could not know whether she was happy, or what made her happy, what she thought about when she shut her eyes at night. I thought of her unbuttoning her shirt and throwing it onto the silk chair in her room, and the pull of skin across her cheeks after she washed her face, but it was like looking at her through a window from across the street.

"And thank you for the money, and the pump, and everything else," I said. "Have some faith in me, Ma." I tried to say it jokingly, but the words spilled out of me in an awkward rush. "The details might not be all there, but the feelings make sense. It feels real. That's important, you know."

"It feels real," she repeated, looking to me. "What does that mean?"

"It feels like what we're doing is right. Can you just believe me that it does? Even if it doesn't seem right to you? We're going to make it work. I love him. We're going to make it."

"I'd like to believe you." She pulled a tissue out of a pack in her bag and brushed any loose crumbs off her lipsticked mouth. "I would."

27.

The morning I went into labor, I crocheted and watched the Movie Channel, thinking it would teach me something about life. I'd finally found the ring, and as I did more of them, I was able to recognize what the ring looked like (it looked like a hole!) and how it changed shape a little after each stitch. After a few hours I finished a yellow, slightly lopsided version of the bikini bottom that didn't look half bad. It was a far cry from the multicolored zigzags I'd pictured, but it was a step.

I decided to walk downtown and across the Brooklyn Bridge because I was a week past my due date and my doctor had told me to walk. My water broke just as I reached the high, arched midpoint. I stopped short and doubled over, and a guy running behind me crashed into me.

"Jesus, watch out," he said. We were both sprawled on the wooden walkway, bikers and cars whizzing past. He was practically on top of me, his flimsy blue nylon shorts draping my leg. Then he saw my huge belly and my wet, streaked jeans.

"Shit, are you okay?" He stood up and held out his arm. "Can you stand up?"

"I need to get to the hospital," I said, dusting myself off.

"I don't have a phone!" He waved his arms frantically around his skimpy shorts.

"I do," I said. I dialed Will at school.

"It's happening," I said. "My water broke. Meet me at NYU."

"Where are you?"

"On the Brooklyn Bridge. I'm going to try and find a cab." I started walking back to Manhattan, the guy in shorts following me.

"I'm okay," I said, wanting him to go away. Nothing hurt yet. "Thanks."

"You sure?" he asked tentatively, looking relieved.

I nodded and started walking faster. My flats made awful squishy sounds as I got to the end of the bridge and then to Chambers Street. I passed a discount store where a guy in the window was blowing up soccer balls and throwing them into a big bin. There were people moving everywhere, stepping on and off the filthy curb to get past each other. I had a stolen, surreal moment, thinking of my high school just a few blocks west on Chambers as the banners in front of the discount store waved at me in the wind. A cab stopped in front of an ice cream store a few feet away and someone got out.

I stood in front of the driver's window so he could see me, wanting a little drama. "Can you take me to NYU Hospital?" I yelled.

He nodded offhandedly, as though he were just another cabbie carting another pregnant woman to her hospital cot.

"You gonna be okay?" he asked when we got there.

"You bet," I said, hauling myself out.

A rush of people crowded around me at reception, and a nurse got me into a room and helped me into a gown. Will showed up just as some masochist attendant came in to do something called "strip the membranes," which shocked me into submission and started me on a runaway train of screaming pain. I got an epidural, but all it did was numb my left leg. The hours crawled and flew, the door to my room swinging endlessly open and shut, Will holding my hand, sitting, leaning by the window, texting, yawning, looking freaked.

At one point toward the end I started to panic.

"I feel like I could die," I said to him. He was standing next to me, holding my foot in the air. ·

"I know you do," he said, "but you're not going to."

"You're going to be fine," said the Irish nurse holding my other foot. "You're doing great—just stay with us and push when the doctor says to push."

I wiped my sweaty forehead and the weirdest thought flashed through my head—Mrs. Weston in the Columbia reception lounge with her serious, urgent, expression: *"Be positive."*

As the head came out, I stared at the ceiling and imagined karate-chopping my way through it. I felt like I was on fire, along with the rest of the world. "It's a boy!" the doctor shouted, and I looked down and they flopped the baby onto my bare chest, slippery and bewildered, looking right at me with wide-open, alien eyes.

"Oh my God," I cried. I said it over and over and over again.

28.

They helped me into bed and I rolled gently onto my stomach, which was like sinking into a forgotten, beloved pillow. The nurse left and I remember Will watching me from the chair next to me and shaking his head and smiling.

"Wow," he said.

"Yeah," I said.

"All that blood. It was like a slasher movie." He held my hand and I drifted off to sleep, wondering where he was, the baby, but I was too tired.

Someone turned on a fluorescent light over my head.

"He's over eight pounds, which means you should try and

feed him every three hours," the nurse whispered, wheeling the baby in, his face slightly magnified from inside the plastic rolling cot. His eyes were open and his mouth was shaped like a Cheerio. The nurse lifted him out, a clump of warm, white flannel with pink and turquoise piping, and aimed him at my boob.

"You want his chin to jut out a little," she said. "That's how you know he's properly on." But his chin never jutted out. We tried, but he kept closing his eyes and drifting off and then waking up and squirming around. The nurse manhandled his head, nudging his mouth to where it needed to be.

"How about you leave us for a while and we'll see if we can figure it out?" I finally asked.

"Fine," she said, picking up a blood-smeared towel at the edge of the bed.

After that it was just me and moon-face, high above town, some lit-up bridge outside our window, and Will, asleep in the bed next to us.

"Hello, little man," I said. "Are you hungry?" He gazed into the space between us, his cheek pressed against my chest. There was something incredible about speaking to him for the first time, even though he didn't understand me. It felt almost as though I were speaking to a part of myself who had just been born and who was in the room with us too.

I spent the rest of the night nudging him onto my nipple. He eventually latched on, squeaking a little as he sucked, and at some point I fell asleep with him splayed across my chest. I woke to the sound of heels clomping down the hallway.

Mom arrived with daisies and a bag filled with Pellegrino, pretzels and Milano cookies.

"All the stuff I would want," she said, looking at Will, who was still asleep. They had not been in a room together since she'd found out I was still pregnant. "I'm only staying a few minutes."

"Can you wash your hands?" I asked. She paused to take off her coat and put it behind the chair, then headed for the sink in the corner.

"I couldn't believe it, what she went through," Will said, sitting up as if he'd just dozed off in the middle of a conversation. "I've never seen anything like it in my life. She pushed for, like, three hours. I thought her eyes were going to explode out of their sockets."

"Lovely," said Mom, drying her hands. "When he came out, did he look angry or did he look worried?" she asked.

"Neither, I don't think." I thought of his eyes, blank and searching, when they put him on me.

"He didn't scream bloody murder? You screamed your head off, but then after a while you got it together."

"I think *I* was screaming," I said.

She peered into the cart, where I'd deposited him at some point when the sky was still dark, and looked at me and Will. "So?"

"We like Ian," Will said. "Ian Galehouse Weston."

"Ian," she said, jiggling the cart lightly with her hand. "You don't think it sounds too much like Theeeeeaaaaa?"

"That's part of why I like it," I said. "Can you like it too?"

"Wasn't Ian the name of that daft road manager in *Spinal Tap*?" She sat down in the chair next to my bed. "How do you feel?"

"Okay," I said. Ian stirred, sticking his hand up out of the blanket he was tightly swaddled in. I reached over to pick him up. "He should eat again."

"He's a furball," Mom said, looking at him and forcing a

smile, folding her hands in her lap. "Where did he get all that fur?"

"He's a baby, Mom," I said, my shoulders stiffening. "Not a monkey."

Will flipped his feet onto the floor, facing us from the other bed. "Did I ever tell you that my name is not short for William?" he asked, looking at both of us. I thought about where I'd seen his name in print: on a list of AP physics tutor volunteers, in the yearbook, on his gray high school sweatshirt, which was suddenly okay to wear now that he'd graduated. The name was always Will.

"It's not?" I asked, pushing Ian's face onto my nipple, which was already sore. He squirmed and butted at me, not latching on.

"My name is actually Willbraham," he said.

"What the hell is that?" I asked. "It's like Baberaham. Baberaham Lincoln. What were your parents thinking?"

"I'm named after a town they rode through on a bike trip," he said, fiddling with the crank at the end of the bed. "They biked through Switzerland on their honeymoon. Can you imagine my mother on a bike?"

Mom crossed her legs and sucked her lips in, which made her lipstick smudge over her lip line.

"Yeah, so . . ." Will stood up and touched Ian's head, looking over his shoulder as someone came in to change the wastebasket. "It was this little town where, they said, everything was very plain, very workhorse, but then the houses all had tulips growing around their doorways and it was really simple and beautiful and . . . crisp. That's the word they used to describe it."

"Like crispy tofu," I said stupidly, looking at Mom. Both of her elbows rested stiffly on the arms of the chair.

"And they spent the night there," Will said. "In some pensione or whatever."

"Some *dieflockerhaus*," I said, my neck starting to hurt from craning down at Ian.

"Yeah, some *dieflockerhaus,* and they woke up and sat at the café and they saw all these people riding by on their bikes and they all had kids, little babies riding in seats behind them or in sacks or whatever, and they thought it was very cute. And my mom said that's when she decided she wanted to have children."

"That's kind of sweet," I said.

"They were such hippies, in a way," Will said. "What the hell is wrong with William?"

"Why didn't they name you after your dad?" I asked.

"Mom didn't want to," he said, winking at me with his good eye.

As if on cue, Mr. and Mrs. Weston walked into the room in matching Dalai Lama–style jackets with silk cord fasteners. Mr. Weston was carrying a basket from Zabar's. "I figured you could use food more than flowers," he said, placing it on the windowsill. "So I believe congratulations are in order."

Mom stood up. "Lynne, Philip," she said tightly.

They all stood there until Will went over to hug his parents. Ian's face was buried behind my nipple and I desperately wanted to cover up, but my hospital gown was stuck underneath me. All of a sudden the room felt too warm and too crowded.

Mrs. Weston searched out Ian's face, Mr. Weston thankfully hanging back. "He's beautiful," she said matter-of-factly, her switch on–switch off smile in action. I hadn't seen them since that day in Will's dorm. "What's his name?"

"We're going with Ian," Will said.

"Ian," Mrs. Weston repeated. "Lovely. Can I hold him?"

"I think he's finished." I yanked my gown across my chest and handed him up to her. "He's supposedly not getting much now, anyway."

"She didn't wash," Mom said accusingly.

"Oh," Mrs. Weston said. She looked at Mom and handed the baby back to me. "I guess I'll go wash, then."

"Thea, can I get you anything before I head out?" Mom asked, gathering her coat from the chair.

"I'm good," I said. "You're leaving?" She was inches away from me, but it felt like miles. I looked at her, trying to draw her in closer. "When are you coming back?"

"Are you sure?" she asked, not hearing me. "Just call me if you do."

Mrs. Weston lifted Ian out of my arms and Mr. Weston was behind her in an instant. "Look at that," he said, jingling the change in his khaki pockets. They looked like your average, over-the-moon grandparents.

"He's got Will's face, from the nose up," Mrs. Weston murmured. She divided Ian's face in half with her hand.

"Definitely his eyes," I said. They carried on gazing as if no one else were there.

"Well, it's a big day," Mom said on her way out. "Thea, I'll ring you later."

I sat back, shrugging my stiff shoulders. Will moved next to his dad. Both were swaying lightly with Mrs. Weston as she rocked Ian.

"I'm just so happy he's out and safe and healthy," I said.

"You should have seen her," Will said. "I had no idea it was going to be like that."

Mr. Weston looked at me, then inspected his watch. I wondered just how greasy and limp my hair was, whether my face was still puffy and if my nose still had red dots on it. Mrs. Weston moved to sit down with Ian, laying him on his back on top of her legs. "Will used to love to lie like this," she said without looking up.

"Did the money land in your account, Will?" Mr. Weston asked, leaning against the windowsill.

Will nodded. "It did, thank you."

"Thank you, Mr. Weston," I said, feeling unbelievably tired all of a sudden. The adrenaline rush I'd had since I woke up was quickly evaporating, but I felt an odd relief I couldn't pinpoint. I opened my eyes and looked at Mrs. Weston, who was still gazing at Ian's sleeping face. She looked up and smiled at me and it was a completely different expression from the borderline-patronizing looks she shot me that day at Columbia, when she called me forth to face my future as a strong, independent woman. Now she pitied me.

After they left, I called Vanessa. She was with her parents in Maine, and then they were driving her to Vassar toward the end of August. "It's a boy," I said. "I was right. I'm glad I didn't find out, but I had a feeling it was a boy the whole time."

"Oh my God, I'm shocked. I was so vibing girl. Tell me everything. How bad was it?"

"It hurt like hell," I said, pulling at a loose thread on Ian's flannel blanket.

"Really?"

"Really."

"What did you do when you first saw him?"

"I don't think I could ever describe it," I said.

"Listen to you," she said. "How was Will?"

"He was amazing. I'm on a cloud. So crampy. They put me on Percocet."

"La, la," she said.

"I know. I'm flying. He's so beautiful, Ness. Not pruny at all. He's the most beautiful baby."

"I know he is, Thee. I'm so proud of you. Will you *please* email me a pic? Or send me one from your phone."

"You know my phone is messed up and can only send texts, no pics."

"Have Will figure it out. Is it weird yet?"

I looked over and smiled at Will, who was sucking on a chocolate milk shake, watching CNN. "Not yet."

"Maybe it won't be."

"Maybe."

I hung up and dropped my head back on my pillow, watching Ian sleep. I wanted to ask the doctor about Ian's head, which seemed squishy and too big for his body. I wanted to ask her about his neck. How he didn't seem to have one. A few hours later my phone buzzed. It was Dad.

"I'd like to meet him. Are you exhausted?"

"Kind of, yeah."

"Well, it's getting late. When are you leaving?"

"Tomorrow," I said.

"How about I pick you guys up and take you home?"

"Okay, if you want," I said.

"I'll bring the camcorder."

I hung up and drifted off to sleep. Will had gone home for the night with instructions to bring the car seat back in the morning. I woke up after a while, feeling acutely sore and spongy, waiting for Ian to wake up, not knowing what to do with myself until he did. Whenever I looked over at him, I got a feeling of déjà vu, like he'd always been there next to me, my little prince, asleep in his plastic throne.

29.

I was bending Ian's ears when the pediatrician arrived the next morning. She woke him up and pulled at his legs, uncurling him.

"He looks great," she said. "You're nursing?"

"Yes," I said.

"How's it going?"

"I'm a little sore."

"That will pass in a few days, just stick with it," she said, passing him from the rolling cot to me. "I don't need to tell you how good it is for him. Is he latching on?"

I nodded.

"Great," she said, watching as he started his butting, squirming, sucking routine. "Looks like you're both doing just fine." She scribbled on her board. "Things you want to look out for—projectile vomiting. Spitting up, even in large quantities, is normal, but projectile vomiting, or vomit that looks greenish in color, is cause for concern. Are you circumcising?"

"No," I said. I blurted it out without thinking about it, but after I did, I realized I'd blurted out the right answer.

She grinned, her thin, lipsticked lips reminding me of Glenda the good witch. "I have my own opinions about circumcision for nonreligious reasons," she said. "I'm glad we'll both be spared that little chat this morning." She glanced at me and looked around the room, and the bluster left her voice. "Who's picking you up?"

"My boyfriend. He'll be here any minute," I said. I would have liked to stay longer. It was safe and orderly there, the nurses with their thermometers and paper cups of Percocet pills and Jell-O.

"Here's my card," she said, brushing my arm with her smooth cotton coat. "Call me anytime, day or night. No question too dumb, and I'll be happy to do the follow-up with you in two weeks' time."

She and Will passed each other in the doorway without saying anything.

"When can you leave?" He stood over me, patting Ian's sleeping, furry, black-haired head.

"Not sure," I said. "I think she has to give the okay and then we sign out." My phone buzzed.

"I'll go see about signing out," Will said, walking out purposefully.

"I just have to finish up something," Dad said. "I can be there soon."

"Okay, but I think we're leaving," I said.

"Call me if I'm not there when you need to go," he said. "But I'll be there."

I hung up, annoyed that I'd have to manage him again. Will didn't come back for a long time and I thought for sure Dad would get there first. I pictured Will hitching a ride to Montana on a Mr. Softee truck, getting a job on a dude ranch. When he finally showed up, he looked sweaty and I wondered if it was too hot outside for Ian. "There was a shitload of paperwork at the desk," he said, setting his jacket on the swinging bed table. "I've been out there forever. This kid is like a minute old. Unbelievable."

I passed Ian to Will and he tensed up a little, the crook of his arm almost swallowing Ian's head. Will looked up at me and for a moment it was like someone had zapped an unbreakable blue force field around the three of us. I collected stuff at the sink and threw them into my bag.

"You think he's eating enough?" Will asked anxiously. "He's sleeping so much."

"The doc said every three hours," I said. "I don't think they eat much the first few days. They said my milk won't come in for a while anyway. Whatever that means."

"What *does* it mean?" he asked. "What does it mean, 'come in'? Why don't you have it yet?"

"I read in the book that I'll know when it comes in because my boobs will get 'engorged.'"

"Sounds scary," he murmured, his face turned back to Ian.

"I know. Engorged. So sexual," I said, untying my gown in the corner so Will wouldn't see my deflated pooch of a stomach. "But the doc said they sleep eighteen hours a day in the beginning."

"You'd think he'd be a little curious, after being cooped up in there for so long," he said. "Can you imagine how boring it must have been? Just sitting there, endlessly in the dark?"

"Tell me about it," I said.

We pushed out of the revolving doors toward the street, and everything outside—the low roof of the atrium, the blowing trees—felt menacing. I saw Dad at the end of the driveway and my heart sank: How were we all supposed to fit in that tiny car? How were we going to get the car seat in? I realized I'd forgotten to call him, and couldn't believe he was actually there. He was pointing a video camera at us through the driver's-side window.

"Glad I caught you."

We walked to the car and Will tried to hoist the car seat up a little higher so Dad could get a look at Ian. It was a weird scene: us standing frozen in front of the car while Dad filmed Ian asleep in the seat. It was like he couldn't take the camera away from his face and just look at him.

"Hey there, little man," Dad finally said, getting out of the car. He paused the camera and turned to study me. "How do you feel?"

"Fine," I said. "Glad we're going home. How are we going to do this?"

"Well . . ." Dad opened his door again and pushed the tan bucket seat as far forward as it would go. I crouched into the back, snagging a hole in the cellophane of the Westons' Zabar's bag, and waited for someone to hand me the car seat. Will was the first to try, angling the square plastic base away from the top of Dad's headrest, but it was too wide for the car seat to get through.

"Easy!" Dad said, pushing the seat-back down, clearly worried about tearing. As I leaned forward, a jar of Bonne Maman jam somehow rolled out of the car and smashed on the curb. Ian's head was dangling in a way I did not like at all.

"Watch his head!" I said.

"He's okay, Thee," Will said, huffing, kicking the jam glass out of their way. The car seat was now completely stuck between the ceiling and the seat.

"Let me have at it," Dad said. He reached in and now there were men's arms and hands groping and grabbing in front of me. I was surprised at how similarly tanned and hairy they were. Eventually Dad nudged Will aside and extracted the car seat back out into the blazing sun, Ian still sound asleep.

They wound up squeezing the car seat, with Ian still in it, through the space between the two front seats.

"Remind me not to get a ride with you again," I said, pushing the seat belt through the holes in the base like the instructions on the side of the seat said. "I'm sure I'm doing this wrong."

Dad put his foot on the clutch and the car lurched out of the driveway. He drove his car just like he drove his boat, as though it had a single stop-start button. I immediately thought of waterskiing, or *not* waterskiing.

"So this is the famous Aston," Will said, stroking the burled-wood window panel.

"This is it," Dad said. "Where am I taking you to again?"

"Ninth Street, between Fifth and Sixth," I said, watching Will push a panel in front of him that revealed an empty slot.

"Don't tell me, this is where an eight-track player used to live," he marveled.

Dad glanced at him, unsure of what he meant.

"I read that you're supposed to walk them around the house and introduce them to everything," I said.

"I'm sure he'll appreciate that." Will smiled, turning back to me.

"You never know how much they can take in," Dad said, his voice weirdly animated, like he was a game-show host trying to psyche up his contestants. I felt a pang of appreciation that he was being such a good sport. "I always thought you were wise beyond your years when you were a baby."

We got to Florence's apartment and hoisted Ian back out the way we got him in. Dad made a big deal of holding open the doors and carrying my bag, looking for things to do. We climbed the three flights, Will gripping the car seat. The stairs were dark except for a bulb with grubby fingerprints on it dangling from the second landing. Dad would be seeing where we lived, where Ian would be living, for the first time. We all watched Ian in his car seat, levitating up the stairs.

Will put the seat down to open the door and Dad picked

it up and walked in, looking around for a place to set it down. He finally nestled it into the crook of the couch, and set my bag down next to it.

"Do you want a drink or something?" I asked.

"No, I should run along," Dad said, fixing his eyes on Florence's hanging wall-quilt. "How about I run out and get you guys a few things first? Something for dinner? Some fruit? A chicken?"

"That's okay, thanks," said Will. "I'll run out later."

"Are you sure?"

"Yes," we both said.

Dad went over to Ian and bent down to kiss his forehead. The kiss seemed to last forever. I made a face at Will from behind him.

"Okay, you guys," he said, coming up for air. "Call me if you need anything."

"Thanks for taking us home," I said, walking him to the door.

"I'm glad everything went well." He opened the door with one hand and threw his other arm around me in an awkward hug.

I shut the door and turned back down the hallway. "What was with that kiss? It was like he was anointing him or something."

"Give him a break," Will said. "It was nice of him. Do you think he was horrified by this place?"

"Of course not," I said.

"He looked horrified to me," Will said. "Considering where he lives, I'm sure it was not up to par."

"You haven't seen where he lives," I said, sitting down on the couch next to the car seat.

"Yes, I have, and it's slightly grander than this."

"You don't know what you're talking about," I said, trying to undo Ian's straps. "He doesn't care about that stuff."

"Bullshit," he said. "You don't have a job like that, you don't work like that and not care. Anyway, I'm starving."

Will went out and came back with four slices of pizza stacked in a white paper bag. Ian slept on a blanket next to me on the couch while Will figured out how to straighten all four legs of the Pack 'n Play at the same time. Dad had ordered it online and had it mailed to us, along with a stroller that carried the car seat, and another regular stroller. After we'd unpacked everything, a mountain of cardboard, plastic wrap and Styrofoam engulfed the living room. I couldn't help but think how lucky we were to have benefactors on our side who had sent us everything we needed. No matter how hard things might get, I thought, we were lucky. I told myself to remember that.

The Pack 'n Play had a plastic U-shaped bar that hung across the basket and shined lights and played music.

"I bet we never turn this thing on," he said.

"You never know," I said, inhaling my second slice.

"There's something very *Rosemary's Baby* about it." He wound it up and moved his eyes from side to side, imitating a marionette. He glanced at Ian from where he was on the floor.

"I have a son," he murmured.

"You have a son," I said.

The Pack 'n Play clicked down and Will leaned over to turn the dial in the middle of the base, his boxer shorts puffing out of the top of his jeans. Every part of his body still struck me in the same way that a piece of art or the idea of heaven did: enduring and pure and a little bit out of reach.

He stood up, fists on his hips, proudly assessing his

handiwork. I went over to him, feeling all banged up and contorted inside, and put my arms around him. "This is totally freaky," I said, "but kind of fun."

He smiled and pressed his forehead to mine. "Yup."

"I can't help being a little happy."

"Me too," he said.

"Really?"

He nodded slowly, glancing at Ian. "He's so cool. His tiny little everything. Did you smell him? When he first came out? I'll never forget that smell."

I put Ian on Will's chest and they both fell asleep in Florence's armchair. After that, Ian woke up every twenty minutes, sometimes to eat or cry. I thought of what Mom had said when I used to stay up late watching old reruns of *The Dick Van Dyke Show,* fixating on the wool furniture and swinging kitchen doors and married life: "Once you lose sleep, you can never get it back." I remembered my old self, how I used to brush my hair by the radiator and make it stand up. How Vanessa and I would lie in bed and talk in the dark, and it was like our universe hung in the air and we were somehow talking about everything and the night would go on and on. An unbelievably loud motorcycle roared down the street and I waited to hear the sound of someone cursing out their window at it, but it never came and then everything went quiet again, Will on my left side in the creaky, lumpy bed, Ian on my right, where he'd fallen asleep at my boob. It seemed easier to hold him there; he cried when I put him down. I couldn't move an inch, but I didn't care: it was warm and still and us.

30.

"Whoa!" I yelled into Florence's empty apartment. Ian's umbilical cord stump had popped off as I bathed him in the battered porcelain sink. It fell onto the floor and I picked it up and looked at the TV and there was footage of a submarine coasting along the bottom of the ocean, sand puffing out of its way. I dipped a Q-tip in alcohol and rubbed it around Ian's belly button like the doctor said, which made him scream his nuts off. I picked him up, featherlight and sweaty, and walked around the room, wondering what Will was doing at his job. Was he sitting at a desk, holding a pencil? Was he doodling a baby's head with a curly sprig on top? The air conditioner was barely working and we were smack in the middle of a heat wave. Was he relieved to be out of our house?

Ian fell asleep and I spotted the yellow, rolled-up bikini bottom sitting on the second shelf of the side table. It felt like a million years since I'd touched it. The last time I worked on it, I didn't have a baby, I thought. I set Ian down in the crook of the sofa bed and silently picked up the bikini. It was time to start the top, so I cast on fifteen chains, like the instructions said, which would be the bottom right triangle. I told myself the top would be easier compared to the bottom because it was triangles, which meant dropping stitches instead of gathering them into a circle. I sat for hours while Ian slept, the bed creaking underneath when I uncrossed my legs, and thought about all the people in the world who had crocheted who were now dead. I felt a sense of connection with all those dead people, with my dead grandmother sitting on another couch in another house in another time with her large, star-patterned, mustard-colored blanket. I wondered what she'd been thinking about as she'd crocheted my bikini. Did she worry about her son, my dad? Did she worry that his life was out of control? That he drank too much and that his wife was a shrew? My grandmother hated my mother. Why did she hate her so much? As I worked, I noticed that my stitches were becoming more even and less lopsided. I was getting better at it, and it felt like the only thing in the world I was getting better at. The rest of the time, I was in a haze, unable to get out the door.

In the movie on TV there was a blond girl with a ponytail and bangs cut very sharply across her forehead, exactly the way Mom used to wear it when I was younger. It reminded me of Mom sitting in a seafood place on the Charter Island harbor with me and Dad when I was younger, around the time Dad had come back from "drying out" in Arizona. I remembered, out of nowhere, I'd asked them where I was conceived. Dad was sitting across from me, but I looked at Mom when I'd asked. "My friend Sherry was conceived in Mexico," I'd said. "That's why she loves Mexican food. Where was I conceived?"

Mom pretended to choke on her popcorn, shocked.

"Interesting question," she'd said. She was about to launch into something, but Dad interrupted.

"Fiona, not appropriate," he'd said.

"What's not appropriate?" she'd asked. The familiar dynamic: Dad gruff, Mom innocent.

He shook his head and said nothing.

"What's not appropriate?" she asked, louder.

"She's twelve," Dad said, not looking at me.

"Oh Ted, relax," Mom said, dismissing him with as few

words as possible. She picked a single piece of popcorn from the basket, crunched and turned to me.

"I was managing the Kettle, my first job in charge, so I was the big stuff, and I knew it and Daddy knew it. He showed up every night. Didn't you, Daddy?" She looked at him, but his eyes were up at the bar TV.

"He would come when he was done with work, at around eleven or midnight, and he always stayed till the last set. In the beginning I thought it was his abiding, unrequited passion for music, you know, the poor, trapped artist inside the banker thing, but soon I realized it was really just a ploy to catch me as things wound down for the night."

A trace of a smile crossed Dad's face, but he stayed on the TV.

"Anyway, he'd gotten into the habit of waiting for me to close up, very gentlemanly. And then he'd take me home to his place on Warren Street. I was afraid of his lift. It had one of those metal accordion doors, and Daddy would start kissing me and I worried I'd get my hair caught or lose a finger on the way up."

"Fiona, can we leave it?" His chin burrowed into his hand. His other hand rubbed his graying, wiry sideburns. He'd let his hair grow out while he was gone.

"She asked, so I'm telling her," Mom said. "What's the problem with that?"

He leaned hard on the table, the weight of his elbow bringing it toward him.

"I don't think it's necessary for her to hear the gory details at this stage."

"Gory? Lighten up, Ted." She leaned toward him, her hair falling across her eyes. For a second I thought she was going to kiss him. "Please don't let this little rehab stint deplete what's left of your sense of humor. Please. Reformed is one thing. Puritanical, another entirely."

"Humor has very little to do with it," he said. "Can you wait on anything? Can you let anything wait?" He was talking in a way where the corners of his mouth seemed to be trying to seal his lips shut. It was something his mouth did when he drank, which confused me because he'd just stopped.

"You're right, Ted, I should just continue waiting. That's what I should do." She picked up the big menu and closed herself behind a pissed-off tent, where she remained, it seemed, until the end. They split less than a year later.

By the time the movie ended, my neck was killing me from hunching over the yarn. I took Ian out for a walk in the scorching August heat, and Vanessa and everyone else from my old life were like ghosts in my head, conversing and vivid, floating and following my every move. A truck emblazoned with the words *Halal—Schwarma Kabob* emblazoned on it stopped at the corner. I laughed with imaginary Vanessa, who by then was at freshman orientation at Vassar—"What the hell is a schwarma?" I imagined her teasing me: "You've lived in New York City your entire life and you don't know what a schwarma is?"

31.

Will came home that night in a good mood because all the summer associates were getting five-hundred-dollar end-of-summer bonuses. "Maybe we can fix up this dump," he said, ruffling Florence's dusty quilt on the wall. "Let's go celebrate," he said.

I packed Ian in the sack and Will carried the car seat to the coffee shop down the street, where he wedged it into the seat of a booth. The waitress made faces at Ian as she took our order.

Will looked around with a self-satisfied smile. "We could get married and have the party here," he said, balling up his straw wrapper.

"In the back room of Aristotle's?" I asked, confused.

"Sure, it'd be fun. Why not? That guy could host." He nodded at the guy stacking cups by the coffee maker, the guy who'd asked me and Will, "How are you, my friend?" through his mustache. I reached over to stick the pacifier back in Ian's mouth. Will had a strange, forced grin on his face. He looked almost embarrassed, like he'd said something he shouldn't have.

"Seriously," I said. "Do you ever think about it?"

"Yeah," he said a little too casually, lifting his spoon to his mouth. "Every once in a while. Not every second, mind you—I'm a guy."

"Meaning what?"

"I'm a wild and crazy guy," he said, bobbling his head from side to side. I stirred the paper cup of coleslaw on my plate with my fork. I didn't understand where he was coming from and it was making me nuts. He was being offhanded and nervous at the same time.

"If you'd really thought about it, you wouldn't have mentioned it like that."

"Like what?" he asked, wide-eyed.

"Like it was nothing."

"Who said it was nothing?"

"Forget it," I said, wanting to dig our way out of the conversation. The truth was, I thought about getting married—or dreamed about it—more than I cared to admit. And I realized as I watched him, mashing crackers into the bottom of his bowl, that he did not. He looked up at me and I could tell he knew he'd been busted. But busted for what? Did the fact that he didn't think about getting married mean he didn't love me? The thought sent a chill through me as I watched the little tabs of phone numbers on the ads for music teachers and cleaning help flutter in the breeze from the door whenever it opened and closed.

At home Will held Ian and watched TV while I tried to catch a couple of hours' sleep before Ian woke up again. I put the pillow over my head, but I could still hear the sounds of buildings exploding and people yelling at each other. I decided I hated TV.

"Can you turn it down?" I asked, watching as one volume bar went black on the screen. "A little more?" Two more bars. I squeezed the pillow closer to my head, starting to get pissed. He rarely offered to hold Ian during the night; come to think of it, he never did. Granted, I had the boobs, but could he *offer*? And why couldn't he deal with the idea of getting married?

"Will, it's too loud!" I hissed, bolting upright.

"What's your problem?" he asked. "Is that how you ask?"

"I asked, and it's still too loud," I said. "I'm tired. I need to get some sleep."

"Whatever," he said. He turned it off and lay motionless in the dark with Ian asleep on him. "Get some sleep, then."

"Oh, screw you, don't make me out to be the big bad bitch." I waited for him to say something, wondering what had gotten into me. "Look, I'm sorry," I said, my hand grazing his shoulder. "I'm just so tired."

When I woke up the next morning, Will had left to register for his fall semester classes without saying goodbye. I got up, put Ian in the sack on my chest, brought the laundry downstairs, drank coffee, took a walk, went to the drugstore, talked to Mom, watched TV, changed Ian, fell asleep with Ian, went to the supermarket and came home, all the while expecting to see a "We're okay" gesture in the form of a text on my phone from Will—which never came.

32.

Vanessa finally came home from Vassar one weekend in September to meet Ian.

"Paposan!" she bellowed as Will opened the door.

"You're past due," Will said, following her in.

"What am I, a gallon of milk?" she asked.

"Mamosan!" Vanessa kissed me and I pulled her inside to where Ian was lying on the couch.

"Oh my God, he's beautiful," she said as I picked him up.

"Thanks."

"No, I mean it," she said. "He's really beautiful, Thee." She hugged me, sandwiching Ian between us. I hadn't seen her since she'd left with her family in July. She looked older; her curly brown hair was longer and she had more wisps and chunks of it flying around her face. She smelled like cinnamon and trees. "I can't believe it. Can I hold him?"

I put Ian in the crook of her arm.

"I can't believe it," she said again.

"I brought you a belated housewarming present." She pointed to a large floppy rectangle in a plastic bag. "Open it."

Will picked it up, letting the bag drift to the floor. It was a horsehair welcome mat that said GO AWAY in big black letters.

"Perfect," Will said.

"I'm totally behind on Ian's hat," she said. "I need more yarn. Can you believe I ran out again? I need to go back to that store."

I smiled at her, feeling resentful that she'd been too busy hanging out, eating pineapple pizza, to finish it by now. Vanessa sat down, holding Ian in the same position as I did when I fed him, which made him root around, darting his head at her chest.

"Uh! Look at that," said Will, as if proving a point. "He wants to eat again. That's all he ever does." He gestured his head at me. "She's the only thing he wants. How's Vassar? Are you a Vassar girl yet?"

"It's good," she said. "Though there are a lot of wonks and posers from the Midwest. Or worse, *California*. Let's see." Vanessa looked over Ian and examined herself. "Black turtleneck, check. Big ass, check." She pulled up her sleeve. "Uh! No marks! Uh, not a cutter. Guess she's not a Vassar girl yet."

"Ew," I said.

"It's all mock," she said. "Like taking aspirin to kill yourself. Everyone is sooooo intense. Fucking Nick Cave, dude . . . bad seeeeed. You guys are Little Mary Sunshines next to them. And you, little lump o' love." She held Ian up to her face. "Make out with me. I love his little male pattern baldness. Sooooo hot. Does he ever open his eyes?"

"Not so much." Will swiveled in the chair, spinning a CD on his finger.

"He opens them," I said dumbly, bringing a glass to the sink. Will's plate from the previous night was still there, untouched, with dry food all over it.

"Will, this is fucking gross," I snapped, holding it up. "If you're not going to wash it, at least *scrape* it."

Will and Vanessa exchanged a "What's her problem?" glance.

"I'm sorry, but help out," I said. "Did your mother show you how to do dishes? Let me guess the answer to that."

"I can't believe *you're* a mother," Vanessa said, quickly changing the subject.

"I know," I said.

"No, I *really* can't believe it. You're, like, crazy out there now. My crazy mother friend. Are you guys all, like, walking around the Village, going to, like, tea salons? Do you wear berets? All three of you? Matching berets?"

Will and I couldn't help smiling at each other. "Yeah, that's us," he said. "We're part of the movement."

"We're organizing," I said.

Vanessa and I went for a walk while Will stayed with Ian.

"So how's it going?" she said, taking my arm in hers and moving in long strides down the street. "God, I miss New York."

"You do?" I asked.

"Shit, yeah. There's nothing to do up there. So navel-gazey."

"But do you like it?"

"It's a lot of lying around," she said, stopping to roll up her jeans. She was wearing jeans with black flats that looked like ballet slippers. All of a sudden I wanted to roll up my jeans too, but I was wearing clogs. It would have looked dumb. "There's a girl, Helen, on my hall, she's pretty cool. At first I thought she was a huge narcey-marcey. Totally self-absorbed. She sneaks into the room as if anyone in there cared, and her eyes dart around, paranoid, like you've been talking about her all day. But she's funny. And she has beautiful skirts, which she wears every day. She only wears skirts. With black tights."

"Is she your new best friend?" I asked. We'd gotten to the small park near Christopher Street and I steered her to a bench. I was so exhausted from being up all night with Ian that my tongue itched.

"I don't know, Thee. A million times a day I wish you were there."

"Awww," I said.

"I'm serious." She dug into her pocket for a shredded pack of gum and offered me a piece. "What about you? What's going on?"

I watched a little girl in grimy pink leggings waiting by the swings with her mother. "It's scaring me how I can love him so much, and yet every second of the day, I think about how I could lose him," I said, taking the gum. "That's the hardest part."

"Will, you mean?"

I shook my head, surprising myself. "Ian."

"Thea, you're not going to *lose* him," she said.

"You don't understand, Ness," I said. "I *could*. He could get sick, he could suffocate, he could just . . . slip away." She squeezed my hand and shook her head slowly, as though she couldn't believe the things I put myself through. Then she popped her gum and I had a sudden memory of the two of us skateboarding down Seventh Avenue, and her stopping at a traffic light with an exploded bubble all over her face, a long, long time ago.

"Anyway, I'm trying to get him on a schedule," I said, "like the books say. Dinner, bath, bottle, bed."

"Almost the same as mine," said Vanessa. "Dinner, read, vodka, sex, pot, pizza, bed."

"Yours is more fattening," I said. "By the way, I meant to ask you, what the hell is a schwarma?"

33.

On the subway with Ian I overheard a woman in a fitted white shirt and piles of cool, long, gold-chain necklaces talking to someone about a miraculous all-natural sweetener.

"I'm serious, I cut out *all* sugar," she said, fingering her chains. "I don't miss it one bit. Whenever I need sugar for tea, or whatever, I just use this. Now I'm never tired."

When I got up out of the subway, Ian was overdue to eat, but I *had* to get that sweetener. It was the key to quashing my unrelenting, insatiable sweet tooth and therefore the key to losing my baby weight. We trekked against the gusty October wind, a few blocks to a health food store on Twenty-Third Street, and once we were inside, Ian started with his trapped squirm thing, puffing his chest out from his stroller straps like a fat Superman. Then I moved down the aisle and the stroller got wedged in between a stack of boxes. I shoved it through hard, and Ian lost it, big bubble tears bursting out of his eyes, his mouth eating up the rest of his face when he opened it and screamed. I gave the counter lady a bunch of singles for the sweetener and bolted without getting the change.

I was pissed when I got home, the usual thing, how Ian ruled and how I couldn't do something I wanted to for three seconds without him flipping out, how I was stuck with him all the time while in the meantime everyone else on the planet had a life. It was harder when Will went back to school—school felt more threatening to me than his dumb summer job, maybe because his job seemed like real life and school seemed more like a "lifestyle." Everyone shuffling around in their flip-flops, off to class with their Clif Bars. I put Ian in his bouncy seat on the kitchen counter and filled a pot of water to boil some penne. I dumped some butter in a plastic container of leftover peas and nuked it. When the pasta was done, I reached across Ian with the pot in one hand to get the salt, because Dad always throws salt on pasta when he drains it. Then my cell phone rang in my coat, making me stop short. The pasta water spilled all over Ian's leg and seeped through the bouncy seat, a steamy puddle rising on the counter.

Whenever his screams get too loud in my head, and they still do, even now, I try to remind myself that I actually dealt that day and that we didn't just both fall down and die right there. I remembered Dad was a paramedic after college and called him at work. I had to run into the bathroom to hear him. The thought occurred to me that maybe I could just go downstairs, out into the street, away.

"Run the shower and put him under it," he said. "Not too cold, or he'll go into shock. Keep him there for a few minutes if you can. Then get him to the hospital."

I held Ian under the shower by the armpits, almost grateful

he was screaming and crying so much because it meant he wasn't dying. At the same time, I noticed a weird thing happening to me, which was that I wasn't panicking. It couldn't have been more black-and-white to me: he was going to be okay. The driver turned off the radio the second we got in the taxi and got us to the hospital. I had no money. He took us anyway.

They pried Ian out of my arms when we got there and disappeared, which was a huge relief. I stood in the hall, pinching the skin on my neck, saying to myself, Please God, please God, please God, please God. The doors swung open and it was Dad.

We followed purple footprints down the hall and around a corner, over to a woman in green scrubs standing by a cot with metal rails.

"I'm Dr. Lyons," she said. "I'm a resident here. Have you given him anything?"

"I tried to get him to swallow some, you know, liquid aspirin," I said.

"You gave your baby aspirin?"

"Tylenol, I mean."

"Good," she said. "You should never, ever, give your child aspirin. It can really mess with the growth of their brain, not to mention it can cause them to bleed internally. So no aspirin. Acetaminophen only. Tylenol is fine."

Ian wailed and writhed on the cot. I waited for the doctor to stop looking at me.

"Got that?" she asked.

"She gave him Tylenol, did you hear her?" Dad shouted. He pushed his hands together, breathed. "Let's have a look at the leg, shall we?"

"What about the pain?" I asked, pinching my neck. "Is there something stronger you can give him?"

Dr. Lyons straightened Ian's leg. They'd stripped him naked.

"Easy," she murmured. She grabbed some gauze pads off the counter and started dabbing. "It looks like the burns are second degree. That's good news. But I want to have someone else check."

Ian started screaming like he had screamed at home and trying to bend his leg under her grip.

"Is there something you can give him for the pain?" I asked again, frantically.

"We can give him something, yes." She pulled a tube out of a drawer. "This is a topical analgesic. It will numb the area for a while, as well as disinfect it." Ian screamed bloody murder, but as soon as Dr. Lyons was done, he calmed down. She looked up at me again.

"Can you tell me exactly how it happened?"

"Well, I was boiling some . . ."

"On second thought," she said, raising her hands to stop me, "I think I should go find someone who can talk to you . . . privately."

"I spilled water on him," I said. "Boiling pasta water."

"Let's wait, please." She tried to smile, but her smile was urgent and then gone immediately and that's when I realized she thought I did it on purpose.

Dad cleared his throat. "That's fine," he said. "We'll speak to whomever you need us to speak to."

"Are you nursing him?" she asked.

"I am." I picked him up as carefully as I could.

"I'll be back in a flash," she said.

"I'm going to step out there and call Will," I said, reaching into my jeans for my phone.

"Go ahead," he said, pulling out his BlackBerry.

"We had an accident," I said, the hallway doors swinging behind me. "But he's going to be all right."

"What happened?" Will asked.

"I was making dinner and a pot of pasta water banged against something and some of it spilled onto Ian's leg," I said.

"Thea, Jesus Christ," he said. Something in his voice said he was expecting this to happen, as though it were inevitable. "What the hell."

"It was an accident," I said.

Dr. Lyons walked past us with an older guy in a white coat. "Whenever you're ready," she mouthed, pointing to the room I'd just left.

"Where are you?" Will asked. "I should call my parents."

"Just come. You can call them later. Dad's here."

"Your dad?"

"Yeah. I called him first because I thought he'd know what to do. He was a paramedic in college."

"Your dad was a paramedic?" he asked, disbelieving.

"Come soon," I said.

When I hung up, Ian was sleeping in my arms. The gauze pads on his leg were soaked through with a mix of ointment and pus. It hit me how badly I'd screwed him up, but I pushed the thought away. I went back into the room where Dad and Dr. Lyons and the guy in white were talking.

"Thea, this is Dr. Evans," Dad said, as if he were introducing someone who had arrived at his house. "I explained to him what happened."

"Hi there." He winked at me. "Maybe it's a good idea to

have a look while he's asleep." He craned his neck to look at Ian's leg as the rest of his stout body stood erect. Ian flinched but didn't wake.

"Yes, folks, that's a burn," he said cheerfully. "But I'm happy to report we're not going to do anything drastic about it. No scary surgeries. We're just going to hang out and watch it and swab it with cream and let the skin do its magic tricks."

Dad exhaled like he'd been holding his breath. "Okay," he said.

Dr. Lyons moved behind me and must have made a gesture directed at me.

"So tell me what happened," Dr. Evans said. "Some kind of freak accident with a pot of something?"

"I don't know how it happened, I really don't," I said, scared that they were going to haul me off. "It just spilled over while I was bringing it to the sink. I feel so stupid." I shook my head while Dad and the doctor hung their heads to the floor. "You understand that it was an accident, right? That's all it was. An accident. I made a mistake. I'm very careful with him, you know. I am. Dad?"

"I know you are, Thea." He sighed, shaking his head. "You just have to be *more* careful."

I thought of all the hours with Ian, the endlessly repeating, looping thoughts about whether he was eating enough or pooping too much. I saw myself tiptoeing and holding my breath when he slept in the morning. How I walked down the street with him in the stroller, seeing nothing else but his face in front of me. The thanklessness of it all numbed me. I burst into tears.

Will came into the room. "What's the word?" he asked, panting.

"I'm Dr. Evans, and I take it you are the father." The doctor held out his hand. The room we were in was full of computers on carts, and a nurse sat nearby reading CNN and watching us. "He's going to be okay. We're looking at second-degree, superficial burns. Lots of blistering and clear fluids, not pleasant to look at, but he'll be okay."

Will hovered over Ian's leg. "Poor thing," he whispered. "Mama's gonna order in from now on. Don't worry." He smiled and looked up at me and squeezed my arm. It was the last time I remember him being on my side.

34.

Dr. Evans said he wanted to keep Ian in the hospital overnight. There was a single room open in Pediatrics at the end of the hall.

"You should go home," I said to Will when we got to the room. "Get some sleep."

He looked at the single bed, at the sole chair where Dad had already parked himself. "You going to be okay?"

"Just bring him a new onesie when you come tomorrow," I said. "The long-sleeved, blue, striped one. And maybe some socks."

Will kissed my cheek, then Ian's. "Hang in there, little guy," he whispered on his way out.

I held Ian, looked at the soaked bandages and winced. Clear fluid was normal, the doctor had said. Normal. Dad leaned forward in the chair, reading my mind, and it hit me with a rush how glad I was to have that sage, stuffy, older life-form that was my father perched in the corner. "It'll heal," he said. "The feeling Dr. Evans gave was that it looks worse than it is, thank God."

"I know," I said.

He forced a tired smile. "You should call Mom."

"You know how she is with gore."

He nodded, like he was enjoying some personal, fond joke about her. Then he closed his eyes and rested his head against the orange leather seat while I dialed Mom.

"How serious do they think it is?" she asked. Her TV blared in the background.

"Can you turn that down?" I asked, hugging Ian closer. "They said it's second-degree burns."

"So he won't need a skin graft, thank God." I heard the TV go silent, and her voice sounded all of a sudden oversized and echoey. "But he'll probably have scarring. I hope for his sake it's not a real deformity. Are you sure you don't want to switch hospitals? Lenox Hill is really the only one in this city worth its salt."

"No, Mom, we're fine," I said. "They know what they're doing."

"I hope so," she said. "Will's there, right?"

"Yeah," I lied.

"Okay." She hesitated. "Do you want me to come?"

"You don't need to," I said. "We're getting out tomorrow morning."

"Good," she said quickly. "Call me when you get home."

When I looked up, Dad was watching me on the phone, playing with the curtain cord. "Well, I guess I should head out," he said. "Let you guys get some sleep." Change fell out of his pocket as he stood up, and it rolled all over the floor. He looked to see if it had woken Ian up. "Sorry," he whispered, gathering the coins. "Call me if you need anything, okay?"

"Thanks," I said as the door swished closed. I angled the small task lamp on the side table away from us, then turned it off. I carefully lay Ian down into the same plastic box he was wheeled around in when he was born, and I lay flat on the bed. It hit me how recently we were all there and how different things felt now. A nurse peeped through the door, saw me staring at the ceiling and went away. I felt a weird, jumpy urge to see if Ian was okay, and as I stood up, watching his blanket move up and down as he breathed, something happened. I stood over him and thought about how purely, wholly good he was and how I was never going to be able to protect him from or make up for all of my mistakes. I wondered what the hell I'd done, not just with the accident, but the whole thing. Having him. What had I done? Why had I brought someone into this world? I imagined Ian in a calculus class, struggling like me and feeling like shit, and I imagined someone making promises to him, about a job or something else, and him getting his hopes up and the person not making good on it. I imagined Ian loving someone like I loved Will and that person dropping dead on the street. I thought about blood and accidents until a cyclone of grief mashed me up and I wondered how the hell I'd ever thought it was okay to disappear that summer with Vanessa. How could I have done that to them? A trolley rolled down the hall outside my room, one of its wheels catching and banging on every turn. It stopped at my door and a guy peeked in.

"No trays, ma'am?" he asked.

I shook my head and the smell of old food seeped into the room as sobs ripped through me. I thought about Mom and

Dad. Was life nurturing, in some inexplicable way, or was it just a never-ending string of losses in different shapes?

I whispered to Ian, "Remember when you were born and I couldn't stop saying, 'Oh my God?'" He slept on his back with his head turned all the way to his shoulder. At that angle his head looked like it could have spun right around. Did infants have ligaments? Connective tissue? I lay down on the bed and fell asleep in a splinter of light shining from the bathroom door, thinking, This sadness, whatever it is, somehow binds me to Ian, and as a result, to this world, like it or not.

35.

The next morning a nurse griped to someone outside our door over the sound of clattering dishes.

"Without saying anything, she just *took* it from me," she said. I opened my eyes and saw Ian sprawled across my chest on his side; he felt cooler, less clammy, and he had a content pucker on his lips. I couldn't remember the last time he'd eaten. Things felt strangely, wonderfully calm between me and him. A feeling hit me that I'd always somehow known him, or if not him, his spirit; I felt like his spirit had always been with me, climbing the stairwells at school, crossing Fourteenth Street, drinking a soda inside the movie theater on Third Avenue. But I wished I could look down and see his leg healed, the damage I'd done erased.

Will walked into the room with his mother a couple of hours later. He handed me Ian's striped onesie and a pair of white socks, then went straight to the windowsill where my jacket was. "Do you have anything else? Mom's going to drive us home."

I lay Ian in front of me on the mattress to change his diaper and get him dressed. The doctor had said to keep his leg uncovered and I wondered how I was going to keep him warm against the October chill. Loose blankets, I decided. Will was staring at Ian's leg from across the room.

"It's okay," I said. "I know it looks horrible, but there's a topical anesthetic in the cream, so it's not hurting him, right? Otherwise he'd be screaming."

"Do you want to go wash up or anything?" Mrs. Weston stood next to the bed with her hands on her hips, at the ready. Be positive, I laughed to myself. I finished changing Ian and handed him to her, my shirt still open, not caring what she saw. "Ooh, poor baby," she said, taking him gingerly.

"Mom, I'll hold him," Will said, walking quickly over. "Why don't you go get the car and bring it around and we'll meet you downstairs."

"One day," I said, on my way to the bathroom, "I'll stop beating myself up about this, at least I hope I will." I tried to catch Will's eye, but he was looking down at the table, at the instructions that came with the medication.

The elevator stopped at every floor on the way down.

"Hi," I said, leaning toward Will. "Missed you last night. Glad we're going home."

"Me too," he said, staring at the elevator numbers as they lit up and dinged.

I got into the backseat, where Will had already laid Ian's car seat. I wondered how the hell I was going to get the strap over his leg.

"Just do one side," Will said. "You don't have a choice." Then he went around and got in front next to his mother. "Take it easy, Mom," he said. "I don't want him banging around back there. He's been through enough."

"Of course," Mrs. Weston said as she sped down Seventh Avenue.

Ian's leg was smeared with greasy cream and covered with thick, gauzy bandages. He looked like a tiny maimed soldier. Someone honked behind us and Mrs. Weston swerved, trying to get out of the way.

"Forget about him," Will said sharply. "Just focus on taking it slow." I remembered Will saying Mrs. Weston was a shitty driver, that she'd point to something she saw out the window and then steer toward it.

"Did they send you home with anything?" she asked.

"Just more cream," I said. "The doctor said I should call if Ian seemed distressed or feverish but that the pain should be subsiding."

"Yeah, half his leg was almost scalded off," Will said. "But it shouldn't hurt a bit by now."

"It wasn't scalded off," I said. "The doctor's more concerned with potential infection at this point. Making sure the leg stays clean. He said any scars from the burn will heal completely within a year."

"Sure, he's young," Will scoffed, turning the radio on. "He'll get over it."

"I think your cells do multiply more quickly, the younger you are," Mrs. Weston said, catching my eye in the rearview mirror. Was she actually sticking up for me?

"Yeah, well, he'll only need a hundred billion or so." Will sat back and gripped his knees.

"Did I ever tell you about when I spilled coffee on Roy?" Mrs. Weston said.

"Uh-uh." Will stared out the window.

"This whole thing made me think of it," she said. "We'd just gotten a new coffee percolator, I think it was a late wedding present, and I was trying to figure out how to use it and the whole thing exploded."

"Oh no," I said.

"Yup. The whole thing blew, and bits of grinds and hot water sort of showered on top of his head," she said cheerfully. "Bits of coffee grinds on his cheeks, it looked like razor stubble."

"How bad was it?" I asked. "Was he burned badly?"

"I don't think so," she said. "I don't remember. I don't even remember what we did. Can you believe that?" She stopped suddenly at a red light.

"Watch it!" Will said, gritting his teeth. Ian jumped in his sleep as the car heaved to a stop. I loved those flinches. Like he was sending out little smoke signals of alertness and life while he slept.

We got into the house and I sat down to give Ian the boob while Will and his mom took the gauze pads and other stuff from the hospital out of the paper bag. I pointed to the big square pillow on the armchair, the one I used to lay Ian across.

"Can you pass me that?" I asked Will.

Mrs. Weston rushed over to get it. "Here you go."

Will went to the sink and threw water on his face and wiped it with the towel hanging on the refrigerator door.

"Are you all set as far as things from the drugstore?" Mrs. Weston sat down next to me on the couch.

"We're all set," I said. I looked at her face, remembering

again how I'd been afraid of her when I'd first met her. Had she changed or had I? *Be positive.*

"Okay." She looked at Will. "You all right, honey? Can I get you guys some sandwiches?"

"I have to get back to school," Will said. "I've already missed too much."

"They'll understand, I'm sure," said Mrs. Weston. "How could they not?"

"Yeah, it's not every day—"

"Can't you stick around for a little bit?" I said, cutting him off. Ian started to scream. The burned part of his leg was brushing up against the pillow, so I flipped him to the other side.

"I really can't," he said, taking some books out of his backpack and stacking them on the desk. "Is he okay?"

"He's okay, he just has to lie a certain way, off his leg," I said.

Mrs. Weston hunched down and kissed Ian's foot. She patted my leg and gave me a "Hang in there" look. "I'm here and available if you need anything, Thea. Please take me up on it. If you need some time to yourself, to take a nap, to recharge, just call me. Promise?"

"Thank you," I said.

She fished through her big canvas tote bag for her car keys. "Maybe you could bring him around this weekend and we could watch him for a few hours. Give you guys a break."

"Let's see how he's feeling," Will said. He stroked Ian's head for a few seconds and picked his keys up from the table. "I'll walk out with you."

When they left, I ordered chicken with broccoli, an egg roll and a carton of rice and ate it all while Ian slept. He slept on and on that night, barely stirring.

I picked up the yellow yarn, still on the lower shelf of the side table, out of a panicky sense of boredom. It had been a while, but I was relieved to find that my stitches didn't look disastrously different from the last time I'd worked on it. I got all the way up to the top of the triangle—it went faster as the triangle narrowed—and then did the series of chains that made up the tie around the neck, which went faster than I'd remembered. At around midnight, the bikini was done. I held it under Florence's rickety, red metal reading lamp, the night dust circling around it like little fireflies, and thought, This is pretty cool. I marveled at the details Carmen had written into the pattern—how the strap that tied around the back was just a little bit thicker than the strap that tied around the neck. And how the band at the waist had started to roll over just a little since I'd finished it a few weeks earlier. I couldn't wait to show it to her.

When I opened my eyes, Will was standing over me and staring. It was one o'clock and I'd fallen asleep with the bikini top splayed across my chest. He picked it up and the ball of yarn dropped onto the floor. He fished around on the floor in the dark, found the ball and put the top and the yarn back on the second shelf of the side table.

"You're still working on that thing?" he asked.

"I finished it," I said. "Not that you'd care. Where were you?"

"Studying."

"You smell like beer," I said, pulling the blanket up to my shoulders.

"Who the hell are *you*?" he asked, throwing his coat on the chair.

"Nobody, apparently. It doesn't occur to you to call? To see how he's doing, at least?"

"I figured you were taking care of things. Like you've been doing so well."

"Subtle, Will," I said, leaning up on my elbow. "We had an accident. Deal with it. *I* am."

"I didn't say anything." He sat by my legs, his sneakers flopping to the floor.

"You don't have to."

"Let's go to sleep," he said. "You're tired."

I lay there waiting for him to drift off, hating him for the stupid, selfish wall he'd put up, hating him for inserting me so deeply and squarely into the middle of the night, awake and alone. Ian woke up and we sat in the chair by the window. He fell asleep at my boob almost immediately and I wondered for the millionth time what to do. Whether to put him back in the Pack 'n Play or wake him up to keep nursing. I peeled the gauze off his leg, praying he wouldn't scream. I nudged Ian and he startled awake, his jaw starting to move, barely detectable, his arm drifting around my chest, banging it a few times, then drifting up in the air behind him. I wondered if his thoughts were as floaty as his arm. I imagined his thoughts as light phantoms that had no names, just floating and settling, free of synapses or endings. His hand finally settled at my collarbone, and I tried to imagine a future moment when Will wouldn't look at me as though he didn't trust me with Ian, when I wouldn't hate him for looking at me like that. If Will mistrusted me so much, why didn't he step in? If I was really doing such a terrible job, why didn't he just take Ian and run away? Ian breathed in sharply; I tried in the dark to decipher the *New York Times* headlines on the ottoman a few feet away, tried not to think of my own crimes, my honest mistakes.

36.

Will's uncle Dave, Mrs. Weston's younger brother, died of a heart attack in Prospect Park while Ian and I were in the hospital. He was fifty-three. I put Ian in the sack and went with Will to the memorial. We walked around piles of wet leaves and vast, muddy puddles toward hundreds of people huddled on a hill near where he'd been jogging. Dave's wife, Carol, stood by a tree in a navy-blue suit, their three kids next to her. Mrs. Weston was on her other side, her gray eyes sunken and red. She saw us and reached her hand over, where it rooted around aimlessly, touching my cuff, Will's knuckles, Ian's bum in the sack. Amanda cupped Ian's cheeks. "So this is Ian."

"This is Ian," Will said. "And this is Thea."

"He's just beautiful," she said. "I'm sorry we haven't gotten over to see you guys."

You guys, I thought. We were not "you guys." "You guys" were bustling, intertwined; they picked cereal up off the floor and went out to the park, swinging their kid between them. We were not "you guys." I looked at Will, who was shuffling his feet, his eyes fixed on the ground. I missed him in a way that felt like homesickness.

"I'm sorry, Aunt Carol," he said, his hands digging stiffly into his pockets. "I really am."

A guy next to us reached for her. "Hello, Carol," he said. "Don't know if you remember meeting a couple of years ago at Dave's fiftieth. Bob Rosen."

She nodded, looking up at the guy, and smiled in a way that unpacked her grief for anyone to see. "That was such a lovely night, wasn't it?" she said.

The oldest son spoke during the memorial service at a club in Brooklyn Heights. He talked about family camping trips and how his dad loved hideous, cheap light fixtures and was stingy with paper towels and toilet paper to the point of ridiculousness. Black candle smoke drifted up to the ceiling and I wondered for the millionth time, How would I be a good mother? What would it take?

Will went to school after the service, and I went home thinking about how I'd stop snapping at Will when he took his socks off in the middle of the room or threw Ian's dirty diapers directly into the kitchen garbage. It was a Friday night and for some reason, maybe to forget about Dave, Will came home later that night with some people from Columbia and a case of beer.

It was Mark and Maggie and Helena from his hall and Lester and Tina and Jason, all in our small room with Ian nursing and sleeping on me. Maggie and Mark had something going on, but she held on to Will like he was hers; she put her hands around his waist when she spoke to him and they swayed to Neil Young in front of me on the rug. I wasn't supposed to mind. Lester sat next to me on the couch and passed a bong around, taking a hit between each person.

Helena swung her leg over the leather armchair and let her foot float to the music in the thin air. "How often do you have to do that?" she asked me.

"Feed him?" I asked, getting up to open a window. "All the time." She looked away, her puffed lips and her spacey, bored eyes telling me how she believed it was her right to be there, taking up space in our apartment. I looked for her hips, tried to trace them toward the middle of her body, but they were hidden from me. Will sat down at Florence's old upright piano, so dark and unshiny it could have been made out of a blackboard, and played something I recognized by Eric Clapton or a band from the seventies that had a one-word name, and although it was short, it took me around the room in a spiral of aching memories of Will and the way we were together, before Ian, while people talked. It was the opposite of listening to a song over and over until it sinks in and you like it. It was inescapable, lilting love. I didn't know he played piano. What else didn't I know? Will's back was to me, but I could see the side of his face, and he moved around on the bench as though he were in a conversation with someone, as though he were talking, and I thought about being the one he was talking to, how nice that would be, and although I understood all of it for what it was, I still felt as though part of me could step into a cloud of sad love for him and stay there, with Will drifting into the cloud and out, visiting me and then leaving me by myself.

When everyone left, Will threw his clothes in a heap outside the bathroom and flopped onto the bed. I pushed his hip to the side and let my hand wander down, hoping to coax him to life. Usually he took two seconds, but that night he slipped through my fingers. "Will . . ." I whispered, wanting it right between us. Wanting to fuse. Wanting. I rolled on top of him and kissed his forehead.

"What's wrong?" I asked.

"I don't feel good," he said. He let his head fall toward the wall, avoiding me.

"Sick?" I asked.

He shrugged. "Just weird," he said, looking back at me.

"What is it?" I said, rolling off him. "Tell me."

He folded his arm behind his head and stared at the

ceiling. "You could have killed him, Thea," he said, as though he were reciting an age-old, unavoidable fact. "He could have died."

Now it was my turn to stare at the ceiling. I gazed up at the exposed water sprinkler, trying to untangle my defensive thoughts from the truth of what he was saying.

"Do you ever think about how crazy it is?" I finally said. "With Ian, I mean? You must. It's so scary, how could you not. It's like, I know we could lose him at any moment. It's on my mind all the time. Something bad could happen at any minute of any day. But I have to believe it won't. I have to believe we'll keep him safe, that our love will somehow protect him." I found Will's hand under the blanket and held on to it. "The thing is, we can't stop loving him just because we could lose him. I'm trying so hard to just . . . be brave. You can't really be any other way." The sprinkler in the ceiling was starting to resemble a prickly black flower. I thought about Ian's little mouth, how it contracted even smaller when he wanted something, and the familiar aching sadness came right up to me, like a bus getting too close when it rounds a corner. "It's sick, how much I love him," I said. "He is so helpless and I just love him so much." I felt the embarrassing tears popping out of my eyes, rolling down the sides of my face toward my ears.

Will burrowed his arm under me and squeezed, which was such a relief I almost lost it. He squeezed and stroked my rib cage, and relief came to me in soft, warm waves. Finally, a connection, I thought. He didn't say anything, but I felt it: he understands what I mean and he feels the same way I do. It's going to be okay, I thought. We are back in this together.

37.

Ian woke up at six the next morning, and I brought him to the bed and gave him the boob till we both fell back to sleep. When the alarm went off, I heard the shower go on, then later the sound of drawers opening and later still, the sound of shoes shuffling around the apartment. Each time I woke, I remembered Will and me, holding each other the night before, and drifted off into a peaceful, happy sleep.

But a while later I opened my eyes to Will standing in front of the bed with wet hair and a stiff face.

"You shouldn't sleep like that when he's in bed with you," he said. It felt like a kick in the stomach. "You could suffocate him." I picked Ian up and stumbled over to his Pack 'n Play, where he remarkably stayed asleep after I laid him down. Will watched me with his arms folded as I crossed the room. I wondered what had happened, how it had slipped away so easily. I thought he'd been right there with me. I stopped at the kitchen trash bin and tugged the red plastic garbage tie to keep it from spilling over. I didn't know anything anymore.

He sat down on the edge of the bed.

"I don't know if I can do this," he said, his voice sounding thick, underwater.

"What do you mean?" I asked. I sat down next to him on the bed, the first inkling that we might not make it plowing through me, spreading fear over me like seeds. "Will, we're *doing* it. We may not be doing it great, but we're doing okay, which is enough for now." I wanted to keep going, to tell him how full of messy hope I was for us, to tell him we had to keep trying because when the three of us were in bed together, Ian kicking up at the ceiling, the two of us sandwiching him, wasn't it amazing? Didn't he wonder how people could ever let go, after being together like that? The three of us on an island, how could you ever say goodbye to those moments? Just let them go? How did *my parents* ever let them go? How was it possible?

"I want to give him up." He stared straight ahead at the wall. "For adoption."

My eyes skidded over to the Pack 'n Play. For a second I felt like Will was going to get up and take him away. "Don't say that," I said. "That's cruel."

"I'm not trying to be cruel," he said. "I don't know, Thea. When I came to the hospital that morning and saw him in bed with you, lying in front of you on the bed . . . his leg looked like it had been blown off, Thea, I'm not kidding. I can't stop thinking about it. It hit me that morning, so hard. It isn't right, what we're doing. I've been trying to tell myself we'll be okay, but this isn't right. It's not right for him."

I knelt down on the floor in front of him and gripped his knees. We were both crying. "That's not true and you know it," I said. "You're hungover and you feel like crap."

"No," he said, shaking his head. The shades were down and the room was dark, but I could still see his eyes. "I really do believe it, Thea."

Over in his Pack 'n Play, Ian's foot stuck straight up in the air, his toe pointed like a dancer's. I thought of that first night, walking to the Seagram Building with Will in the freezing cold, the fiery orange squares of office lights, how they sort of exploded inside me, little pops of bright, burning sun. I believed they were also exploding inside him. That first night, he told me he was an optimist and I believed him. I looked at that face, into those uneven eyes I didn't know yet, and believed he'd do anything. From the very beginning, I'd thought, This is a guy who'll do anything.

Ian started his coughlike cries. Could Will take him away from me? I stood and went to pick Ian up as Will gathered his stuff for school and left.

38.

"I think he knows the word *poo*," Dad said, dropping the high chair, still in the box, near the sink. I'd spent the day letting the morning's scene with Will play out in my head a thousand times. I would talk him out of it when he got home, I kept telling myself. When Dad buzzed that evening, I panicked for a moment, thinking that Will had called an agency and that they were coming to get Ian. I'd forgotten that Dad was coming to drop off the high chair so that Ian could start eating "real food." I'd told him that it was still a couple of months too early to start with the food, but he'd insisted on bringing it over anyway, "just in case."

"I swear I heard him say 'poo' when we were in the hospital with his leg that night," Dad said, leaning the large box against the coffee table. "Did I tell you that?"

"He's not even three months old," I said.

"Well, he's advanced," he said, ripping through the packing tape with his keys. I rolled my eyes. "Seriously," Dad countered. "The way his eyes dart around when someone enters a room or when that Noah's Ark thing snaps shut. He's very alert. Unusually so."

"Okay, well, take it easy," I said. I was in a black fog, but I couldn't help smiling. "He's got his whole life to buckle under the pressure."

"Of course." He smiled, leaning over Ian, who was on his back on a blanket. "I'm sorry it's taken me so long to get this over here. Better late than never, eh? How is he?"

"He's good," I said, folding up the bed in a hurry. "His leg looks much better."

Dad looked at me, pushed my hair off my forehead. "You all right? You seem . . ."

"I'm okay."

"You don't sound okay."

"Will's still upset about the accident." I stared at Ian on the floor, unable to look anywhere else.

"It was a very rough thing to go through," he said. "But he'll come around."

"I'm not so sure."

"Look, you're giving this everything you've got," he said. "Not everyone is as capable as you are, at your age, you know. If he doesn't realize that . . ."

I escaped to the sink to rinse out glasses and lost it. Horrible, embarrassing, convulsing crying.

"Thea?" Dad walked toward me like he was walking toward a sick animal.

"It's okay," I said.

"Really. What's the matter? What's wrong? What's he doing?"

"Nothing." I was afraid to tell him that Will thought we should give Ian up because I was afraid he'd agree.

"Honestly, this situation . . . ," he muttered, his voice trailing off. He started to lean against the pillar with his hand. Instead he bounced himself off the pillar and then smacked it.

"It's not your fault," he said. "It's not your fault." He leaned his hands up against the counter, just like Will had done that morning, and we both faced the sink.

"I'm fine, Dad," I choked. "It's okay."

"This isn't working here." A quick, embarrassed smile crossed his face as he raised his arms to encapsulate "here." "You look so unhappy. Not just today. How long have you been feeling like this?"

"Since Ian's accident, maybe before."

"Look, just come stay with me for a while, Thea, okay? Take some time apart and figure out what's what."

It made sense, I realized, to be the first one to go. To get out first, like Mom did, before he could take Ian away from me. So I said okay, setting the last dripping glass on the rack.

part four

39.

We got a cab with as much stuff as we could carry, and I sat holding Ian and watching the trees thin out as we made our way west toward Dad's place on the river. Mom called when we were stopped at a light on Tenth Avenue.

"I can't find my black leather belt with the rivets," she said. "Do you have it?"

"No," I said.

"Are you sure?" she asked.

"I'll double-check when I get a chance," I said, moving Ian's fingers away from his mouth. "I'm with Dad, on my way to his place, actually. Will and I had a fight."

"Oh no . . . ," she groaned.

"What do you mean, oh no?" I asked. "You want us to stay together now?"

"I just . . . Wait, how did Daddy end up in the middle of all this?" she asked.

"He brought over a high chair," I said.

"And?"

"And I agreed."

"Agreed to what?"

"We just decided that I should stay with him for a while," I said. "It's not forever, it's just a break."

"You could have called me, you know," she said, sounding strangely forlorn.

"I know, it just happened." I couldn't tell if she really wanted me to go home to her or if she was simply miffed that Dad had "won." "Anyway, we're here now, let me call you later."

"Okay, don't forget," she said.

My room was dark, and as I walked in, I could see the mean queen, elongated by the light from outside, sneering at me from the ceiling. I dumped my bags onto my bed, thinking of all the times I'd dragged Vanessa with me to Dad's to avoid being alone with him. Vanessa always lightened it up. She was so good that way. "Where are we going to find you a good woman, Mr. Galehouse?" she'd say. "What's your type?"

Dad would wince and make a pathetic attempt to play along. "I don't know, uh, Vanessa, your guess is as good as mine."

She set him up once, with Jana, a very blond Czech masseuse. We told Dad she was a *physical therapist,* and that she worked with people with sports injuries.

"Honestly, it made me want a drink," he said when I asked how it went. Vanessa's mom said Jana thought he was cute but that they didn't click and that Jana didn't like that Dad didn't throw his popcorn box into the garbage when they left the movie theater.

"So what? Who cares?" I said, thinking, How cruel. My poor, hopeless, littering father.

When Dad dated Nancy, the violinist, Vanessa and I had made fun of the way her nose twitched like a nervous rabbit's, and the fact that she was twenty years younger than Dad and not even remotely hot.

"He's handsome and rich," Vanessa said. "He could have anyone he wants, and look what he does. Goes for the cellist with stringy hair. King of the midlife-crisis freaks, that one."

I put my mess of underwear in the top drawer, before Dad could see it strewn all over the bed. I stacked Ian's Pampers in a row on top of the dresser, thinking about all the nights sophomore year Vanessa and I did our faces in the bathroom and drank vodka out of Diet Coke cans until I was spinning by the time we went out the door, only to stand in line at some club, get in and walk around, dancing and scream-whispering and drinking more vodka Diet Coke, until we stumbled home. Dad waited up at first, but by the end of sophomore year he was always in bed, Nancy long gone.

And now Vanessa was gone too. I had a flash of her slumped in the corner, drunk and sneering, the tinkling sound of bangles on her wrist as she rolled a joint. Dad tiptoed into my room with Ian's Pack 'n Play. Ian kicked his legs at the ceiling from a blanket on the floor, and for a second I thought Dad wouldn't see him and would step on him.

"He's a happy little guy, isn't he?" he said, hunching over at him. "You done with these?" He straightened up and pointed to the empty duffels.

I nodded and he picked them up and folded them until they were a quarter of their size, then lifted them to a spot in the hallway closet. The room was a large rectangle, one you could easily fit two double beds into, and I wondered what would happen when Ian got older, whether Dad would let Ian take the third bedroom or whether we'd still be in there like siblings. Or whether Will would come to his senses and rescue us. Dad tiptoed into the kitchen and I stayed in the bedroom as long as I could, feeling how slowly the minutes went by when you were stuck in a house with someone who believed you lived your life carelessly.

I called Vanessa and immediately started sobbing.

"I took Ian to Dad's," I said. "I left Florence's."

"Oh no," she said.

"He wants to give him up for adoption," I said.

"He what?" she shrieked.

"Can you believe that?" I said. I put my hand on Ian's stomach as he squirmed and gassed on the floor. "He said that ever since the accident, he hadn't felt right, or whatever. Vanessa, he can't make me give him up, can he?"

"Jesus," Vanessa said. "It's like he has postpartum depression or something. Crazy. No, he cannot make you give him up. No matter what."

"Really?"

Dad appeared in the doorway, looking like a timid puppy. "I was going to make some penne with pesto," he said. "That sound okay?"

I nodded at him, trying to smile.

"Really. You're a *great* mom." Girls laughed and doors slammed in the background.

"What's that noise?" I asked.

"Nothing, some idiotic tea party. Have I mentioned I hate it here?"

"Vanessa, what am I going to do?" I whispered.

"I'm so mad at him." She sighed. "I'm sorry, Thea."

I hung up, wondering if Will had gotten home yet, whether he realized I was gone. I couldn't imagine speaking to him, so I sent him a text. Whenever I thought about what he had said, about giving Ian up, I felt sick to my stomach. "We went to Dad's," I typed. "Don't do anything. Let us go."

Out in the kitchen Dad blasted water into a pot and the showering sound filled the apartment, drowning out my shaky sense of connection to anything.

40.

I woke the next morning at 7:22, stunned that Ian had slept through his 3:00 and 5:30 a.m. snacks. Maybe there was an upside to being at Dad's after all. Maybe my room had secret powers. Maybe the mean queen on the ceiling had cast a spell on Ian. I tiptoed out into the foyer. Dad's shoes were gone from under the chair and there was a note on the table and money: *Home tonight. Pick up some sirloins?* I envisioned another night with him and felt instantly done-in. There were Christmas cards from people who worked for Dad lining the chest by the wall. Young guys, all with short crew-cut hair, all smiling with three kids. I thought of how things had been a year earlier, when Ian was just an about-to-be-aborted grain of rice and Will and I lay on his bed at Columbia, studying for the SATs. I remembered Will's face when I was going down on him after we napped. I missed his body, missed it wrapped around mine. John and Yoko. I looked at the marble bust of a woman on a pedestal in Dad's corner, her arms, legs and head chopped off. I felt like her.

Ian woke up, his wails streaming hollowly down the hallway. I leaned over his Pack 'n Play and picked him up, wondering if it was possible for cheeks to be any chubbier, and held him above me, making him fly. Will's voice blew through me like a cold gust. *"I want to give him up."*

I remembered what Vanessa said and tried not to think about anything else. "Let's go get some yarn today," I said to Ian. I nursed him for a long time, then bundled him up, cramming him into the sack and walking the fifteen blocks to Stash. We clanged the cowbells right after it opened.

Carmen popped up from behind some shelves by the window.

"Thea!" She beamed. Her hair was down and in a jagged, punk-looking part. I wasn't sure, but I thought she'd put streaks in. "It's been ages. How are you?" She crossed the store and peered into the sack. "And look who you've brought!"

"Hi, Carmen." I was so happy to see someone outside of my normal cesspool of a life that I could have kissed her, and did. Ian lifted his head and kicked, also finding it hugely refreshing.

"Oh my God, what a butterball," she said, giggling. "Wow." She made an O face and Ian was transfixed, unblinking.

"So I finished an attempt at the bikini," I said, pulling it out of the bag and laying it on top of a white shelf. "It took me long enough, right?"

"Well, I can imagine your hands are a bit tied." Carmen said, still ogling Ian. I remembered the last time I was there, she said she'd been trying to get pregnant.

"Now I want to do one with teal and royal-blue zigzags," I said. "It's funny how you get these urges, right? I'm, like, possessed now. I have no intention of wearing it, but I *have* to make it."

"I know what you mean," she said, nodding vigorously, studying the bikini. "It's like once the urge takes hold . . . But this one's fantastic."

"Really?" I asked.

"It's fantastic," she repeated. She picked up the yellow top and draped it across her white tank top. "I love how it turned out. It looks homegrown but in this very cool way. It looks like it would sell for five hundred dollars at Barneys."

"You think?"

"Yes! Totally," she said, strutting around with the top. "The Brazilians? Who are always waxing themselves silly? Some rich Brazilian would snap this up in a second."

"They like skimpy stuff more, no? To show off their waxes?"

"Yeah, but I could see them, you know, wearing it a little stretched out, maybe even bunching up a side." She bunched up her own fuchsia underwear, under her skirt. "The thing about crochet is that it drapes so nicely. It's got the whole drape-hug thing going for it."

"Maybe I should try and sell it," I said.

"I'll sell it for you!" she exclaimed. "Believe it or not, I sell a ton of stuff in here." She pointed to the hats with colorful nubs and the baby sweaters hanging from the rafters on hangers attached to fishing wire. "I know it seems like no one's ever in here, but some days I make more money from the clothes than the yarn." She held the top up to the window, seesawing it back and forth in the air. "I'll sell it for you. Not for five hundred, though. Three hundred feels like the right price point to start. Two ninety-five."

"Whatever you think," I said. "It's a much more compelling prospect than trying to lose twenty pounds."

"You just had a baby," she said, looking me up and down. "You look great."

"Thank you," I said, running my hand along the pudge hanging over my jeans, the pudge that wouldn't budge. "I'll just say thank you."

"You know," she said, arranging the bikini top on the shelf and folding the ties over, "self-loathing is the evil curse of the twenties. I see that now that I'm thirty."

"You'd really be willing to hang it up?"

"Definitely. Like I said, I love it. I'll put my money where my mouth is. And how about I get ten percent if it sells?"

"At least that, you designed it, after all," I said. "Thank you."

"No, thank *you*," she said with exaggerated politeness.

She helped me pick more colors—a bright teal, a gorgeous spectrum of oranges and reds and a purple and green that went strangely well together—exactly the colors I'd imagined in my head, only better.

"I can see how you'd get obsessed with yarn," I said. "Some of them are so beautiful, and they're so different, how they're made, how they hold dye. Even if you make something in one color, there's so much to look at with the variations."

"It can get addictive," Carmen agreed. "I have women who come in here and buy tons of yarn, you know, for later projects, but then they don't do anything with it. They just have to own it."

Ian started to squirm around in the sack, so I undid the clips and pulled him out.

"So how's it going?" Carmen asked. "Do you like being a mother?"

"My dad once told me the best way to answer a question you didn't know how to answer was to compliment the question," I said. "Interesting question."

"You're right, what was I thinking, asking that?" She pushed Ian's sock, which was close to falling off, over his ankle. "Can I hold him?"

"Sure." She took him, gripping his bum. "God, what an angel," she said. "Such a yum. He's got the perfect-shaped little baby face. Like a Gerber baby. I'll bet everyone says that, right?" She brushed her cheek against his head. "How's your boyfriend?"

"Not so good," I admitted. I rolled my eyes and she made a sad face. I'm not crying in front of her, I told myself. I'm not. It was important that she thought I was tough and could handle things. "Anyway, thank you again," I said pointedly. "Thanks for offering to sell it for me."

"Fingers crossed," she said.

41.

The weekend rolled around and Dad pushed me to go out. "You deserve a break," he said. "I'll watch the kid." So I called Donna to hang out. Donna went to Barnard. She was more of a quasi-friend—she was really closer to Vanessa—but I called her because I couldn't think of anyone else who was still in the city other than Will.

I got Ian ready for bed, praying he wouldn't poo since I didn't think Dad could handle it. I pumped milk with the machine Mom had given me for the first time, the repetitive sucking noises sending me into a trance. "Ya homesick, ya homesick," it chanted over and over. Ian was fed and cleaned up and when I left, he and Dad were lying on the floor under Ian's mobile, jingling the terry-cloth hearts.

"We won't wait up for you," Dad said.

Donna lived in a ground-floor apartment on 104th and Amsterdam. A girl wearing magenta tights and motorcycle boots that fit her calves like gloves answered the door. Her hair was impossibly thick and messy—some of it had to be extensions—and she had on a plaid miniskirt with some sort of rainbow sweatshirt material squeezed around her midriff, clashing flawlessly with the skirt.

Before she could say anything, a guy yelled to her from inside.

"Cloudia!" he said, then something about a *"bacio."*

Cloudia, whom I guessed was Claudia to mere Americans, couldn't be bothered with introductions. I thought, This girl knows how to dress in a way I never will. I took comfort in the knowledge that I could recognize, understand and accept that fact as I watched her backside swing toward an emaciated guy in leather pants.

Donna was on the phone in the kitchen. It was weird to see her living here, actually inhabiting Manhattan. When we were in high school, she was a tourist, with her black leggings–black sneakers combo and her iPod wires always hanging off her, helping her bide her endless hours on the R train from Queens. But ah, how things had changed.

"Oh, please," she repeated into the phone. "Oh, please." Her eyes crinkled with a self-confidence I'd always found off-putting. I imagined it came from growing up with the kind of family who were very clear and straightforward about how they loved her. A lot of kids from Forest Hills had that.

Eventually she hung up.

"How are you?" She reached out from halfway across the room for a hug.

"I'm good, really good," I said, my enthusiasm nowhere near hers.

"Come," she said, grabbing a tray with a bottle of wine

and some glasses. "Ginny's in my room." Ginny was Donna's best friend from high school.

"Ginny's here?"

"She just transferred to Barnard in the beginning of January. You didn't know?"

"No, I didn't," I said.

"Claudia, come have some wine," Donna called to the living room, where Claudia was playfully straddling Emaciato.

"Your roommate?" I whispered, though it was obvious. I couldn't think of anything to say. Ginny was sitting on the radiator in Donna's room, hunched over in an attempt to blow smoke out the window.

"Hey, Thea, how's mothahood?"

"Hey, Ginny," I said. Ginny's big, stiff, blue-black Queens shag remained intact in spite of the wind blowing in. I looked at her and felt the instant affection I'd always felt toward her. Why weren't we better friends? If we'd spotted each other on the street now, we would have just waved and stayed talking on our cell phones.

"Donna, I am not living in this dump, I will tell you right now," Ginny said, laughing her husky laugh. "You've got termites or something, I'm telling you. You see this dust?" She pointed a magenta pinky nail toward the windowsill.

"I'm trying to get Ginny to move in with me," Donna explained. Claudia slinked in, poured two glasses of wine and left without a word.

"My mothah won't have it," Ginny said. "Not when she sees this." It was an interesting comment, given that Ginny's mother worked in the garment industry and barely noticed Ginny was alive—at least, that was what Donna used to say. Donna's family was Ginny's surrogate family. That was the lore.

We went to a Columbia fraternity party. Part of me wondered if I'd see Will there, but I knew there was very little chance of him showing up at a party like this. It wasn't exclusive enough for him. They played music from the eighties and there were guys in big plaid shirts with the sleeves cut off and greased-back hair, jumping and fist-popping like I remember people doing at Mom's club. It reminded me of Mom sticking shoulder pads into her black silk blazer and going to work.

I ended up getting rip-roaring drunk, sitting bored at a cafeteria table where Donna and Ginny glommed onto some guys from Long Island. Later on I found this guy Florian and made out with him in the stairwell while people trudged by us, their rainy shoes stepping on our coats.

For a while it was nice to kiss someone new, to erase Will from my lips. Florian had a rich, spicy smell that I attributed to his being Greek, and he wanted me to come back to his room, pulling my face toward his in a wonderful need-you, need-sex way. But I played coy. The truth was, I thought of Ian and that little spot under his chin I loved to kiss, his God-spot, and what if Florian was an ax murderer and killed me while we were doing it, leaving Ian motherless. Donna and the cheesy guys ended up going to a club in the West Twenties. I bullied the cab driver into letting five of us ride, thinking I might go too, but I ended up bagging and was home by one, and even that felt too late.

42.

"How was the night?" Dad came out of the kitchen with a plate of cheese. He'd been at work all day, working on a deal, which he rarely did on Sundays anymore. "How's your friend Donna?"

"Okay." I eyed the cheese and thought of Mom with a plate of Brie resting on her chest, how she'd dig at it and keep it lying around on her bed all night. Dad always precut his cheese and put a predetermined, matching number of crackers—in this case, six—on his plate. Then he would sit down purposefully to eat, as though it were an eating "session."

"How's she liking Barnard?" He swiveled in his chair. The only thing Dad knew about Donna was that she went to Barnard.

"She didn't say," I answered, relishing the first few moments of an Ian-free room. He'd finally gone to sleep after a never-ending stream of hungover hours I'd spent feeding, changing and entertaining him and trying not to call Will. As much as I wanted to talk to him, I didn't know where he was with the adoption thing—how much he was going to push it—and I was afraid to find out.

"What did you guys do?" he asked, a chipper lilt in his voice. I didn't know why he thought seeing Donna would make me feel good about things.

"Not much, Dad, we just went out. Hung out." I picked up a *New Yorker* and leafed through it, trying to find the movie reviews. "The whole college thing makes people very smug, doesn't it?" I asked. "Is everybody just so damned happy with themselves? Their schools? Their jobs?"

"What do you mean, smug?" Dad asked, watching me carefully.

"Just, you know, just very, very pleased with their little lives. Donna's doing some integrative studies thing. She thinks this somehow makes her very, very special. Her prof this, her prof that. She's reading St. Augustine. So what?"

"Is she enjoying it?" Dad asked, inserting a stack gingerly in his mouth.

"Yes, she's enjoying it," I said. What an asshole, I thought.

"Sometimes smugness, if I understand what you're getting at, is just another way of dealing with anxiety."

"Huh?" It occurred to me that I'd never complained about my friends to him. I'd preferred to let him think we were sophisticates; any dirty laundry was too cool to be leaked to outsiders.

"Most people have a lot of anxiety, Thea," he said. "Even when things are going well."

"What does that have to do with it?" I asked. "I'm just saying she's being annoying. Her GPA and how it's the highest in her seminar, blah blah."

"Maybe she doesn't want it to end," he said, sweeping crumbs to one side of his plate.

"Doesn't want what to end?"

"Whatever success she's experiencing at the moment." He picked up another cracker and held it pensively in front of his mouth.

"What, is something up at work?" I asked.

"No, it's okay." He leaned back. "Not great. It's been a tough year. I'm only down thirty percent, better than some, but I've still got lots of layoffs."

"Are you going to get the ax?"

"Who knows?" He sighed, setting the plate on the ottoman. "I'm sure I'm on someone's list."

"You're being very cool about it," I said.

"Not cool, just resigned, maybe. Now, how about that salad? I've got some Parma ham and I've boiled some eggs to throw in." He got up and went to the kitchen with his plate.

"Great," I said, stretching my sore, hungover muscles on the couch.

"In the meantime, it's no fun having to fire a bunch of people. A lot of them have kids Ian's age."

"Do you call them into your office"—I lowered my voice, trying to imitate him—"Look, I have some bad news. . . ."

"It's not a game, Thea," he said, turning around from the kitchen counter to glare at me.

"I didn't say it was. It's just that you never seem to be . . ."

"To be what?"

"I don't know, too engaged in what people think anyway."

"What kind of thing is that to say?" His back was to me again and he was making big sweeping motions with his hands, tossing the salad.

"Well, why don't you have any friends? How come you're alone so much?"

"Am I alone? I wouldn't describe it that way."

"Besides us, I mean, and work."

"You take up more of my life than you realize." He pulled the plastic string on a bottle of olive oil and the wrapper popped off. I had a guilty pang that came in a rush. What was that supposed to mean? Were we really that much of a burden? Then I immediately resented him for pinning all his social failures on *us*.

"Look, Thea," he said. "Don't take this the wrong way, but

I'm not that interested in what a twenty-five-year-old kid starting out has to say. Why does he need to get up on the table and do the Macarena, or whatever."

"What are you talking about?" I asked.

He peeled an egg and dumped the shells into the garbage. "Why does he need to make an impact that way? Moreover, why does he need to tell me, to *explain* to me, that that's what he does at parties? Why is this a defining feature for him? One he needs to tell people about? Tell *me* about?" He shook the new olive oil into the bowl.

"What's your point?" I asked. "That you don't care?"

He made a shooing motion with his hand as he carried out the bowl on two plates. "I don't know what the point is, maybe I *am* intrigued by these people, these young guys who come in so eager and giddy, with their elephantine egos, their inflated, fragile sense of self." He shook his head and sat down at the table. I dragged myself to the chair in front of him. "Maybe I'm even fond of them. From afar, ideally." He rubbed his hands together. "Salad du chef."

We chewed in silence.

"Maybe we should go wake up Ian," Dad said. "He'll cheer me up."

"Wake him and die," I said. My phone rang and I reached for it on the table.

"Thea, please, don't answer the phone at the dinner table." He scowled. "You don't see me doing that."

I hit the green button. "Your bikini?" I recognized Carmen's slightly scratchy voice. "It sold in less than an hour. I remember looking at my watch. It was, like, forty-seven minutes after you left."

"No way," I said quietly.

"I think she was Brazilian, I'm not kidding. I was going to

216

call you right after, but I had to catch a train to Wellfleet for a family thing and I ran out of juice. I just got back. Anyway, you should make more. How long did it take you to make that one?"

"A while," I admitted. "But I think I can ramp it up."

"Well, why don't you do, like, two or three more and bring them in. You have the yarn, right?"

"Yup," I said. Dad was glaring at me, but I put my hand up, gesturing, Wait till you hear this.

I hung up, my heart racing, some weird baroque music sounding in my brain. I felt like a window had opened up in my head again, cool air blowing through it, the same way I felt in Carmen's shop when I was first there with Vanessa.

"So something really exciting just happened." I looked at Dad, picking up my fork.

"What's that, Thea?"

"I sold a bikini."

"Bikini?" Dad focused on stabbing his last lettuce leaf.

"Vanessa taught me how to crochet, and I made this bikini, just like one I had when I was a kid—there's a picture of me at the beach on Charter, Nana made it. Anyway, this woman Carmen helped me, a lot, actually, and then she sold it in her shop. That's what she called to tell me."

"I didn't realize you made swimsuits," he said, standing up with his plate. He either wasn't listening or was really dense.

"She sold it for three hundred bucks," I called after him as he headed to the kitchen. He turned toward me and paused at the mention of money.

"That's great," he said. "That's terrific, Thea." He continued to the kitchen, looking befuddled and slightly worried, as though my earning three hundred dollars were potentially illegal. "Some more salad?"

43.

My life and Ian's in the shitter, I drowned myself in crochet.
I brought it with me everywhere—on the subway to Ian's doctor; to coffee with Mom, where it calmed me as she told me
things were heating up with Alex the married guy; to the park,
looping and twirling while Ian stared at the branches over us.
I'd grab it whenever Ian slept, and when he woke up, I'd do
just a few more stitches. Sometimes I'd push it, listening as his
sharp cries changed to long, low growls. Just a few more
stitches. I'd pick him up and he'd scream into my ear, showing
me how mad he was, and I'd mash his cheek against mine and
beg forgiveness.

It had taken two days to finish the first teal and royal-blue
zigzagged bikini. I crocheted from six a.m. Thursday until two
a.m. Friday, stopping only to put Ian on the boob for ten minutes a side. When he wasn't nursing, he lay next to me in a
nest of blankets I constructed to help him sleep. On Friday I
started again at nine a.m. and went until midnight. By midnight my eyeballs were swollen and frozen in their sockets and
my index finger felt like a burnt twig. But Saturday morning I
started right in on the second one.

The second bikini had the hardest design—a red, orange
and yellow sunburst pattern. It took me almost five days of
nonstop crocheting to finish it, and I was feeling so good about
it, I thought for sure Will would call before I finished to say he
hadn't been thinking straight. He didn't.

The third bikini's pattern was almost identical to the bikini
I had when I was six, and as I cast on the first few chains
of green, I pulled out the original photo of me, in glorious

red, white and blue, that I'd kept in an envelope. I looked at my Mona Lisa–smiling face in the photo and remembered how miserable I was after that fight Mom and Dad had had in the middle of the night, and how hard it had been to smile for my grandmother, who was snapping photo after photo of me on the beach. How long after that had they gotten divorced? Six long years. I did the first row and all the slipknots, remembering the day I found out.

"You know, I was thinking," Mom had said, standing in my doorway, "last night when I picked you up from Kyra's and you were running down the hallway to the elevator . . . your pants are too short. Your ankles are starting to show again." She'd sat on my bed and examined a chicken pox scab healing on my cheek. "When did I take you to that horrible place for jeans? September, when school started. And already they're getting too short."

"I don't want new ones," I'd said. She always started an argument with me as I was just waking up.

"Sweetheart, you look like Twiggy."

"Who?"

"Never mind. Let's just get you a couple more pairs and you can at least alternate. Wherever you want. Your choice. We'll get some breakfast first."

"Daddy too?" I'd asked.

"He's got errands," she'd said. "Just us."

I don't remember what I had. It was gray and windy and there were puffed-up plastic bags in the tree outside our booth window. Mom brought the paper and she read it while we fought about letting me go to some movie that she didn't want me to see. Then we went to an army-navy store, where I got a pair of black corduroys.

"How about we go look for dresses for Aunt Cecilia's wedding?" she'd offered. Her face was bright but tense, the way some people looked after snorting cocaine.

"It's not till July," I'd said. A strange, open-ended feeling had started taking over the day.

"We don't need to buy," she'd said. "Just look and think."

So we went to Barneys. We walked around the second floor and Mom picked up sleeves of black jackets and long-sleeved shirts and dropped them. She tried on a pair of brown suede boots.

"Let's get a coffee, shall we?" she'd asked. "Are you hungry again? I love the café next door. Let's go."

It was starting to fill up for lunch and we sat down at the last free table.

"Aren't we lucky," she'd said, straightening her place mat.

It was one of the few times in my life I remember her sitting still. She held the menu up to her face and read it for a long time. Then she put it down.

"Thea, there's something I need to speak with you about."

"What?"

"It's about your father and me."

She called him "your father" instead of "Daddy" and I knew right away. She went back to calling him Daddy again after they got divorced. She still calls him Daddy and he still calls her Mom when they're with me.

When we got home to our lobby, Dad was talking to Tom, the doorman. He was standing with a suitcase between his legs, the same way he stood when he waited for the elevator. He turned around and looked at me, all of a sudden a stranger.

As I started to cry, Mom asked Tom if the mail had come, and Dad hugged me, not saying anything. I thought about how good everything had been since he'd stopped drinking. How he'd helped me do my homework and made popcorn in the lobster pot and did crosswords under the black lamp. Every single night he was Dad instead of the sleepy-eyed, drunk imposter who'd come home late from work and fling his arms around in the air whenever he said anything. But for some reason that I couldn't for the life of me figure out, the fact that he'd finally quit made no difference to Mom.

"Where are you going?" I'd asked.

"I'll be close by," he'd answered, and as I looked at his face, I thought I could see disappointment as big as mine.

Ian stirred and scrunched his face next to me, burrowing his head into my leg. I put down the crochet hook and picked him up as he opened his eyes. The questions that had plagued me since I'd left Florence's crowded the air around his head: Did he know Will was gone? Did he miss him? Would I be able to love him enough to make up for not having a dad? I kissed him and held him, letting his warm cheek sink into my neck. It was all I could do.

44.

I took my new green-and-purple-squared bikini with me to the moms' group I'd read an ad for on Craigslist, thinking it would facilitate hanging back, not getting caught in the fray.

Ian and I were the first to arrive at the restaurant, which somehow confirmed that I had no friends. I sat down in the middle of a long, narrow farm table as Ann and Hilary, the preexisting friends who'd started the group, came in together with their babies. They saw me and parked their strollers by the door.

"Are you Thea?" Hilary shook my hand overly hard, jutting out her Sigourney Weaver jaw.

I nodded, getting up. Ian was in the sack, his head nestled against my chest.

"Don't, you're in kangaroo mode." She smiled, nodding at Ian.

"Thea, this is Ann. Leah and Kate should be here any minute."

"Hi, Thea," Ann said in a nasal voice. She grabbed the menu. "Eggs, I want eggs," she said. Her baby reached for the brown sugar packets.

"If I have another coffee, my head's going to explode," Hilary explained. Her baby stood on the floor in a jean jacket, leaning on her, swatting her legs. "He's just standing, as of yesterday."

Hilary was an associate at a law firm and had taken a year off, but she'd just hired a nanny because she was "going back." She was having trouble relinquishing control to the nanny.

"I feel like she can't do it I like I can," she said, banging her empty latte cup on the table. She glanced at me crocheting away. I tried to catch her eye every so often to not seem rude. "We're working on it."

"You know what will make your life so much easier when you're working?" Ann asked urgently, licking her thumb and sticking it on the table to sop up the spilled sugar from the packet.

Hilary and Ann started in about a meal delivery service. I watched them, wondering, How did I used to make friends?

How did I make friends with Chris Fontana from Staten Island, who I had nothing in common with other than pre-calc? We laughed about Mr. Kushman's shoes and made fun of the way he rolled his *l*'s, as in *l-l-l-evel*. We'd write notes back and forth—"What did you do last night?" "Went to the mall with my mother, she picked out something for her date with the butt doctor." And then all of a sudden you knew each other, you could ask specific questions—"How was the date with the butt doctor?" "Sucky, poor Mom," and so on. It was easier then, I thought, watching as Kate, too pretty for me, arrived in boho-chic perfection, a binky-sucking boy slung on her hip.

"Thea, you're the new girl," she said, holding her free hand away from me. "I won't shake," she said apologetically. "He's got something."

"No problem," I said, nodding earnestly, then smiling at the baby. He turned his head as far away from me as it would go, and I decided I hated making small talk with other people's children. My knees bumped up against the table as I watched her saunter around to the other side, to a seat next to Hilary. Kate had a nice, direct way about her, and she was wearing a cute embroidered-leather belt. But there were pots of jam and menus, nestled between hunks of bread, blocking our way, and I just felt too tired.

I loitered at the table after they all left, pulling my hook and yarn out of the bag, annoying the waiters seating lunch customers. I ordered another coffee and crocheted until my fingers were white-knuckled and sore, my arms aching from holding the whole thing over Ian's sleeping body. I slipped the last loop off the hook just as someone placed my check squarely in front of me. It was Friday—exactly two weeks since I'd started. I was done and ready to haul my new stash to Stash.

My phone rang as we got outside.

"Hi," Will said.

I leaned my shoulder against the traffic-light post on the corner, the ticking noise from inside it reverberating through me. I couldn't speak. It had been almost three weeks since I'd left Florence's. Cars clunked over a manhole in the street. I wished I could sit down someplace quiet where I could hear him better.

"How are you? How's Ian?" He sounded distant. All business.

"He's fine." Everything I looked at took on a surreal quality. I had no idea how I felt or how to "be" with him.

"Thea, I'm sorry I haven't called. I needed to think."

"About what?" I mumbled.

"Listen, I want to talk to you about something and I want you to really think about it. Do you want to meet someplace?"

"What is it?" I asked.

"Maybe we should meet."

"Just tell me, Will," I said. "I don't want to wait."

"I talked to someone at an adoption agency. They were incredibly understanding and . . ."

The light had turned green, but I stayed put. "No," I said.

"You can't just say no without talking about it first."

"Yes, I can."

"Well, I want to talk about it."

"There's nothing to talk about. If you don't want to be a part of it, that's fine," I said. "There's nothing to talk about beyond that."

"Thea, please . . ."

I hung up the phone and crossed the street. The first thought that went through my head was that I was going to have to change my cell phone number. I caught our reflections in the window of a sushi place, my puffy black down jacket, Ian in his checked hat, broadcasting whited-out loneliness in the flat winter sun.

After that, Will became the enemy. I wondered how far he was willing to go. Would he plant drugs on me? Would he lie about me? What was he capable of? I walked around to the front of the stroller. It was almost as if Ian's whole body broke into a smile as he looked at me. If anyone took you away from me, I don't know how I could keep living, I thought. How could Will even consider it? How could he know me and know how I felt about Ian, even when it was tough and I was in a bad mood—how could Will even begin to think about doing what he was doing?

"Just go on with your life," Vanessa said when I called her right afterward. "He's powerless and he knows it."

"I'm so scared, Vanessa," I said. I'd gone one block while I was on the phone with her, staring the whole way at the whirly pattern of Ian's knit hat. When I got to the next corner, it hit me how quickly things changed. How sharply and un-waveringly betrayal could sink in.

45.

Ian kicked in his stroller the next day, knocking a box of matzo off a shelf. It was starting to dawn on me that he really didn't like food shopping.

My hand was in a plastic bag, about to grab some lettuce, when Carmen called.

"They're gone," she said. "All three. Sold today."

"No way," I said, debagging my hand.

"Saturday is always my best day, but this is nuts. I think you've got something, Thea. People looove them."

I spotted Dad standing by a refrigerator, pointing to a bottle of juice in a strangely shaped bottle, gauging my interest, the Saturday crowd jostling past him to get at the roast chickens. I shrugged at him, my heart racing.

"They're just unique," Carmen continued. "I don't like that word, but that's what they are. The cut . . . I admit I tried the teal one on. It just lay on the hips so nicely. Even on *my* hips. If I could buy one, I would."

"I'll make you one," I said.

"The last one to sell was the fiery red and orange. The customer even asked if there were other colors, and when I said there weren't, she bought it anyway. That says something to me."

"What sold first?"

"The teal one, of course. Then the purple and green."

"Wow, Carmen, I can't believe it."

"Nine hundred clams, baby, believe it! So what next? You need to make more. A lot more. I could put you in touch with these women I know in Brooklyn, they're seamstresses who do everything—knit, crochet, whatever. Maybe you could work something out with them. Do you have any money you could . . . you know, start something with?"

"I might," I answered.

"Well, I could hook you up with them," she said. "They do great work. Let me know. In the meantime, congratulations! Come by and I'll give you a check."

My first thought was to call Will and say, *"See? I actually did something. You thought it was stupid and you were wrong. You're wrong about everything."*

I found Dad on the line, pursing his lips at a woman in front of him who was digging into the bowels of her wallet for change.

"So guess what!" I asked, almost ramming the stroller into the checkout station.

"What's that, Thea," he asked, placing two artichokes on the belt.

"All three bikinis sold today. I dropped them off at Stash yesterday and they all sold today."

"You don't say." Dad smiled, distracted. He pulled a credit card out of his wallet and gave it to the cashier, who nodded and motioned for him to swipe it.

"Carmen said she could hook me up with some women in Brooklyn who could help me make, you know, more of them than I could alone."

"Who's Carmen?" he asked, swiping his card in the black groove.

"The woman at the knitting store I told you about, remember?"

"Vaguely," he said. The cashier motioned for him to do it again, which he did, but it was the wrong way. I grabbed it out of his hand and turned it around.

"She said these women could help me make more than I could just by myself."

"What is it, like a sweatshop?" he asked. He looked at the cashier, annoyed. "Do I have to sign?"

"No, not a *sweatshop,*" I said quickly as the cashier shook her head at him, shooing us down the line. "Do sweatshops even exist anymore?" I hung one of the bags on the stroller and we pushed through the big green doors.

"Are you kidding?" He laughed, looking at me sideways.

"There are laws in this country, right?" I asked.

"Well, how many workers do they employ? How much do they make an hour?"

"I don't know, Dad."

"Well, that's something you'd want to research."

We headed west on Broome Street, past the soot-stained cast-iron buildings and I wondered how I could bring myself to ask him to help me again, when he was already helping me out so much. The truth was, I hated asking him for anything because it made me feel guilty. Especially since I'd gotten pregnant and was now living with him. What was more, the idea of asking him for things always reminded me of when I was little and he, bombed out of his mind in the middle of a Saturday, took me to the toy store on Charter Island. We'd wheeled a shopping cart around the store as we piled stuff in—a Barbie makeup head, Barbie outfits, games and more games, a red soccer ball. Bright orange, see-through plastic water guns with extra-long barrels. A badminton set and extra birdies.

"What about a skateboard?" he'd asked.

"I have one in the city."

"Yes, but did you bring it?" He'd plopped a red plastic skateboard onto the heap. Its wheels were too small, but the thrill plodded on.

At the register I'd waited to hear "Thea, we've overdone it—put this one back, why don't you." But it never came. I watched as everything went into shopping bags, excited beyond containment at my luck. But after Mom and Dad split, the scene that replayed in my head was of me cashing in on all the crap that had been going on between them; I got a Barbie makeup head because Dad was on the verge of a nervous breakdown. Then, when I got older, I'd just sneak or take what I wanted instead of asking, like when I snuck off to Europe.

As we crossed Sixth Avenue, I told myself that I'd bring it up again at dinner, hating the fact that after all he'd done, I still needed his help. But when we got home, he went into the kitchen and threw himself into making dinner, grunting at me when I asked him where the Diet Coke was as he whisked together a marinade for the steaks and cut up paper-thin slices of garlic to grill them with.

"Table twenty-four enjoying their jar course, I see." Dad walked slowly out of the kitchen with our plates and utensils in one hand, steak sauce in the other. He'd nicknamed the high chair "table twenty-four" and he called Ian the Machiavelli party. It was after nine o'clock when we finally sat down, and by that time I was too undone from starvation and accumulated-over-the-day depression about Will to have a productive conversation about anything. And then, with Dad's impeccable sense of timing, he threw me a curveball.

"So listen, Thea, I spoke to Tom Davidson this afternoon. His office needs someone while his assistant is on maternity leave."

"What's his office?" I asked, pulling my napkin out of its ring.

"What do they do, you mean?" He threw so much pepper on his steak that the top was almost black. "Pullman Capital. It's a midsize private equity firm. They do some derivatives work for us. What's wrong?"

"Nothing," I said, wiping Ian's mouth.

"Thea, I think this could be a good thing," he said, cutting his steak methodically into small bites. "You could do this until you're ready to go to NYU. It would be a good thing to have on your resume."

"Despite the fact that I have no intention of going into

finance," I said. I'd been with him all afternoon. When had he spoken to Tom Davidson? Had he pulled this idea out of his hat because he thought I was getting too caught up in my little bikini dreams? Resentment rushed over me. He wanted me to do something and it didn't matter whether I wanted to do it or not; if I loved him or, more importantly, if I wanted his love, I had to do it.

"What about Ian?" I asked.

Dad leaned forward on his elbows, in serious mode. "Bonnie Whelan gave me the name of an agency that places domestic help. She found her nanny through them and she's been with them for years. Apparently there's only one agency you want. That should be your plan this week. To find a nanny."

"You mean an agency? Like St. Mary's?" I asked.

"No," Dad grunted, shaking his head. "These women are professionals. They do this for a living."

"Remember Bridget?" I said, rubbing it in. My parents had funny luck with babysitters. They'd gotten them all through a Catholic agency next to the church down the street. There was Elishka, the nudist; Patty, the pyromaniac; and Bridget, who took me with her to O'Neal's Pub to meet her boyfriend. She sat on his lap, letting him stick his tongue through her hoop earring, while I hid in the booth with them, seeing how many times I could tie her incredibly long gum-wrapper chain around my neck. The bartender gave me a ginger ale with about seventy maraschino cherries in it. When we got home, Dad was standing in the living room with two cops.

I thought for sure he'd at least smile at the memory. He sat there waiting, his shoulders slumped, for my enthusiastic response.

"Do I have to go there?" I asked.

"No. You call them up and they send over a few people to interview."

"All at once?"

"One by one," he said, rolling his tongue across his teeth. "Is this how you're going to be?"

"What do you mean?"

"You're behaving helplessly."

"I am not," I said, prying Ian out of his high chair. "I'm trying to figure it out. It's not that easy to just stick him with someone. He's pretty attached. Or maybe it's me who's attached to him." I squeezed Ian's soft, springy foot and thought of Will again with a weird combination of fear and missing him. I stopped myself from imagining for the millionth time that someone was at the door, ready to lift Ian out of my arms. I wanted to kill Will for making me feel so vulnerable. But if I killed Will, they would definitely take Ian away.

"A little separation will be good for both of you," Dad said in a way that hinted he thought Ian would be a wimp if he was attached to me. He crunched into a green bean, sat back and crossed his arms. It started dawning on me that he was going to force the job issue. "Your mom loved working, remember?"

I remembered and was suddenly homesick for her.

"What?" Dad asked. "What is it?"

"I kind of want to pursue this bikini thing," I said meekly. "I think I could really make something happen with it."

"Thea, it sounds like a little more than you can chew at the moment," Dad said impatiently, throwing more pepper on his steak.

"Well, I'd rather do that than private equity," I said, laying Ian on a blanket on the couch.

There was a long silence, then Dad said evenly, in a way I knew there was absolutely no room for argument: "I think we should give this opportunity at Pullman a chance."

"When does it start, this opportunity?" I asked.

"As soon as possible," he said, sauntering victoriously into the kitchen. "But I bought you a week because I knew the nanny would need taking care of."

"You bought me a week? Is that like buying me a vowel?" I followed him, dumping my half-full plate in the garbage.

"It's an exciting place," he said. "See where it goes. That's all I'm thinking. You can't sit home with Ian. I won't have it. Eventually you'll start college, and this is a perfect way to bide your time until you do. It will help give you options in the workforce after you graduate."

"Workforce. It sounds like a branch of the military." I took his plate and yanked open the dishwasher as he made a beeline for his room.

46.

Joy was from the Philippines. It struck me about halfway through my conversation with her, when she told me that she loved "working" with babies, that I was in the middle of a job interview. That she was there to get hired.

"So you're currently working for another family?" I asked.

"Yes." Joy smiled. "Two girls. One is ten, the other, seven." She folded her hands primly on her knees, anticipating questions. "They're in school now. Mom Melissa doesn't need a full-time nanny anymore. Just part-time." The tone of her voice seemed sad, and I felt bad for her. She had so little control over it, kids getting older.

Adelle came, followed by Yvonne an hour later. Adelle had three grown kids. Yvonne from the Farrell Agency said she was "seasoned." I thought she seemed seasoned too, by the way she reached for Ian right away and made a big deal about him, his long eyelashes, his dimpled chin, but his eyes kept darting toward me.

Monica was from Barbados. When I opened the door, she glided in with a beautiful scarf tied tightly around her head, which made me wonder about her hair. She was getting a degree in criminology at night and wanted to be a detective. She looked me in the eye more consistently than I could look anyone in the eye, and she walked with a fun swing to her butt. She had long legs and a formidable presence. She looked like she'd be alert and on-the-ball enough to prevent Will from running with Ian out of a park.

I barely remembered how she was with Ian, just that her smile seemed real, and that she had the air of someone who was doing worthwhile things with her time. I told Dad when he came home that night, and he was overly proud of me for making the decision so quickly. "Your mother was always amazed at what good child care was available in the city," he said, which forced me to consider whether Monica might actually be an ax murderer.

He smiled at me from the foyer, slipping his shoes off and lining them up under the red silk chair. Ian was lying on a mat by the dining room window, reaching for a drape near his hand by the floor.

"Ian, don't," we both said at the same time, and Ian turned

toward me with a sweetly defiant look on his face that was so Will it made my whole body ache.

"I appreciate what you're trying to do, Dad, I really do," I said, grabbing my coat from the red chair and hanging it in the closet. "But this bikini thing could be interesting. Don't you think?"

Bikini thing. I realized how silly it sounded, especially to someone like him. He paused and looked at me, then walked purposefully to the fridge and pulled out a bottle of Pellegrino, giving me the impression that he was mulling it over. He struggled to twist the bottle, sticking it between his knees, but it wouldn't budge. He grabbed a dish towel and after more struggling he opened it, then downed it straight from the bottle. "Aaaaah," he said. At that point it was clear he'd forgotten what I'd asked, and I was once again too tired and disheartened to bring it up again.

47.

Monica arrived on my first morning at work and pulled a beaten-up *Goodnight Moon* out of her purse after I handed Ian to her. I wondered if she thought we didn't have enough books in the house, and if she was going to read him *Goodnight Moon* because she wanted him to nap all day. I headed to the subway, thinking about Will colluding with Monica to steal Ian, traveling with him for miles, across borders. How would I get him back? I imagined my legs moving through water, or running in slow motion in the air like in a dream. I wondered if I'd ever hear from Will again.

Pullman Capital was in a tall, narrow building on Sixth Avenue, or Avenue of the Americas, depending on your mood. When I got to reception, the guy behind the desk phoned someone named Sue and motioned for me to take a seat on a black leather couch. After a couple of minutes I picked up the front section of the *Times,* just to peruse the headlines, because I hated getting interrupted in the middle of a story, like I always do in a doctor's office. A few more minutes went by and I caved and started at the back with an obituary about a children's book illustrator, which made me wonder when I should start reading to Ian. I finished the article and still no sign of Sue. Hopefully this is what the job will be like, I thought. Hopefully they'll just install me in some cubicle and forget about me and I'll be free to crochet under the desk. I'd take my six hundred dollars a week after taxes and save it toward a production deal with the women in Brooklyn. If they left me alone, I could actually ramp up production to two or three bikinis a week, sell those and prove to Dad how lucrative it could be. But I was interrupted.

"Thea Galehouse?" A boxy woman in a black pantsuit and glasses with beaded croakies stood by the reception desk.

"Hi, yes, that's me, nice to meet you." I stood up, straightening my too-tight Gap pencil skirt.

"Nice to meet you, I'm Sue. So follow me. We're going to need you to help out in client services, if that's okay." Sue pushed through both glass doors, giving us a wide berth, and led me to a room with a bunch of long, wide tables, the same size as the lunch tables at school, pushed into a large U. She launched into a synopsis of the meaning of Pullman Capital and explained, in incredibly unspecific terms, what I'd be doing there. Every second or third seat had a computer screen, and some of the screens had men sitting in front of them, but most did not.

"Why don't you have a seat here and make yourself comfortable," said Sue, exiting the room in long strides across the carpet. "You can hang up your coat in that closet, and Malcolm will be with you soon."

Now I had nothing to read. I noticed that my spot at the U didn't have a phone. I hoped I had cell reception but wasn't optimistic because the room was windowless. What if Monica needed to reach me? A guy next to me was enunciating something into his phone, and at first I couldn't figure out why I was having trouble understanding him—I thought maybe it was another language—but then I realized he had a speech impediment that made him lose all of his s sounds. Each time he said "Seabrook," it sounded like "Heabrook." He also talked very fast and it made me sure that only those who had an intimate relationship with him could understand what the hell he was saying. I prayed he wasn't my boss because I would definitely offend him.

He was, of course.

"You're Hea? Nie to meet you," he said, wheeling over to me. "I'm Malcolm. Terrific you're here."

"Hi," I said. It looked like his tongue was missing. I was immediately, painfully conscious of trying to act normal in front of his disability, positive he could tell. But he was gallant. Later on, someone alluded to the fact that he'd had cancer in his jaw.

"I'd like you to tart, if you would, with organi-ing hom of our pre-entation folder," he said.

I nodded, relieved I understood.

"We have heven department at Pullman Cap, each of which is repre-hented in the folder. You'll find a page for each of the heven loaded on and in-hide that con-hole over there."

I spun my chair toward the console in the corner. The job would require getting up and down a lot.

"Come." He got up and motioned me to the presentation station.

Together we put a folder together, taking a packet from each pile and sliding it in.

"Not the moht eck-hiting thing, but we need them dehperately," he said, throwing his arms dramatically in the air.

"No problem." I smiled, wondering how many folders I'd have to put together before I could work on the bikini under the desk.

"Fabulouh," he said, exiting the room.

I wondered if I could cheat and bring seven little stacks back to my chair and stuff them into folders from there. Surely Malcolm didn't expect me to stand at that console all day. I'd do five or six standing up, get my bearings, and then bring it over to the desk, where I'd do twenty or so, and then I'd crochet three or four rows on my lap under the desk.

I opened drawers, looking for an empty one to hold my bag. Someone snickered behind me.

I turned around and saw a guy with jaw-length, shiny black hair slumped in his chair, his shirttail hanging out. "We'll need ten thousand of those today," he joked with a pronounced English accent, flicking back his hair. "And they all need to be FedExed. We'll get you the list."

I shot him a dirty look.

"What's your name?" he asked, grinning.

"Thea. What's yours?"

"Daniel," he said. "Good luck. You'll be at it for decades. Careful of paper cuts. Nice top, by the way."

"Thank you," I said, trying not to appear embarrassed or antagonized.

237

"Paisley always makes me think of the Beatles," he said.

"It's my mother's," I said as I glanced at the door, half expecting Malcolm to appear and shush us.

"She must be very chic," he said, flipping the pages of a huge loose-leaf binder.

I'd never heard a boy say "chic."

"She's into clothes," I said, pulling my sore, blistery heel out of the black flat I hadn't worn in months.

"Into clothes?" he drawled in a cheesy American accent, flicking his hair out of his face yet again.

"She enjoys shopping for and purchasing women's wear. She's a fashionista. That better?"

I got up and went to the stacks at the console. Men, no women, came into the room throughout the morning, mostly to check the computer screens or to buzz someone on the intercom, and then they'd leave. I sat and stuffed, listening to Daniel on the phone—he was talking to someone named Elle who was having a party and wanted him to bring a bottle of Pernod, and to someone named Cass, who I took to be his girlfriend in London.

"Fly here this weekend, babe," he kept saying. "Study for it on the flight. I can't bear it, darling . . . you know I can't . . . I've got no money." At twelve-thirty he let out a loud yawn. "Thea, let's trot out. I'll take you to meet Mr. Spaghetti."

I went with him down Fifty-Sixth Street to a guy standing in front of a takeout place with a platter of tomato bruschettas.

"So I have this mental picture of you in my head," Daniel said, taking a bruschetta off Mr. Spaghetti's tray and spilling it down his chin as he ate it. "Tell me if I'm right. You had a breakdown during your, what do you call it here? Sophomore year, so you've dropped out to take some time to collect your-self, to 'find yourself' as you Americans say, and since someone owed Daddy a favor, you're now biding your time in the hal-lowed hallways of Pullman Capital. Am I right, darling?"

"Why do English people call everyone darling?" I asked, popping a bruschetta into my mouth as we stepped into the takeout place and onto the long line. I was tempted to just tell him my True Hollywood Story but wasn't ready to part with the idea of free-and-easy Thea yet.

As we paid, he motioned to the cashier, saying, "See that woman? She's mad for me." The receptionist in the front hall of Pullman was also mad for him. On the way back he let me listen to a dance track on his iPod, made by a guy from some club in Dubai or St. Bart's. "I like my music long," he said, and something about the way he thumped his head back and forth reminded me of a turtle. He told me he was living in the East Thirties for six months, on some kind of break from Oxford.

We got back to our desks and ate. He pointed a breadstick in my direction.

"No, thank you," I said. He smiled over some secret little joke to himself and turned back to his desk.

48.

Ian finally started sleeping through the night—really sleeping—from seven or eight p.m. until seven in the morning, after I let him cry for fifteen million hours over the course of two days, like the book said. It worked. As the weeks went by, we fell into a routine: Woke up at seven and messed around on our favorite spots—my bed, the floor in our bedroom, under the mobile. Dad would feed Ian while I jumped in the shower before Monica showed up at eight. When Ian was around five months old, Dad got very into making some recipe he'd concocted with watered-down oatmeal and mashed-up bananas. He would make a big bowl for breakfast and share it with him. "I forgot how much I love bananas," he said almost every morning, alternating a big spoon into his mouth, a baby spoon into Ian's.

Mom took me to a media-elite Italian place for lunch one Friday after I'd been at Pullman for a couple of months. We sat down at a tiny two-top and dove into a bowl of olives as Mom spied on the people next to us, trying to listen in. She looked back at me and I swore I saw a trace of a wince.

"Did I tell you we are finally, finally, closing on that Astor Place apartment tomorrow?" she asked, tossing a pit into a zebra-striped wooden bowl. "I never thought it would happen. The buyer made endless demands—replace all the windows, redo the floors—it was ridiculous and I never thought it would happen, but it finally is. My first closing. I'm really pleased." An undercurrent of spite trailed under her voice, like I hadn't been involved enough throughout the transaction, the whole undertaking.

"Maybe you've found your calling," I said. "Remember when I looked at all those places with Daddy? We could have used someone good, someone who's good at figuring out what people want."

"It's fun, but it's a lot of work." She browsed the menu. "I'm craving pasta. Isn't that strange?"

I pulled the hook out of my bag. It was becoming almost

like a compulsion, the crocheting; I couldn't figure out if it was helping me engage or disengage. I just felt compelled to do it.

"What is that?" she asked, peeking out from behind her menu.

"It's a bikini. You like it?"

"I have to first come to terms with this ludicrously domestic picture in front of me," she said, blinking dramatically. "First you get yourself knocked up, now you're knitting."

"I'm crocheting. You've seen me do it before. Vanessa taught me, remember?"

"Whatever," she said, setting her menu down. "Knitting, crocheting, they're all dowager sports." She scraped her chair out and crossed her legs. "I'm convinced sometimes you must be someone else's daughter. But then I remember . . ." She frowned and made horns on the top of her head. "Evelyn Galehouse . . ."

"Chill out, Mom," I said, tucking the yarn into the crook of the banquette. "It's not a big deal. Just because you don't do it."

"It's more than I don't do it. I'm unnerved to see you doing it. It's so . . . retro in a not pleasant or inviting way."

"Well, what if I told you I'm making money from it?"

"How?"

"I'm selling bikinis for three hundred bucks a pop at this knitting store," I said. "You'd like it, it's trendy, not crafty. This woman Carmen, the owner, she's been selling them and she wants to hook me up with some women in Brooklyn who can help me."

"Who is Carmen?" she asked suspiciously, as though I were utterly incapable of conducting business.

"She owns the knitting store on Charlton Street. Vanessa took me."

"Of course she did," Mom said, rolling her eyes.

"She thinks I should try and not mass-produce them but work something out, like a production deal, and sell them to small boutiques."

"Do you notice that I clench my jaw?" she asked. A large plate of pasta with mushrooms arrived in front of her and she passed a bite over to me, dripping oil across my plate of ravioli.

"You're changing the subject," I said.

"This awful dental assistant who did my cleaning last week at Dr. Church's," she continued, ignoring me. "She asked me if I ground my teeth. Just from her asking it, it was like she made it true. I'm a tooth grinder. A jaw clencher." She took a pocket mirror out of her bag and examined her mouth. "I hate it when someone insinuates something and then somehow you start believing it. Daddy used to do that."

"What do you mean?" I asked, letting the buttery ravioli melt in my mouth.

"Oh, he was so critical. Every little thing. And it always came in question form." She hissed the "sss" in "question." It hit me how pissed she was, still. "Do you think your bangs are a little long, honey? I can't see your pretty eyes." She looked at me and closed her lips. "Anyway, never mind. How's it going over there? How's the old codg adjusting to modern parenting?"

"He's trying," I said, cutting my ravioli in fours in an attempt to eat it slowly. "He's home by seven most nights now."

"Unbelievable," she said, shaking her head. "Maybe he's finally getting his head in the right place."

"Hey, I just thought of something," I said. "Doesn't your friend Christine work at *Bazaar*? Maybe you could call her and tell her about the bikinis and she could do a little write-up about them."

She picked up the lemon wedge hanging on the rim of her Diet Coke and bit it, her red lipstick staining the rind. "You're really thinking about this."

"I am," I said.

She plunked the lemon into the glass. "I haven't spoken to her in ages, but I'll see what I can do. Can I see it?"

I wiped my hands, picked the bikini off the banquette and handed it over. This one was off-white with a turquoise and gold zigzag running vertically down the side of each hip.

"Where on earth did you learn to do this?" she asked, stretching the bottom out.

"I've told you before," I said. "Vanessa taught me."

She handed it back. "I'll see if I can track down Christine." She took a slice of baguette out of the basket and swished it around her plate. "So where is Will these days?"

"He's still at Florence's, I guess—I haven't heard from him in a few weeks." I forked the last quarter-ravioli and put on a brave face. "In a way it's easier without him."

"Sure," Mom said, laying down her fork. "One agenda. But is it over?"

"What? No," I said too loudly. I felt sick from the butter and oil. First he turns on me, then he disappears. I didn't know what I was more angry over—the fact that he so badly betrayed me with the adoption bullshit, or the fact that he'd then just dropped it, and dropped out of our lives. And the worst of it was the unavoidable reality that I still loved him.

49.

Daniel cast his wide-set, hazel eyes on the woven leather bag that I'd filched from Mom a while ago.

"Tell me, sweet Thea," he said, flicking his hair. "Why do American girls carry such big bags? Where I'm from, girls don't try to carry the world around with them like you do. What do you have in there?"

My phone rang before I could answer him. It was Mrs. Weston.

She'd called the house and gotten my number from Monica.

"I hope I'm not bothering you." Her voice sounded higher-pitched and more whispery than I'd remembered.

"You're not at all," I said. "How are you?"

"I'm well, thanks," she said, sounding nervous. "I'm having some trouble with my mom, but aside from that."

"Oh no," I said.

"She's just had a hard time, you know, losing my brother. She's not herself. She's suddenly afraid to go outdoors, afraid her freckles will burn, she's sort of spiraling."

"I'm sorry," I said.

"Yes, well, she's in Calabasas, in California, so hard to manage from afar." She cleared her throat. "Thea, I don't want to keep you. I'm sorry this is so hard for Will. I'm sorry that you probably feel let down."

"Yeah, well." I could barely get the words out.

"Well, I'm glad you're moving forward. You've found a job, that's wonderful."

"Yeah," I said, "Dad's idea."

"In any event, Thea, we still want to help you in any way we can with Ian. That still holds true, needless to say."

"Thanks," I said, wondering what Will had told them. Had he just said we'd broken up? Had he told them he wanted to give Ian up? "Would you like to spend some time with him? He's with the nanny while I'm here, at work. You can see him anytime you like."

"I'd like that. I have her number now. I'll call her to set up some dates, if that's all right with you."

"That would be great," I said, hoping that spending time with Ian would effectively wipe out any talk of adoption.

"Is he eating solid food yet?"

"He is," I said authoritatively. "He loves to eat."

"I want to bake him something yummy," she said. "Something with mushy apples."

"I'm sure he'd love whatever you make," I said.

There was an awkward pause as I couldn't think of anything else to say, but then Mrs. Weston responded, her voice somber and serious. "You're going to make this work for you, Thea," she said. "I can tell you are already. You're a strong person. I admire you."

"Thank you," I mumbled, not sure what to make of her attempt at a pep talk, another version of her famous "Be positive," wondering why she had ever scared and intimidated me so much. Was it just because I was so desperately in love with her son? Did he have that much power over me that he could transfer it to other people? The idea that I could have forged some kind of relationship with her if Will hadn't busted everything up hurled me into a black hole.

I hung up. Daniel was zoning into his computer screen. I was enjoying a harmless flirty thing with him to pass the time

245

and didn't want him to hear. There was an empty, closet-sized room down the hall with a phone in it that no one ever used. I went to the room and dialed Will's cell phone. He'd see the number and not know it was me and pick up. It was three o'clock on a Thursday and his last class ended at one-forty. It had been over a month since we'd spoken.

"I haven't heard from you," I said when I heard his voice.

"I know," he said. He sounded totally caught off guard. "How's Ian?"

"Ian's fine," I said. "But why do you even get to know that?"

Silence.

"What's going on?" I asked.

"I'm sorry."

"Sorry for what?" I was scared of what he was going to say.

"Just sorry."

I held my breath. "You know I'm not giving him up, right? I'm never giving him up."

"I know." He sighed.

I ran my fingers over the back of the linty-wool chair, relief washing over me in the dark room. Outside the glass door, a man with red hair deposited a large plate of black-and-white cookies on top of a file cabinet. He glanced at me disapprovingly and turned back down the hallway.

"So you're going to leave it alone, the adoption thing," I said.

"I don't have a choice, do I?" There was resentment bordering on nastiness coming out of him. I wanted to take those cookies, break each of them at the exact mark where black met white, hurl them at the ceiling and shatter all of the hot

246

dog–shaped fluorescent lights onto everyone. I was working so hard and I was doing a good job.

"You know what, Will? I'm a good mother," I said. "The fact that I even have to say it, to justify myself to you, it makes me sick. You make me sick, Will. You make me sick."

My throat felt jammed. I slammed the phone down and banged the desk like a two-year-old, stinging my hand. After I got it together, I went out and made my twelfth green tea of the day and brought one to Daniel.

"I'm so bored," he said, leaning so far back in his chair he was almost lying down.

"It's boring here," I said, my voice hollow. "You'll get no argument from me."

"Good, because I couldn't bear to have you cross with me." He slumped and wriggled, one pod of a headset in his ear, the other traversing his flat, almost concave, chest. "You look blue. Come to the supply closet and I'll cheer you up." He looked up at me and winked. "It locks."

"I thought you were gay," I said.

"Now, that's a cheap shot, Thea." He blew into his tea. "Surely you can do better than that."

I glanced at the door and looked at my watch. 4:20. I'm going to do something stupid, I told myself. I'm going to do something stupid. "You're sure?" I asked as I followed him, feeling achy and already full of unruly remorse.

He turned a metal lock near the floor. "Alone at last," he said as he backed me into a corner shelf, kissing me so hard I could feel his teeth behind his lips.

"You kiss like a dog," I said.

"I do?" he asked. "Well, you have a lovely mouth. Your lips are so smooth and thin and pained. Such a slant to those

247

pained lips." We crammed ourselves down onto the minuscule floor space, and I thought about something Will said once, how I always kept my eyes open.

"Do you have . . ." I asked, half hoping he didn't.

"As luck would have it." He smiled, reached into his trouser pocket and pulled out a condom.

A poster of a smiling Asian girl with doughnuts flying around her head stared back at me from the wall. I was imagining how great it would be if Will could just be brave, like me, and throw doubt to the wind in the name of love, as Daniel tore the edge of the condom wrapper with his teeth. The closet was black with my disappointment. Daniel moved around on top of me, his black hair hanging down, kissing my cheeks and forehead.

"Forget it," I said, wrestling out from under him and standing up. "I can't do this, sorry."

"You're joking," he said, still on the floor.

"I'm not," I said. "Sorry." I opened the door. It felt like we'd been in there forever, but when I got to the table stacked with marketing packets, the clock said 4:35. Daniel appeared and immediately got on the phone, ignoring me, and when it was time to go, I grabbed my bag and my coat and left without looking at him.

Someone shoved the revolving door downstairs, speeding it up and ejecting me onto the granite-flecked sidewalk. I turned the corner and passed a hot dog vendor, who smiled at me from under his baseball cap. I looked down at the black garbage bag hanging off his cart. I hadn't done it. That was good. But I wondered if it was possible to feel any emptier.

50.

When I got home, Monica walked toward me holding Ian in front of her. He was facing me, flailing his arms.

"Someone's happy to see you," she said.

"Hi, boo," I said, kissing him under his chin. I took him and he looked at me and smiled, quickly squirming around, wanting to get down. Monica left for school, and Ian and I headed into our room so I could lie down and figure out our next move. Ian didn't want to go, but I put him down on the rug next to my bed anyway. I stared up at the ceiling and saw the mean queen take shape within the shadows and light from outside. As Ian groped my sheet, I looked down at him and noticed a triangle-shaped bruise on the lower part of his cheek. It hadn't been there when I'd left that morning. I reached into my bag and texted Monica: *Did I. have a spill?*

Something started brewing as I waited for her to respond, the same rage that had been percolating all day, but now more distilled, honed. Monica was not taking as good care of Ian as I could. Monica was probably texting some friend as Ian pulled himself up the coffee table and then fell back down, banging his cheek.

I don't know how much time went by before I heard a key in the door. When I heard it, I had a split-second moment of thinking it was Ian's mother, finally coming home; that she'd give me my money and send me on my way.

Dad was on the phone telling someone he'd "circle back" to them after "the due diligence." I wondered how he could stand doing what he did all day. I got up slowly and brought Ian out to the living room, feeling voraciously hungry. Dad was in the kitchen, rinsing a cucumber, a bag of spinach on the counter.

"I don't want spinach salad," I said, getting a glass out of the cabinet and letting it slam shut.

"I wouldn't dream of making you spinach salad," he said offhandedly. "I was going to sauté it in some garlic."

"What's that?" I pointed to a cucumber on the cutting board.

"I believe it's a cucumber," he said, holding it up and turning it around, examining. "I was just going to slice it up to dip in some hummus. That all right?"

"I'm starving," I said. I filled the glass with water, letting it fill up too quickly to overflowing. My lonely life settled onto me like soot.

"Ian has a giant bruise on his face," I said, ripping off a paper towel. "I texted Monica because I want to know what the hell happened, but she hasn't responded."

He put the knife he'd been cutting the cucumber with down and went out to the living room to look at Ian's face.

"I don't see it," he said.

I stormed out of the kitchen. "Right there," I said, pointing. "How can you not see that? It's getting darker by the minute."

"Oh, that," he said, straightening up. "It doesn't look too bad. Just a little nick."

"No, well, I've got news for you," I said, my brain starting to tighten. "He's not safe! He's not safe, Dad, and you don't give a shit!" As I said it, I wondered what I was actually screaming about. I didn't want to watch Ian all day. I liked being away from home, escaping, even if it had to be at Pullman. I picked up a square plastic block Ian had chucked under the couch, understanding deep down that my emotional turmoil was much vaster and murkier than I realized, and that only pissed me off more.

Dad held his hands up and went back to the kitchen. "You're blowing this way out of proportion. Whatever happened, it's a small bruise. Given what happened with his leg, you must realize that accidents happen. To everyone. Including you." He pointed his finger at me.

"Now *you're* going to start with the irresponsible Thea bullshit?" I said.

"I didn't mean it as an attack," he answered, his voice growing tighter and more monotonous as he went back toward the kitchen. "Just be careful."

"I am careful!" I screamed, making him fumble and almost drop the cucumber. "I'm nothing but careful. Why is nothing I do ever good enough for you?"

He started to say something, then turned stonily back to the cutting board. Then he looked up again, gritting his teeth.

"C'mon, Dad, out with it!" I yelled, shaking. "What else? Anything else? Let's hear it. You think I'm a complete screw-up. Trust me, you don't have to say it."

"Thea, I suggest you collect yourself," he said, pointing the knife at me. "I certainly didn't come home early to hear this."

"Who asked you to come home early? You think I want to spend every freaking night with you? Please, go find a client who wants to have dinner, for once. Please!"

He looked at me, his mouth tightening into a little ball, which only spurred me on.

"I wish I could be anywhere *but* here, believe me."

"Great." He thrust his arm out at the door. "Then go."

I shoved past him and grabbed Ian off the living room

251

floor. He was wearing a onesie with blue stars on it. I'd have to get Ian dressed. We both looked at Ian. My whole life with Dad rose in my throat, our awkward, silent dinners, all the empty time I spent alone at his apartment when I was younger and he was at work, flipping through the pages of his photography books while I waited for him to get home, just so that I could say goodnight and finally go to bed—how I always, always waited up to say goodnight just to make it feel like there was a purpose to me sleeping over.

Dad stood frozen in the kitchen, the knife at his hip.

"Mom was right," I said. "What the hell was I thinking?"

51.

I had the key but I rang, which felt weird. Mom opened the door in her black silk bathrobe. She leaned forward, gripping the half-open door, and kissed me, smelling like sugary grapes.

"Sorry I didn't call," I said, hoisting Ian higher on my hip. "Dad and I had a fight."

"You did?" she whispered. "Alex is here."

"The married guy?" I asked, disgusted. She nodded. There were mascara smudges under her eyes, but the smudges somehow accentuated them. She looked pretty.

"I won't keep you." I threw our bag onto a dining room chair. "We just need to crash here." There were stacks of glossy real estate brochures held together in thick strips of white paper covering the table.

"What happened?" she asked, tying her bathrobe tighter.

"I don't even know. It was stupid." Ian wriggled to get down. Part of me expected her to pull up a chair and devour any gory details.

"You'll work it out," she said quickly. She glanced down the hall at her door, then turned and headed to the kitchen.

"He doesn't want to come out and say hi?" I asked, following her with Ian. "Meet your grandson?"

"Now's probably not the time for that," she said, looking skittishly at Ian. "Where's he going to sleep?"

"Don't worry, I'll rig something up." As I said it, it dawned on me: Ian had never been there.

"Okay, well, it's getting late. You guys should get some sleep." She looked nervous, like she wanted us to clear the area.

"Do you have any food?"

"Take a look." She opened the fridge, letting it hang ajar, and darted out of the kitchen before I could ask her to take Ian while I scavenged.

Ian had just started sitting up. I put him down on the kitchen floor with a toy and found a takeout container of brown rice. I dumped some soy sauce in and ate ravenously, spilling out dry rice clumps onto the floor. Ian spotted some rice near him on the floor and reached for it, but instead fell back on his head, his feet sweeping into the air. There was a long, deep pause before he screamed. His pipes had really developed and he seemed much louder, all of a sudden, than he used to be. I wondered about the neighbors, the Chesleys, next door with their stupid dachshund. I scarfed a few more bites and chucked the container into the trash, then grabbed Ian and scooted down the hallway to my bedroom.

Everything looked the same: my bed neatly made with my

white duvet and little lace pillow squarely in the middle of my two bigger pillows. How long had it been since I'd been there? I pulled Ian's blanket out and lay it on the floor. He fussed but grew quieter once I found the pacifier and shoved it into his mouth. I took his clothes off and put on a clean onesie, counting out loud with a stretchy mouth to keep him distracted. I took off my clothes down to my underwear and tank top, picked up Ian and jammed his head down on my shoulder as I walked him around singing "Twinkle, Twinkle." He was asleep within a minute, like he'd breathed in a magical rose in a fairy tale. I turned off as many lights as I could and pulled the covers down, figuring I'd put Ian between me and the wall. I did and he stayed miraculously asleep. I got my hook out of the bag and sat down at my desk, but I couldn't bring my hands to move. I looked around the dark room, at the line drawing of the Eiffel Tower above my bed and the stack of old jeans on the floor in the closet. There was something really sad about being there, as though time was passing and things were changing too quickly. I got into bed.

In the middle of the night I woke up in a panic, wondering if there was a chance that the fight with Dad would make him go down to the deli and buy a couple of six-packs, drink those, go down again for two more six-packs, drink those and pass out. The idea of him drinking again was almost as scary as the idea of him dying. I fell back to sleep, but then Ian woke up crying. I picked him up and walked around in the dark, squeezing his body across my chest, biting the inside of my cheeks, worried he was going to wake Mom and the cheater. He went on and on, calming down, then starting back up. He kept looking at the door, wanting to go, I think. At one point Mom peeked in.

"What's the matter with him?" she whispered.

"I don't know," I said, nudging the door closed. "He'll be all right. Go back to sleep."

In the morning I woke to the sound of drilling outside on the street and the sound of Mom's voice, telling someone on the phone, "Cancel it. I don't need it."

Ian was sleeping soundly after finally falling back at six. I pulled the duvet over his little shoulders, put my teddy next to him and snuck out, covered in a heavy, almost painful blanket of fatigue. When he woke up, he'd need to eat. There was a mango in the straw basket on the kitchen counter. I picked it up and squeezed, wondering if Ian could gum it down. Mom appeared, showered and with her hair combed back off her face.

"Did you get *any* sleep? she asked.

I shrugged. "He doesn't usually do that anymore. He's been really good at night."

"Guess I got lucky," she said. "Alex slept through it—how, I don't know. I think all men sleep like the dead."

"I think it's being in a new place," I said, cutting the mango into tiny pieces. "Is he still here?"

"He snuck out earlier."

"Of course he did," I said.

"He's not so bad, Thea." She swiped a piece of mango and popped it into her mouth.

"How would I know, right?" I asked. Ian woke up as I was plating the mango. I put the plate down on the dining table and went to my room. He was wedged into the crack by the wall, trying to roll onto his back. "Good morning, shuggi-buggi," I said. "I have mango." He looked up and around, wondering where the hell we were now.

"So what happened with Daddy?" Mom asked, eyeing me as I sat down with Ian.

"What are you looking at?" I asked.

"Nothing," she said innocently. "Did you see the flyers?"

"What flyers?" I asked, only then registering the piles of flyers covering the table. I picked up a stack and, with my free hand, slid the white sleeve down to the bottom so I could see what it was: a quadrant of photos, backlit and shot with a wide angle, of our apartment. HUGE, TRADITIONAL WHITE-BOX LOFT—TWO-BEDROOM IN THE HEART OF CHELSEA, read the banner across the front.

"Two million dollars?" was the first thing that came out of my mouth.

"That's what we valued it at," she said, standing yoga-ready straight, obviously proud.

"Wow," I said. I picked up a piece of slippery mango with my fingers and found Ian's lips. "Do you think you could have talked to me about it?"

"Oh, it's nothing, really," she said, sitting down on the living room rug in front of us. "I just thought I'd cast the net, see what little fishies I caught." She looked at Ian, watched him pick a piece of mango up by himself. "He's so sort of self-sufficient now, isn't he?"

"Mom, where would you even go?" I asked.

She lay down and flexed her red-toenailed feet. "I don't know," she said. "Maybe Gramercy or Tribeca. It's time for me to downsize."

My phone rang. It was Dad. "Look, Thea, I'm sorry about last night."

I put Ian on the floor next to Mom and scurried back to my room, ignoring his cries. "Why did you ask us to come and stay with you when it's clear you don't want us there?" I asked.

"Of course I want you here." His voice was a confused muddle. "What makes you think I don't want you here?"

"You just seem like you'd rather be alone."

"That's not true."

"Dad, you grunt. I ask you a question when you're cooking and you grunt."

He sighed.

"And I can't wait till nine o'clock to eat," I said. I smiled in spite of myself. "I just can't."

"Then have a snack, for Christ's sake."

"I can't. You make it impossible to set foot in the kitchen. It's a no-fly zone when you're in there. Face it. If you don't want us there, I don't want to do that to you."

"I do want you here." He said it so quietly I could hardly hear him. "I do. Can you come back? Before I go to work? I'll wait for you."

Back in the living room, Ian was lying on the rug, swatting at a playing card Mom was dangling in front of his face.

"I've forgiven him for last night," Mom said. "That was Daddy?"

"He wants us to go back," I said, stabbing a piece of mango.

Mom lay down on the rug, swaying her knees from side to side, the morning light delineating the deep smile lines around her mouth, her "parentheses" as she referred to them. "You two'll work it out," she said, yawning.

"Wait, I'm not done talking about this," I said, waving the flyer. "I think this is weird, just selling this place out from under me, without even *discussing* it first."

"Thea, I *told* you, it's just to see if someone bites."

"And if they do?"

"Then who knows." She tickled Ian's belly and he laughed, rolling onto her arm. "You've got such a cute little giggle, who knew?"

I asked her why she didn't seem that interested in hanging out with Ian.

"Of course I'm interested," she said. "I see him."

"You haven't seen him in at least a month."

"I haven't?" she asked, overly surprised.

"Yeah," I said. "I don't get it. He's your grandson."

She grimaced. "Don't remind me, please."

"But don't you want to see him growing? He changes every day. He's so bright-eyed. How could you not want to see him?"

"Of course I want to see him," she said, playing peekaboo with Ian. "Maybe I've been a little distracted with this real estate thing. I have four listings now. And I think I'm about to get another one."

"That's great," I said.

"Don't be so defensive," she said.

"What?" I implored. "It is. I mean it. I miss you, though."

"Well, I'm *around*, Thee." She rolled her eyes. "It's not like I'm not here if you need me."

"If you don't like seeing him, if he just reminds you of how I'm a failure, just say it. You can tell me, you know. That's kind of what it feels like. It's what everyone seems to be feeling these days."

"It's nothing like that," she said quickly. "I'm proud of you. You're making your own way. With any luck you'll end up in better shape than the Vanessas of the world. Maybe this will show you early on that it doesn't come easy. We can hope, right?"

She covered her face with her hands and said, "Huzzah!" when she took them away. Ian watched, delighted, waiting for her to do it again, and she smiled at him, but her eyes darted around the room restlessly. I'd seen that restless look so many times in my life and it occurred to me, maybe she'd gotten restless with *Dad*. Maybe, after all the fury around getting him to stop drinking, and after all the crazy anger she had about Bill Mindorff getting him to stop and not us and how Dad cared too much about work and making money, maybe all of that was just an excuse. Maybe she just hadn't loved him anymore.

She straightened her legs in front of her on the floor and stretched while Ian stared at her, awaiting her next move. "Anyway, Daddy always said I wasn't a baby person. And he might be right. I think I'm better when they speak."

52.

Dad opened the door and shooed us inside, as if he were pulling us into shelter from a tornado. "I worried about you two all night. Where did you go? Where did you sleep?"

"Mom's," I said, putting Ian down on the living room floor with the pack of playing cards Mom had given us. It seemed like I was always plopping him on the ground, like a sack of potatoes.

He looked at me intently. "Well, I'm glad you're back." He shifted his glasses up to the bridge of his nose. "I think we both could have handled things last night a bit better, don't you? I think we *both* have some apologizing to do."

"I guess so," I mumbled. Inside my head I was saying to myself, *Come on, be an adult. Apologize.* But I couldn't get the words out. Ian flung the cards all over the rug, and Dad and I watched as he tried to bend them back into the pack.

"Thea, you've got to bear with me," he said, leaning against the living room wall. "Your mind works at this clip. So like your mother. I didn't mean that, exactly. Christ, I don't know what I mean. Just that it's hard with you sometimes."

"What's hard?" I asked. "I'm doing everything you want me to do."

He shook his head vigorously, as though trying to clear his head of my voice and gather his thoughts. "You've got to stick with it, kiddo."

"Anyway, that doesn't matter," I said, kneeling on the floor. "Last night doesn't matter. What matters is, I have to make this work for me. I can't go crazy. I can't lie down and die. I'm his mother, and I love him and I'm a good mom, no matter what anyone says. But I have to dig myself out of this hole."

"You're in a hole?"

I laughed. "Isn't it obvious?"

"Well, I don't like to hear you say that."

"You can take it," I said.

He started to say something, but his eyes fixed on a *Newsweek* on the coffee table. For a second I thought he was actually starting to skim an article the magazine was open to. But then he looked up. "I don't understand how we got here, Thea," he said, searching my face. "I try and figure out how we all got here." His eyes crumpled into something I hadn't seen before and he hid his face behind his big knuckles, like I was the sun and he was shielding his eyes from me. He retreated with his hands like that till he reached the hallway, then turned around and went to his room.

"Dddddsss," Ian said from the floor, sprinkling spit down his chin. I reached over and wiped it with my sleeve, the living room weirdly silent and empty. After a few minutes Dad came down the hall with his suit jacket on and the features of his face in their usual placid formation. "Okay, well, I should get going." He paused in front of us on the floor, tugging his shirt sleeve.

"Dad, you know what?" I blurted out. "It's not the end of the world, what happened last night."

"I know it isn't." A quick, almost embarrassed smile flashed across his face, but his eyes stayed fixed on me; it was like an understanding passed between us that we both, in some hazy way, had been thinking of Mom and the old fights.

"You're really not enjoying that job, are you?" he asked.

"Uh, no," I said. "But enjoying it's not the point, is it?"

"Well, it's not meant to be torture." He laughed stiffly. "I just want you to get a glimpse. It's not always patently obvious to people what path they should pursue, based on their talents or skill sets or what have you."

"It's patently obvious that I don't want a career in private equity," I said. "It's patently obvious to me that I want to sell crocheted bikinis. And maybe crocheted skirts. It may sound silly or frivolous to you, but it's not."

"Let me ask you this, Thea," he said, clearing his throat. "How long does it take to make one swimsuit?"

"One bikini?" I said, standing up and taking my jacket off. "A couple of days. I'm getting really fast."

"And theoretically, how many orders would you expect to receive?"

"I'm not sure," I said. "But those three that just sold, and that first one I made, they all sold very quickly."

"How much do you think you could sell them for?"

"They each sold for three hundred," I said. "Remember, I told you?"

He brushed the shoulders of his suit jacket. "So if you made, say, ten a month, to be safe, that's well under three thousand dollars, given store commissions. Pre-tax."

"Yes, but there are those women in Brooklyn who could help."

"How many could they make?" he asked. He took a drink from a glass of water sitting on the stereo console, probably left there the night before.

"I don't know, fifty a month?"

"They'd make fifty," he said evenly.

"I'm not sure of the numbers yet, but that's what I was thinking."

"All of this is irrelevant since we're not clear on the numbers," he said, picking his briefcase up from the chair in the hallway. "But the point is, how much do you want to make on every swimsuit? You'd have to figure out how much you could sell the swimsuits for and then how much you can afford to make them for. Depending on how many stores have interest in your swimsuits and whether you could get someone to make them for as little money as possible or whether—"

"I don't have those answers yet," I interrupted, his repetition of the word *swimsuit* making me crazy. "Is this how you are with your clients? Someone comes in with a great idea and you just . . . shove it right up their asses?"

"You might say that." He smiled, fiddling with the lock on his briefcase. "That's what they pay me for." He opened the door and looked back. "You going to be home tonight?"

I nodded, thinking, How could it be any clearer: we had nowhere else to go.

When Monica arrived, I jumped in the shower, got dressed and kissed Ian goodbye. Monica had left her phone at our apartment, on top of the fridge, so she'd never gotten my text asking about Ian's bruise, which was barely visible at that point, so I decided to let it go. I got to work and Daniel ignored me, giggling into his headset. I couldn't believe I'd almost had sex with him. Malcolm didn't make an appearance all morning, and when I finally asked Daniel, he murmured something about his being in Canada.

Sue from Human Resources came by and said I could leave early if I wanted to, so I neatened the pile of forty files I'd just put together and left at three. I let Monica go and took Ian to the park in Union Square, where I pushed him in a swing for the first time. As I pushed him, his body flopped backward and forward inside the black rubber swing, and he had a sort of anxious look in his eyes and a tightness in his lips that made him look alarmingly like Dad. A bunch of little kids ran around with big sand-filled balloons, and the whooshing sound surrounded me as they punched them into the air. I remembered Dad, spouting his wisdom about my bikinis that morning, and thought, Maybe he wasn't critiquing my bikini dreams for pure sport or to make me feel like shit. Maybe he *was* trying, in his that's-what-they-pay-him-for, tutorial way, to help me.

53.

Mrs. Weston called me at work a month later.

"Will mentioned to me that it's your birthday Sunday. I thought I'd offer my services if you want to spend the day celebrating."

Even though I hated Will and thought he was the world's biggest traitor, wimp and asshole rolled into one, I took comfort in the fact that he had remembered my birthday.

"Thank you, Mrs. Weston," I said. Spend the day celebrating. I pictured myself leading a parade of drunken revelers down Broadway, waving silk streamers and banging oversized kettle drums.

Vanessa took a bus from Vassar on the big day and met me for lunch at a bistro in Soho we used to go to late night during our dancing days.

"I haven't been here since before I met Will," I said as I dove into the dark-wood banquette.

"Amazing, isn't it?" Vanessa chirped. The waiter sloshed water into our glasses.

"Am I a total loser, Vanessa? Living with Dad? Ian? Is it all just too much loserness?"

"You're only a loser if you feel like one." She opened her bag and pulled out a box wrapped in polka-dotted paper. "Do you feel like a loser?"

"Sometimes yes, sometimes no," I said, waving the box away.

"Well, I'm in the same boat. Vassar has a small amount of loser-stink on it. But it's okay."

"You sound like Mom," I said, putting on her voice. "School is for bloody wankers. . . ."

Vanessa laughed. "Remember how pissed she used to get at you when you said the word *wanker*?"

"But she could say it whenever she wanted." I nodded.

"God, I love this bread," Vanessa said, unfolding the cloth napkin that covered it. "Remember how much of it we used to . . . just . . . basket after basket?"

I picked up my present and opened it. It was for Ian: a stiff little black dog with a red leather collar.

"I thought it was adorable," she said, chewing.

I put the dog on the table, facing her. "You know you're a grown-up when you don't even care if presents aren't for you," I said. "Means I'm a good mom, right?"

"That's right," she said, flashing me a wink.

"He loves that other dog you gave him, by the way," I said, remembering how much I resented it when she first gave it to me at my makeshift shower. "He holds it to his chin by its ear, and the other day he made me take it outside with him. It's his favorite."

"I knew it would be when I saw it," she said gravely. "I had a feeling."

After lunch we walked around Soho, checking out clothes we couldn't afford as she told me about a preppie guy from Michigan she was obsessed with. It was a relief to hear her drone on and on, like a radio broadcast, about how he wasn't her type, about his ruddy cheeks and short, square body and his hands, blistered from playing lacrosse. It was a relief to be taken out of my dull, slightly worrisome existence. I asked her to stay over and she pretended to be tempted but then mentioned a party that night at school she "was supposed" to go to.

"You need to come visit soon," she said, sounding offended as she kissed me on the cheeks. "I can't believe you haven't yet. Give the boy a kiss for me, okay? From his auntie Ness?"

Vanessa got in the cab to Port Authority and I went to pick Ian up at Starbucks, the meeting spot Mrs. Weston had established in the two or three times she'd come to get him. She was always very accommodating about coming down to me from the Upper West Side, but she'd made it clear that she didn't want to pick him up at Dad's. She'd established the meeting spot right away—"Isn't there a Starbucks near you on Thirteenth Street?" she'd said, which made me think she'd figured it out before she called. I was a few minutes early, so I bought a massive cookie with M&M'S in it and sat down in a dirty velvet chair.

"Happy birthday, Mommy," I muttered to myself. The espresso machines screeched as I picked the M&M'S out of the cookie and thought about the fact that I didn't have any friends other than Vanessa. I would have to work on that. Even Vanessa was in a different place, as nice as it was to see her smiling, confident face.

She'd looked different. Her eyes seemed by turns more jaded and more excited, as though school had somehow intensified her reactions to the world. Was that what college did to people? Or maybe she'd always been like that and I'd just noticed it now. There were things that seemed new about her. Like the way she fired off texts with lightning speed instead of slowly hunting and pecking like she used to. And I hadn't seen her twirl her hair behind her shoulder once the whole day. It was an age-old habit of hers. I was trying to remember when I'd last seen her do it when the door swung open and Ian rolled in, asleep in his navy-blue sack. He was being pushed by Will.

I stood up. Will's head did a slow pivot across the line at the register, the tables, the corners. His hair was shorter and he was wearing a gray coat with tattered, unraveling cuffs, which I'd never seen. When he spotted me, a nervous smile crossed his face and quickly vanished, just like smiles appeared and vanished on his mother. He headed to the back in long, purposeful strides. I'd forgotten how tall he was. My legs were shaking.

"Hey," he said. We stood in front of each other for the first time since I'd left.

"Do you see him a lot?" I asked, my words rushing out as if we'd been midconversation. "When your mom gets him, do you see him then?"

"Sometimes, yeah," he said, crossing his arms. "That's okay, isn't it?"

"It would have been nice to know, that's all," I said. I put my hand on the stroller, starting to make a move.

"Can you stay a minute?" he asked.

"What for?"

"Just to talk."

"What about?"

"Come on, Thea," he said, forcing a smile.

"Come on, what? What is there to say?"

He tapped the velvet chair across from the one I'd been sitting in and then grasped my shoulder. "Sit."

I sat on the arm of the chair, staring at the door. I hated him, and at the same time I also wanted to crawl into the dark cave of his coat and spew and sputter my misery out.

"I just"—Will sat down and leaned forward—"I want to try and explain to you what happened. I still don't have a handle on it."

"Go ahead," I said.

"Look, Thea, I just, it was too much. I felt trapped."

"I didn't trap you," I said.

"I'm not saying it was right. I agreed to everything that went down, I know it. But that's how I felt."

He turned his head to the counter, where a crowd of people stood waiting for their drinks. "And when Ian was hurt, it sent me over the edge. I don't know how else to explain it. I panicked."

"It's one thing to panic," I snapped. "It's another to threaten and torture me."

"I know," he said quickly.

"How could you do that to me?" I asked. He leaned over and held me in a tight, awkward hug as I felt myself dissolve into sobs. I looked at Ian over his shoulder and allowed myself to feel it for the first time—how scared I'd been.

"I wish I could be as brave as you are," Will murmured. "You're so brave and you're a really good mother. I know you are. What I did was unforgivable." He pulled away and sank back into the velvet chair. "Thea, I feel like a failure on so many levels, I don't know where to begin."

A mom waiting by the bathroom opened up a bottle of juice, making the lid pop, and handed it down to her daughter. I didn't know what to say to Will. It seemed like there was nothing to say.

Will eyed the mangled cookie on the table. "Why didn't you just buy some M&M'S?" he asked, smiling weakly at me. "Happy birthday, by the way. Mom says you have a job."

I nodded. "Ian has a nanny." I couldn't help smiling. It sounded ridiculous.

"So did you know I'm thinking of getting my eye fixed?" he said.

"Fixed?" I asked. "How?"

"There's this thing they can do with a laser. I still won't be able to see out of it, but I'll be able to move it. It'll follow the other one."

"Wow," I said. We're so young, still, I thought. There's still so much to fix.

"Wow, what?"

"I think I might miss it."

"You'd miss my lazy, wandering eyeball?" He sat back and his good eye crinkled with something that I recognized for the first time in a clear, straightforward way. Will loved me. Despite what was going on, despite the fact that we couldn't be together. I had a flash of the way I often used to feel when I was with him, without even knowing it—rudderless and lonely—and I realized something: That was *me*, my emptiness, my cauldron of crazy, bottomless need, it wasn't him. Will *loved* me.

The kids behind the counter were starting the closing process, running water in the sinks, talking earnestly about whatever, laughing. We watched Ian sleep for a long time without saying anything, a storm of pride and desolation ripping through me before the fumes from the floor cleaner chased us out.

54.

"Ian, watch!" Dad calls from down the beach on Charter Island, where Ian is hobbling around, knee-deep in the water. Ian is two now. Even though his arms are immersed in the murky water as he digs for rocks, I can see how the crescents of fat around his wrists are dissolving into defined strokes of arms and hands.

Dad skips a rock seven times, almost all the way out to the raft. Ian looks up, too late.

"Yay!" Ian shouts, even though he missed it. A flock of geese sits on the water, out by the diving board at the end of the bluff. One by one they circle out from behind the rocky pier, forming a wide, moving arc.

"They're like dancers on a stage," Dad says, moving behind Ian and holding him by the shoulders to keep him from falling backward. "See that, Ian?"

I stand behind them on the beach, trying not to get my feet wet, fishing my camera out of my bag. I pull it out and turn it on, flipping back to the shot of Will and Ian I took a few days ago on the rocks in Central Park. Ian was trying to climb, but Will was smiling at the camera with his thumb in the belt loop of Ian's jeans. The confident father. We meet every weekend now, the three of us, and usually spend the day—but never the night—together, and at the end Will walks us to Dad's and gives us long, lingering hugs outside the building before he heads down the street.

"Can you take one of us?" I ask, handing Dad the camera and kneeling down next to Ian, who is bent over trying to dig a rock half his size out of the sand. Dad walks backward, in the water.

"Ian! Hoo hoo!" Dad calls.

I squint into the sun, just like I did on the same beach when I was six and Nana took that picture of me in the red, white and blue bikini. Sometimes when Dad and I fight, about the usual things—how I leave those plastic milk tabs lying around that always get tangled up in the garbage disposal, how I'm not taking any steps to enroll at NYU even *part-time*—I'll catch a flash of the same confused look on his face that he had sometimes with Mom, and I remember how angry and lost he seemed when I was younger, like he was kind of wrecked. Men are very fragile, it turns out. It's hard to bounce back from rejection. Once I understood that about him, it got easier for us.

I'm still working at Pullman. I graduated from the internship to a salaried position with benefits. Even though it is still mostly paper-pushing, I have my own desk. It actually makes me proud to flash my medical insurance card with my own name on it.

A few weeks ago Mom's friend Christine at *Bazaar* finally came through after Mom kept bugging her for me. In the June issue, next to a small photo of a model sitting on a beach ball in my all-time favorite red, white and blue bikini, Christine wrote that "Galehouse's designs" were "unique in their modesty," and that she could imagine them kicking off a "fresh, slutty-conservative trend in swimwear." I'd tacked up a website right before the article ran, and two weeks later I had 312 orders. Mom then took it upon herself to get in touch with her old friend Graham, who used to bartend at Fiona's and who's now a buyer for Barneys. That's when I sat Dad down in front of my laptop and we did the math.

"Ninety-three thousand, six hundred dollars," he said coolly. But I saw that jump-start his eyes did when he was discussing anything that involved a profit. It wasn't hard to miss.

"So what about helping me?" I'd asked matter-of-factly. This time, I was not the drunken slut crashing my rental car into gas stations in Europe, or even the little girl with the too-big shopping cart at the toy store. I was a mother who wanted to support her kid doing something she loved. This time I was channeling Ian. Ian Galehouse Weston, my albatross, my savior. I had to go after what I wanted, or neither of us would stand a chance. "I can't crochet three hundred bikinis all by myself. Can we please go to Brooklyn and meet these people?"

Dad shifted in his chair, clicking the tip of a pen up and down. "Okay," he'd finally said.

The shop was in a one-story, tan brick building in Red Hook. Carmen and I got there first and went up a flight of stairs, into a dim room with a square table in the middle of it. The table was covered with brown paper, with streaks of masking tape running along the sides and bottom, and five women were sitting around it. They all had long, black hair, and all but one had it tied back in low ponytails.

"Thea, this is Dalma, Lydia, Elizabeth, Josie and—I'm sorry I've forgotten your name," Carmen said. "You're new, aren't you?"

The woman nodded and smiled. "I'm Jade."

"Josie and Jade," Carmen said. "So this is Thea and she has designed a beautiful bikini, which everyone wants to buy."

Dad walked in as they said, "Ahh, bikini," giggling, in unison.

"What's so funny?" he asked.

"This is my father," I said to Carmen.

Carmen shook his hand vigorously. "Nice to meet you." She waved her arms around the room. "Yeah, so we're trying to set Thea up with a . . . production situation."

Dad glanced at me skittishly, nervous about what he was getting into. "Right," he said. "And are these the women who would be helping?"

Carmen nodded. "They're wonderful. Very skilled and very meticulous. I love their work."

"How does it go, then?" Dad said. "They get orders from designers and fulfill them within a certain time frame?"

As if on cue, a man with his hair combed over in a short-sleeved button-down shirt stepped out of a door in the narrow corridor at the end of the room. He walked up to us and introduced himself.

"I'm Mr. Silva," he said. "We charge by the hour. If the order is a large one, sometimes by the piece."

"Or the two-piece." Dad smiled at me. "Get it?"

One of the women was sliding the bikini onto a white plastic mannequin.

"It's so nice," the woman said. The others nodded enthusiastically, then dipped their heads back to their needles.

"It *is* nice, Thea," Dad said, surprised. "There's a pretty cut to them. I was expecting them to look more . . . showy."

"That's the whole point," I said.

"She's got a very specific sensibility," Carmen interjected. "She knew exactly how she wanted them to look."

"Hmmm . . ." he said, turning to Mr. Silva. "Well, how do we do this? Is there some sort of contract?"

"You tell me what you want and I write something up for you," Mr. Silva said.

Dad looked at him and rubbed his mouth. I could tell he was put off by Mr. Silva's vagueness. "Well, you need to make three hundred," he said, turning to me. "Is that right, Thea?"

I nodded. "Three hundred and twelve, so far, but I can do the twelve."

"We have to factor in shipping costs." Dad put his hand on my shoulder and paused, watching the women.

"And work out some kind of wholesale deal for the yarn," I said.

"I can help you with that," Carmen said quickly.

"And are you . . . looking for anything?" Dad asked Carmen.

"Me?" she asked, putting her fist to her chest. "Oh, no, I'm just helping her out."

It hadn't occurred to me that Carmen would want a cut. "Thank you," I said. "Really, thank you."

Carmen smiled at me and put her hand on my back. "You deserve it, kiddo."

"I have no idea what the margins are in the garment business." Dad frowned at the floor. "Mr. Silva, what if we offered you twenty thousand dollars to do the work?"

Mr. Silva looked away, smiling passively. "Three hundred pieces?" he said, gesturing at the women. "Twenty-five."

Dad looked at me. "When do you need them by?"

"Two weeks?" I said. "Is that a reasonable amount of time or will you have to hire more women?"

"We'll see how it goes," Mr. Silva said.

"Shall we put something in writing, then, to that effect?" Dad said. "I can write you a check today."

I heard a garbage truck groan outside as Dad started to follow Mr. Silva. "This will all be in addition to your work at Pullman," he said sternly. "And you're going back to school someday."

I nodded as he turned down the hall. Carmen winked at me and shot me a subtle high five.

"I'm going to make Dad proud," I said.

Now I watch as Dad turns the camera horizontally, then vertically, then horizontally again, my eyes almost tearing from the setting sun, trying to hold Ian still as he fends off a patch of seaweed coming toward him. I wonder if we'll just go on together like this forever, until Dad's an old man and I'm a spinster, long forgotten by Will, and Ian's a punk in the park. About a year after we split, Will and I started talking on the phone, late at night, when the rest of the world was shut down and far away, the way we used to when we first met. I learned some new things, mainly just *how* afraid he was of failing. I tried not to think about the irony of it: he was so afraid of failing and yet he'd failed *us* so completely. But as time went on, I realized that part of being a healthy, well-adjusted adult meant not holding on to stuff that made you so angry you couldn't see straight. There was no point.

Will is coming back to us someday, I think, as Dad finally clicks the shutter. He is, and if he doesn't, more power to me for believing that he will. Once I'm hooked, I don't let go. So sue me. I'm not holding my breath—I've got things to do, a luxury crocheted-accessories business to build. Department store contracts to win.

I splash seaweed out of Ian's way and let him throw about fifty more rocks into the water until it starts to get dark. "We should get back to the house," I say, imagining all the things I wanted to do once Ian went to sleep, like think about designs for a collection of crocheted skirts. "It's getting late."

Dad wades onto the beach and rolls down his khakis. I pick Ian up and we climb the steep steps and cross the street into the parking lot, where Dad helps me strap Ian into the seat on the back of my bike.

"So I'll see you two at home," he says. He is running into town to pick up a pizza. A car drives by, too fast for Dad's liking, stirring up the sandy pavement.

"Slow down!" he yells after the car, taking a few indignant steps out into the street. "Jesus!" he mutters, turning back to me. "Should I get a salad?"

"Only if you want," I say. "It's too hard to think about salad when there's a pizza staring you in the face." He smiles, the creases on his forehead relaxing, revealing little white lines. "You're a little sunburned," I say.

"Am I?" he asks, wiping sand away from Ian's mouth and tightening his strap. He heads to his car as I start to pedal out of the parking lot, getting ready for the hill that leads to our house. Dad passes, waving his arm at us out the window, and I have a strange thought—the weird, hard-to-connect possibility that Dad loves me in the same, dumbstruck way that I love Ian. When we reach the top of the hill, Dad's blinker fires shots of red into the dusk as he turns the corner. His car stretches farther ahead of us, his blinker still on, a flickering, distant star, here now but not forever.

Catherine Greenman grew up in New York City and lives there now with her family.

II